THE BRIDGE COMMITTEE

KIM WESTRUP

Published in the United States of America

Brilliant Books Literary
137 Forest Park Lane Thomasville
North Carolina 27360 USA

ISBN:
Paperback: 979-8-88945-257-7
Ebook: 979-8-88945-258-4

1

The day had started out hot, and by the looks of things, it was going to end the same way though by three o'clock, Glenn Becker's day was far from ending. The bell had sounded, sending four-hundred-plus students on their way home, and Glenn, as always, thought momentarily of that Friday in November when he had had to tell these same kids what had happened to their president as he was driven through Dallas, Texas.

They would remember well into the twenty-first century where they were and how they heard about the assassination. He turned his attention back to the present. He still had a meeting with the Drug Study Committee, an appointment with the computer coordinator, and his son's Little League baseball game to attend. This was the order in which the events would occur but certainly not the order in which Glenn looked forward to them. He would be glad to get the Drug Study Committee out of the way since he couldn't see that it would be able to accomplish much. He had set up the committee under pressure from a single teacher who thought the drug problem was out hand. As far as Glenn could tell, there was no significant drug use at the school; but since a committee had been formed for the absence and tardy problem, one for intramurals, another for discipline, why not one for drugs? He would provide the forum and see what happened. Jim Parks talked little, but usually what he said meant something. Glenn would let him have his say.

Preparation for the meeting with the computer coordinator occupied most of Glenn's thoughts and his desk. He knew she would listen and make notes of all the scheduling ideas for the whole school, existing staff, and students for next fall. Within a few months she would tell him those which were feasible, what could be altered and possibly used, and those which simply could not be scheduled on a computer. His job was not to sell her on a particular program. What he would have to decide was how much of one idea would he be willing to sacrifice in order to gain another. Clearly flexibility with as much individual student choice as possible was what Glenn had decided was top priority and was what West Junior High needed most.

After only one year as principal, Glenn had come to realize that computers are not too long on individual choice. He had found this out at second semester when an awful lot of computer bargaining would have had to have been done to allow freshmen to pick between two science courses. Finding himself faced with going to three lunch periods, the third of which would not have had access to the gym on stormy days for recreation during their noon recess, he had backed off, and earth science was still mandatory. There had been lots of stormy days.

Jim Parks entered his office with a sigh and a nod. The nod was about the only greeting anyone got from Jim. His briefcase dropped to the floor.

"I think we'll need a scheduling committee," Glenn quipped as he gathered up the papers strewn across his desk. The committee concept had become something of a joke in his one year. He liked the idea getting the feel from the faculty, and it seemed the teachers generally appreciated some voice in matters. He had become aware of the joke only when he found on his desk a poster from the science department: When All Else Fails —Form a Committee.

"Is that what you're doing?" Jim had seated himself comfortably and was watching students scurry across the courtyard outside the window.

"What I'm doing is getting hot. My god, is it always like this around here?"

Jim chuckled, "Yeah, it warms up a bit about this time of year. Don't you get this in Minnesota?"

"Not in May. In July, maybe, but who cares then?"

"It's not the heat," Jim started absently.

"It's the humidity. I've heard that. Hell, it is."

"You goin' home this summer?" asked Jim as he brought his attention back inside the office. Mary Dennis had slid in under an armload of books. Jim wondered why a speech teacher needed to take home so many books.

"Hi, Mary," said Glenn. "I don't know. I'd like to, but I may got to hand scheduling if the computer backfires. I should know by tonight. Let's see, Don was going to be here."

The noise in the hall swelled as if electrically amplified. There was something about it which told Glenn a fight had broken out. He also knew by the sound. It was between two Black girls. Fights were not frequent—at least not as much so as he had been warned—but the warm weather seemed to be having its effect.

Neither teacher moved; Glenn himself always tried to play down fights. He looked at them more as a spectator problem though he hated to see girls fighting. He had rolled his chair over to an intercom. "John, let's get 'em out of here."

"Right," came the muffled reply from the assistant principal.

Easing back in his chair, Glenn reflected briefly. In that terse command, he had said so much. "Get 'em out of here" meant we don't care to know what the fight is about, we don't try to prevent its breaking out again on the way home, and no one is to be expelled by the assistant principal.

Can we show these kids this kind of behavior is just a nuisance? Glenn wondered to himself.

In that fleeting instant, he recalled his first meeting with a parent at West, Mrs. Walker. She had harangued quite a while about the assistant principal. "No matter that he is Black," she said repeatedly. "He just doesn't know how to handle kids. He comes on too strong, too loud. They think Mr. Bemis is a joke."

Glenn realized he had gradually eased John Bemis from the foreground. He was relegated to attendance problems, lunchroom procedures, and other less crucial functions. *No matter that he is Black*, Glenn reflected.

Mary was making her acknowledgment of the heat and somehow trying it in with the disturbance in the hall. Don Mills arrived and sat down, looking at his watch. He rarely stayed long after school hours but could be counted on to be in his room in the morning well before any of the others.

"John will be right in, and we can get started," Glenn announced.

"We hope," added Don. Whether this comment was aimed at starting soon or John's ending the fight soon was a little unclear. Glenn opted for the first.

"What's the trouble out there?" he asked, displaying half interest.

"Veda and somebody else were going at it. John got to them before I could," said Don.

"Same old thing," Jim added, and Mary's nod showed everyone knew what was being talked about.

Glenn jotted down "same old thing / Jim Parks" and underlined it on a scrap of paper. He would have to find out what the "same old thing" was.

John was saved the embarrassing duty of explaining the fight to his White colleagues—and they were spared the equally embarrassing duty of listening—when Glenn got the meeting underway.

"So…we've got a drug committee," he said with a smile. He eased back in his chair and swiveled, facing Jim. "I have to admit, I don't know too much about the extent of the drug problem here, but it seemed worth looking into, and I appreciate your willingness to do it with me. I can think of several reasons you are here—maybe just because you felt obligated to be on some committee—but seriously I guess we fall into one of the two groups. We either know something about drug usage here, or we want to know about it. I'm in the second group." He was smiling now at Jim. "I don't want to put anyone on the spot, but, Jim, where exactly do we stand?"

There was a pause as Jim crossed his legs and settled into his chair. I don't claim to know exactly where we stand," he began slowly. "I will venture that each of us teaches at least one kid a day who is stoned. I think we could find some grass, marijuana"—he looked at Mary—"in a dozen lockers if we looked right now."

Glenn listened, realizing Jim was dropping bombs just as he had done the one day in class when Glenn had visited. This young history teacher had a knack for stirring up his listeners while staying so deliberately calm himself. His slow, precise speech indicated authority.

"The important thing," he continued, "is not what the percentages are nor how often they use the stuff. The question is what do we do about it? Suppose we had a list of a dozen known users of marijuana—or fifty or a hundred—what would we do about it? That's what I think we need to talk about."

"Well, what are our options? Let's crank 'em out, good or bad, without making any judgments," Glenn suggested, reaching for his pen. "Rose, send in some Cokes, will you, please?"

"Inform parents," offered Mary to get things started.

"Call the police," was Don's.

"Set up an education program just for these kids," Mary suggested. "And include their parents."

"Suspend them," said Glenn with his usual smile. He realized the controversy his three-day suspension policy had caused. He had stuck with his guns on this one, explaining to any critics, "I'd rather get them out of here and worry about how to get them back in than worry about how to keep them in." Usually "how to get them back in" involved parents coming in for a conference before readmission, his critics arguing that the vast majority of suspendees don't, for one reason or another, live with their parents.

"If we're just listing options," said Jim. "We could ignore it."

Glenn was writing but paused to thank his secretary, who entered with refreshments. He saw to it that everyone was served.

Finally, John spoke, pushing his glasses back on his nose as he always did when he began to talk. "Couldn't we do something to talk with these kids—find out why they're using it? Seems like it would need to be done on an individual basis, and I don't know what we'd call it or how we'd fit it in…but counseling of some kind."

This was what Jim wanted to hear. Its source was a bit of a surprise to him, but he would gladly team up with the man to get such a program though he was already thinking far enough ahead to realize

John Bemis would do more harm than a good once such a program could be started.

"Okay, now help me kick these around," Glenn said. "And for now, let's not consider cost."

This last statement confused Jim. Perhaps, he thought, Glenn already had a plan—or at least favored the only suggestion that would really cost money.

"Read the list, will you?" said Don.

*****

It was hot also where Jack Flemming was working. A warehouse job just didn't seem right to him after a college education and two years as a soldier, but he had taken what he could get after his return home, and for now, at least this was what he got. This was the time of year he would like to be getting his stock car ready for the season.

But that was one hobby he could not yet afford. Maybe by the end of the summer, he would be able to return to the track. For now, it would have to be working in a warehouse for next to nothing and coaching a kids' baseball team for nothing at all. He glanced at the clock, which told him he had another hour and a half before picking up hamburger on his way to batting practice before the game. Pitching to ten-year-olds was about the extent of his recreation, and Jack didn't like it that way. He found himself looking forward to the games, though; and while his early record was far from impressive, he knew the boys on the team idolized him, and he enjoyed them and several of the families involved.

On nights when Janice, a stewardess, was out of town, his social life was pretty well limited to visiting with whoever would invite him over after the game—some he enjoyed more than others—and it had nothing to do with the kids. Only once did he feel that an evening in a home was designed for purposes other than radiating appreciation for his efforts, and even then, Jack could have misinterpreted some of the things which were said. He had left with the distinct impression that his host felt his son deserved to play more frequently. Jack could be philosophical though. Everyone has an ax to grind, and anyway, was he himself not seeking to improve his own lot? He was job hunting as surely as he was consuming his host's refreshments every time he went into someone's house. A coaching job is what he wanted, and who knows when he might be talking to someone influential with the school board? Monotony was the main problem now. Standing all day behind a metal desk inventory, he felt the coming and going of hundreds of electrical appliance parts got to be pretty old. An electric fan droned above his head, and Jack was too hot and too bored to even turn on the radio he kept on a shelf behind him. Had he, it would have snapped his boredom. It would have told him of flight 491, which crashed short the runway in Los Angeles, killing all passengers and crew.

*****

It was a clean break which sank one ball and gave Dan another shot. Russell calmly chalked his cue stick. It was a grudge match, but then every day it was a grudge match for Russell. Having for so long been undisputed pool champ, it was difficult for him to see anyone threatening his kingdom.

Dan had beaten him before, and the news spread quickly. So far, there wasn't much crowd, just Jean, who lay draped over a couch near the corner. The only movement there was when a fan rustled her hair as it panned back and forth as if watching the game and then looking at Jean. The fan had a definite assignment, however. With the basement windows open, its job was to blow the smoke out so that it would not become trapped in the stairwell leading upstairs—not that Mrs. Carter didn't know about the marijuana in the basement. It was just simpler to avoid the whole issue if she weren't reminded of it daily. If the kids in the basement were happy with the pool table, she was happy upstairs with the television and an occasional drink. The marijuana could be worried about some other time, and since her husband wouldn't be home until late, this was not the time.

Russell crouched low, lining up his first shot. A click and a thump told Jean he had sunk his first. She hoped he would win. If he lost, he was sure to play again, and she preferred him on the couch. On the floor beside her lay his algebra book, and upon it rested a joint, smoldering. She closed her eyes and thought back to the first time. How attentive Russell had been to her that day! He had coached her so carefully and made her feel relaxed. Whether her first marijuana hit had actually had an effect, she didn't know, but she was delighted with the attention and concern she found with it. Never before had anyone talked so understandingly with her as Russell had that day. Somehow, he had made her feel that he was proud of her and glad that she trusted him. She felt no strong desire for the grass itself, but from then on, she knew using it might restore the beauty of that first day.

Since that time almost a year ago, things had changed. At least times were prosperous. Just look at the joint smoldering away unattended. It used to be that the gang sat in a circle, passing the joint around, this being the most efficient way to consume it. It was as if every whiff of smoke had a special value and had to be used by someone for the good of the group. It was no good unless they were all stoned. By now the whole scene was relaxed. A joint was no big deal. No one any longer came over to Carter's to get stoned as they had in the past, but everyone got stoned or came that way—it was understood—only now, they came to play pool, listen to tapes, the grass incidental. The results were the same.

Jean liked what was happening. Not that ceiling tiles each was a different shade of blue, not that the fan was singing to her, not that she was consumed in bubbles, floating, but all these experiences channeled her mind back to the warmth of that first time when Russell had radiated that mysterious pride in her; and now he was there on the couch with her, whispering to her and touching her. The fan was singing to both of them as they floated, immersed in bubbles. It didn't matter that he was also a few yards away, playing pool. That was some imagination that didn't need to be explained. She was loved. She was happy. The afternoon could pass slowly or speed by; she would be oblivious.

*****

Time was most critical to Glenn by now. His next appointment was fifteen minutes away, and no decision had been made by the committee. The feeling seemed to be that the school had some responsibility to kids and parents but that this responsibility did not include searching for drug offenders nor taking legal action against them. Jim had convinced everyone that there was cause for concern, and though no names were mentioned, Glenn felt sure he had ample evidence to back up whatever he said.

"This has all been very interesting—perhaps alarming. Just to wrap up what we've said, let me see if I get the correct message thus far," he began. "I'm sure you're all anxious to get on your way home." He paused and looked at Jim. "What I hear you saying is that one, we have a drug problem which isn't going to solve itself. Two, we as teachers might be able to help through an education program, and three, more important than education will be some kind of counseling. Is this more or less what we agree to?'

Jim was quick to amend. "We don't need an education program for the kids I'm talking about. They could teach us." His soft tone and gentle smile turned sneer left no room for argument.

"So you place importance on the counseling end?"

"Yes."

"Let me put two questions to you, then we'll break up. By the way, could we get together next week?" Seeing a collective nod, he continued. "First, what are some realistic goals? In other words, what are we after—what are we trying to accomplish? And secondly, if we went the counseling route, what kind of person would we use? Would we need an expert in the drug area or someone more personable with the kids? Another thing to think about, I guess, is whether, assuming we could get someone, would he be known as a drug counselor or would he or she come in under some other title?"

"Whoever it is better be used to losing," Jim said as he stood to leave. Don was already out the door. Mary parted as she had arrived, talking about the weather.

*****

Warner Field was already showing the signs of neglect—at least lack of water. The half inch of soft dust pleased Benjie. Several contrails hung in the still air around him, slowly settling to earth, the golden sun's rays cutting through them. Benjie always got to ball games first—that was his only distinction from a coaching standpoint. He scooped up huge hands full of the dust and heaved it skyward to watch it arch and plummet to the ground. There was no one around to stop him, and within a few minutes, he had most of the infield engulfed in a golden smog all of his own creation. He loved jets and considered a trip to the airport just about the greatest way to spend a day. This love is what caused him to race around the bases, arms outstretched, with dust dribbling from each fist. It was beautiful, he thought. He could even look back and see where he had banked his turn at first base.

His finale was a performance on the pitcher's mound where he whirled in place so that he was surrounded by two corkscrews of glittering dust. A screeching bicycle brake interrupted him.

"What the hell are you doing?" It was one of the Ryley twins. The other was carefully cantering his bike down the rough slope to the ball diamond where he coasted behind the bench.

"Looks like a hurricane!"

Benjie walked toward them, a little sad that his privacy had been breached. Soon others would come and begin their wait for Jack to tell them what to do—though they all knew anyway. Before long, balls were sailing about, and the team was looking ready to play ball.

It was not until the fifth inning that Benjie had managed to scoot over so that he sat next to Jack—not that he thought this would get him in the game any sooner. Benjie had other aims.

"When are you going out to the airport?" he finally asked.

"Tomorrow after work." Jack had not stopped chewing his gum, had not stopped scanning his fielders who were trying to come back from a two-run deficit. There was a long silence, then Jack turned and smiled. As if there was no ball game at all, he said, "She gets in at four thirty. I'll leave right after work. What time do you get home from school?"

"I'll be home by then. Can I go?"

"You check with your mom. I'll come by on my way. If you can go, be in front waiting, and get ready to go in to right field next inning."

That's all there was to it, but Benjie's whole evening had changed, and he knew he would have a hard time tomorrow waiting until they would leave. He liked Jack's girlfriend too. She had shown him around the airport the last time he went with Jack to meet her and had promised sometime to take him into a plane. He wanted to ask about it now, but Jack's attention was back on the game, and Benjie knew his own should be too.

✶✶✶✶✶

Glenn was pleased with his meeting and once again satisfied with computers. West Junior High would schedule by quarters rather than semesters, and a form of ability grouping would be possible within certain required courses. The big question remained about the changing of teachers at the semester break. Was it better to leave the students with the same teacher all year or switch off for the second semester? He would ponder this as he watched the ball game. Traffic was snarled, and he realized the game would be half over before he reached the park. He hated even the short trip across town. The time needed to get from one place to another always bothered Glenn. His plight irritated him less when the newscast reminded him that others had to travel more than he. Anytime he heard of a plane wreck, he was glad his job required no travel. He didn't—he couldn't—realize how closely this particular wreck would affect him in the next few hours.

He was proud to see Tom on the mound as he wheeled into the parking lot, but a second look showed him his son was in trouble. His pitching was always poorest when runners were on base. Two were on now, and Tom was wasting his arm with snap throws to third. Glenn knew well how the runner there felt diving back to the bag way ahead of the throw, smiling from ear to ear as he wiped off the dust.

"Get the batter," he yelled to his son—more to let him know he was there than to give any real advice. He found his wife and daughter. As usual they had an extra folding chair for him.

"How are we doing?" Glenn asked, picking up Jenny playfully before sitting down.

"Not good," his wife, Helen, answered. "Nine-seven."

"Tom been in all game?"

"Not pitching. He started in center."

A wrinkle of surprise crossed Glenn's forehead. "Any hits?"

"A double, a single on an error, and a strikeout. We're in the sixth."

Glenn looked at his watch then settled to concentrate on his son's pitching. A swell of excitement and fear rose within him with every windup. The man on third was still a problem to Tom.

Then the batter went for a high two-and-O pitch, and it shot straight up in the air. Tom was calling for it and holding his arms out as if in complete control.

Glenn's body tightened. The ball seemed to hang there above the field. It plummeted earthward and toward Tom's glove where it smacked loudly and stayed. Glenn sat back and stretched out his long legs. Tom and the rest of the team trotted toward the bench.

"Well, how did the meeting go?" Helen wanted to know.

"Which one?"

"You know which one." They had discussed for weeks the chances of getting away for the summer versus the likelihood of having to stay in town while Glenn tediously scheduled each student according to his own choices.

"Oh, the computer one?" He was teasing now, but she knew how to handle it.

"I'd just as soon not go back home anyway. It seems like an awful waste of money, and the kids have—"

"I think we can make it. It looks real good."

Just then Mary Foreman walked past, chair in arm.

"Leaving already? We haven't lost yet," Glenn quipped.

"I've got to pick John up at the airport. I wish I could stay."

"Can we take Johnny home?" Helen asked.

"No, he's got his bike, and Grandmother is there. Thanks."

"Okay, we'd be glad to."

"Well, I'll remember. We may need to do it that way. Thanks again."

After she had gone, Glenn turned to Helen. "Was John out on the coast?"

"No, it's usually New York, I think." There was a long pause. "I know why you asked. Have you heard anything lately?"

Glenn shrugged. "They were all killed. I don't know how many. Was it landing or taking off?"

"Landing!" Helen said. "From here."

By now there were runners on first and second with one out.

"When does Tom bat?"

"Not for a while. He just struck out last inning."

A ground ball to the first baseman moved the runners to second and third but cost another out.

Glenn looked to see who was next batter. He saw Benjie. Benjie's uniform was a bit too large, and his hat was well down over his face, bespeaking a hat size too large also, but there seemed to be some confusion—on the part of Benjie. It wasn't his turn to bat. Jim Riley was up.

"Get back on the bench and play with the dust, would ya!" Jim yelled as he strode to the plate.

"That poor kid," Helen murmured.

Glenn chuckled understandingly, "It doesn't bother him a bit, honey." Then he dropped his voice. "And he'd rather be back on the bench playing in the dust anyway."

"I just wish they weren't so rough on him. I don't see how or why he stays on the team."

"The reason is coaching third base."

The third pitch to Jim was in the dirt and got away from the catcher. Jim leaped back as the runner from third crossed the plate. Jack held the next runner at third. Jenny wanted a snow cone and knew whom to ask, but Helen answered, "No, honey, we'll be leaving in just a few minutes."

"Oh, that's right." Glenn was on the edge of his chair now. "They only play seven innings. This is it!"

With a three-and-one count, Jim stood like a rock for the next pitch, which cut inside and low. He was on with a walk.

"Who's going to pinch-hit for Benjie, I wonder," said Glenn, sitting back with his hands clasped on top of his head.

"Benjie is going to bat," said Helen, looking tenderly at the tiny right fielder carrying his bat to the plate. Jack was trotting down the third baseline toward Benjie.

"Oh, no, he isn't," stated Glenn. "This is tough thing to do."

Jack had crouched down and was looking up at the boy. Benjie nodded twice, and he looked at Jim on first. He nodded again. Jack swatted him on the rear and jogged back to the coaching box at third.

"Oh my god," murmured Glenn.

"Come on, Benjie!" Helen's voice cracked, and Glenn saw her bite her lip.

"He's putting a lot on this kind," Glenn said. She nodded but didn't answer.

"Benjie, come on, honey." Her voice was a whisper.

With the windup, Jim started for second. Benjie looked ready but didn't swing.

"That's what that little conference was about," Glenn said reassuringly.

The next pitch was low, but the catcher came up with it. The runners raced back to their bases.

"Has he gotten a hit yet this year?" Glenn was trying to keep his voice calm.

"He doesn't get to play much," scolded Helen. "Come on, Benjie, get a hit!"

"A hit's all it will take."

On the next pitch, he swung and looked bad. Glenn dropped his head and stared at the ground. Curiosity made him find Tom among the team on the bench. There he was, hat off, head up, shouting and clapping. Glenn wouldn't give up if he wouldn't. "Okay, Benjie, rap one, boy."

The next pitch was right down the middle. Benjie didn't move.

"Stee-rike," yelled the umpire and walked off the field.

Helen stood up and started to fold her chair. Glenn threw his arm around her waist, saying, "I wanted that one too."

"Just imagine how he feels."

"Jennie will go with you. I'll bring Tom and Jack if he'll come. I'd like to talk to him…if you don't mind."

"Sure, have him bring Janice if she's in?"

"We'll, they may have plans. We'll see."

Glenn moved toward the bench where he would stand at a distance to listen.

Jack had congratulated the opposing coach briefly and caught up with Benjie as they neared the bench.

"Still want to go to the airport tomorrow?" Jack asked as cheerfully as possible.

"Can I still go?"

"Nothing will change that. So you struck out." There was a long pause until they neared the bench where the team had gathered. "Get 'em next time, huh?"

"Why couldn't we put in a pinch hitter?" Jim was whining, not really talking to anyone in particular. "We know he can't hit."

There was silence as everyone waited for Jack's reply. It was obvious he had heard the complaint. Jack put his right foot up on the bench and leaned forward. Addressing Jim directly, he said, "You guys get to decide how the game is going to be played…I get to decide who. Besides, I know only one other guy who only made one out tonight." It was settled that quickly.

Jack stood up straight. His tone of voice changed; he smiled. "That was a good game. I like 'em close. Next time we'll win it. I'll be here a half hour before the game so we can get a good warm-up, have some batting practice. If you're going to be here with me, it's time we go over and congratulate the winners. If there's any other complaints or problems, I guess I'd better stick around and hear those too. Keep your chins up on the way out of here so I'll still know you've got class. See you Saturday."

It was a slow, dutiful exit attended by much dust kicking. Glenn was glad to see Tom leading the way over to the other bench. He then gave his attention to Jack. "Can you come over for a while? I've got something to talk to you about. I'll pick your brain of you'll let me. Bring Janice if you want."

"No, she's out tonight. I'll be right over. Thanks."

*****

With the coming of dusk, the pool gang had dispersed, individuals and subgroups going their own way so that Carter's basement was again quiet with only the fan droning and forgotten. Jean couldn't figure out why the pool games were so important to everyone. It all seemed artificial or something. She now sat in the doorway of the hardware store, there being no hurry to get home. This particular doorway had become a favorite of late. She could count on a bedraggled cat to put in an appearance here nightly, and that made it a satisfactory hangout. She almost felt cozy there, but she didn't know whether she was happy or not. The beautiful part was it didn't matter, and if people walked by and looked at her, that didn't matter either. How could things like that matter.

She was talking to herself now. "So what if people look at me and pool! Big deal if you win or not. These people like to go crazy over stupid pool game. Sure, I like to play as much as everyone else, and I can probably beat everybody else—except maybe Russell—but I don't go crazy over winning. I wonder what's important to me. Russell. Russell has big shoulders. That's important." She pulled her knees up close and rested her head and arms upon them. She did not see the cat slither around the corner and approach her. "There's nothing wrong with Russell. If he likes pool, that's okay. I'm glad he won today. Danny's all right, though, but nothing like Russell."

She was startled as the cat squirmed into her lap. "Well, what's important to you? Food. That is the only thing wrong with you, your food. It's wrong to eat meat, but you don't look at it that way, do you? I'm glad I don't have to, but you—that's all you know to eat, isn't it?" She stood, held cat close to her for a moment, and then dropped it to the sidewalk where it stood looking up at her. "I think I'll paint you. Would you like that?"

Just then a car pulled up, and the head of Mike Keller leaned out the window. "Want a ride?"

"Where you goin'?"

"Anywhere…nowhere."

She looked back down at the cat and stroked it before climbing into the car.

*****

Glenn had kicked off his shoes and had stockinged feet propped comfortably upon the coffee table. "Tombo," he called out to his son who was in the kitchen. "See if you mother still has some pretzels in there, will ya? And this time, put them in some kind of bowl." He teased.

Jack had remembered the last time when a bag of pretzel crumbs was all that had been in the house. "We had a kind of meeting today which has gotten me to thinking a little, and like I said, I'd just like to see what your reaction would be. Thanks, Tom. Do you have any homework tonight?"

"No, I got it done already." He was already seated on the arm of his father's chair as if he was going to stay and listen to the conversation, but Glenn was too quick for him.

"Well, you take your shower now, then come on down in your PJs and have a quick soda with us. I think we have time for that if you snap to."

Tom started across the room and looked at Jack. "It would have been pretty neat if Benjie had got a hit, wouldn't it?"

"Yeah, well, you got a lot of class. I know what you're saying, and I thank you for it. See you after your shower."

"Anyway, some of the teachers got together this afternoon," Glenn continued. "And we talked about the, quote, *drug problem* there at West, and I don't know whether there is any consensus of opinion yet—or if there ever will be—about what we are going to do next. Apparently, it is worse than I had thought, and I guess we're going to have to try to do something about it."

The conversation stopped as Helen brought in two large glasses of iced tea.

"Can you join us?" Glenn prompted.

"I'll be in in a few minutes. I've got the dishes to do still."

"Thank you for the tea, Mrs. Becker." Jack was eager to hear what more Glenn had to say.

"There's plenty more. Yell when you need a refill."

"But I guess what is in my mind is someone who can get close to the kids on this thing and maybe, through some kind of counseling, figure out if there is anything we can do. Just thinking out loud now, would something like that interest you? I think we could do it under a federal grant. You can do anything under a federal grant as long as you write it up." His smile told Jack more than his words did about the tentativeness of this whole proposal.

Jack shifted nervously. This was turning into the job interview he had always been hoping for, and yet he wasn't quite ready for it. "I can't say that I know anything about drugs personally except what went on in school and the service. Yes, I'd be interested. Do you have any thoughts about what exactly this would involve? I don't have a certificate, you know."

"All right, at this point, we don't want to worry about the certification part of it. I don't think I'm looking for a drugs expert, so to speak. I'd rather have somebody who can get on with the kids. They already know too much about the drugs, if you ask me. This isn't a teaching activity as much as it would be a…" He shrugged. "I don't know what to call it—*counseling*, for lack of a better term—but of course, you can't hope to sit in a counselor's office with a sign up that says DRUG COUNSELING either. But let's say for now that that is my problem—how to get you to the kids or vice versa—would you be willing to get that close to kids so that they might talk? You're the best bet I can think of. You know how kids think and"—he smiled—"you must know what they think about you."

"Getting to the kids is no problem, is it? As long as you like race cars and baseball and your hair covers your ears. It's really kind of a cheap shot, but I know what you're saying. If you think I could do something, it would beat working in a warehouse. That isn't what I mean either." He ran his fingers through his hair nervously. "Sure, I'll do it as long as you think I can fit in to whatever your program might be. It sounds exciting, as a matter of fact, the more I think about it…"

2

Helen came into the room, wiping her hands on the apron she had just taken off.

"Finished? Great. I was just telling Jack about a meeting…"

"No." Helen lowered herself to the front of a chair near the corner of the room. Her hands folded in her lap, twisting the apron. "I was listening to the radio and was reminded again about the accident out on the coast. I thought Janice had flown out there today. Jack might want to make certain she is all right."

Her words hit Glenn like a thunderbolt. A glance at Jack showed him he didn't know anything. Glenn's eyes went ceilingward as he slouched back in his chair. "Yeah, there was a plane wreck of a flight from here this morning."

"What airline?" Jack blurted out. His drink kept his hands occupied.

Glenn nodded. "Will you let me phone for you? I'm sure we can get all the information. What was the number of her flight?"

"Four ninety-one. I've got the phone number I always call to see if the flights are on time coming in. Here, call this one, would you please?"

"Sure, it will just take a second. Sit tight."

Tom bounded down the stairs, hair plastered against his head, to see that the mood had changed. He didn't need to be told to keep quiet. He went into the living room and moved to the rocking chair near his mother. Jack was staring into his near-empty iced tea glass.

"That was a quick shower. You don't mess around." Jack's warm grin was welcome to the boy who didn't yet understand to sobriety.

"If you want something to drink, you can fix whatever you like, honey. You pitched a good game. How does your arm feel?"

"Okay. I don't want anything to drink."

"I prefer my suspense on the ball diamond," Jack said, gritting his teeth so that the words all came out as one.

"What's the matter?" Tom ventured.

"Honey…"

"There's been a plane wreck, and maybe Janice was on it. Your dad is calling to find out."

"I'll turn on the TV."

"No, Tom." Helen was surprised by her own quick abruptness.

"No, no. I'll keep at it. I just thought…" He was back in the kitchen. The living room was silent until Glenn returned.

"I got a recording, a message stating that this flight was the one involved in an accident on landing at Los Angeles. It gave some other numbers to call for more details but not as yet. Why don't you just stay here for a while?" Glenn's voice cracked in a way Tom had never heard it before. He continued, "Jack, I don't want to jump the gun, but you could have heard the same thing I'm going to tell you on the radio. I'm sorry, but it didn't sound good. The reporter said he didn't see much chance for survivors. It crashed and burned."

Jack slumped back. "Oh, God."

Glenn got up and took the glass from his hand. His other hand had draped across his eyes so that his face was hidden except for his mouth. Tom noticed him biting his lip as he had seen him do before that evening.

"Let's get to bed," Helen said, standing, her hand on Tom's shoulder.

"You think about this moment so often, but when it gets here, you're not ready for it at all." Jack was sitting up now, his elbows on his knees. He looked at no one. "I better call her parents. Good night, Tombo."

"I'm awful sorry about the wreck and all. Maybe she'll be all right."

Hearing his son say the words he himself had wanted to say filled Glenn's eyes with tears.

"Good night, Dad."

Glenn nodded, but no words came. Tom followed his mother from the room.

"Hey, Tom." Jack fought to control his voice. "There's one thing…could you tell Benjie…" His voice broke, and he buried his face in his hands.

★★★★★

The shopping center was deserted by now as Jack strolled across the parking lot from his car. He somehow wanted to be a part of this loneliness, to be swallowed up by it. He did not have to think because he couldn't. He sat on the curb, staring at the pavement, unconscious of time, unaware of noise or the humid heat which the still-warm parking lot radiated beneath him. He was suddenly startled by something squeezing its way into his lap. He sat bolt upright but couldn't get away from a cat which looked straight into his eyes. Both sat motionless until Jack stroked the animal slowly. It settled across his legs as if it knew this would be the reaction for which it had patiently waited. Reality and consciousness were unwelcome, but they came with that cat. Jack realized his sorrow and maddening hollowness within him while the cat showed no signs of its own loneliness. How everything had changed! He thought about his job, about Glenn Becker's offer, about the baseball team. Nothing seemed to matter; the future was as unwelcome as the cat which had so rudely intruded.

Headlights splashed across him from across the lot, and a car sped closer.

"See ya tomorrow," a girl whispered to someone inside as she closed the door.

"See ya!" The car moved on, and Jack's privacy was once again broken.

"Hi." Her voice was so soft, almost sad sounding, not obtrusive. She seemed to be asking him for a reply, not forcing one.

Jack nodded. "Hello." *The party is growing*, he thought.

"Is that your cat?"

"Pardon!" He looked into her face and was captivated. Her look was one of apologies for her intrusion. It was as if she knew of his troubles or was used to her own.

"Is that your cat?"

"No. It just sorta come here while I was sitting here. I don't know."

"It's always around here. I see it all the time. I'm going to paint a picture of him some time.

"Good."

She sat nearby and shared the silence. Both were motionless until Jack slowly turned toward her for another look.

"Bad one, huh?" she whispered.

"Right."

"How long ago?"

"Not very."

"What was it?"

"Bad news." Again his voice failed him. He managed a whisper softer than hers. "Bad news."

"I've got a joint…if that would help." Her voice was asking a question. Jack didn't have an answer. For a moment, nothing made sense.

He drew in a deep breath and looked at her. He felt himself smile and was pleased that he still could. Finally, the words came. "I guess we're not talking about the same thing. Maybe you think I'm tripping or freaked out or whatever you want to call it. Well, little girl"—his voice again dropped to a whisper—"my kind of bad news is the kind you can get over the telephone, and I don't think your joint is going to be able to help much…but thanks anyway."

He placed the cat gently in her lap and stood to walk toward his car. "Good night," he offered.

Her reply was a whisper. "Good night."

⋆⋆⋆⋆⋆

Glenn lay in bed thinking yet trying not to. The day's events were a puzzle to him, and he, for once, didn't know what his next move should be. The telephone startled him, and he switched on a light. He caught it on the second ring.

"Dr. Becker, this is Jack."

"Oh, yeah, what can I do—"

"Is that job still open?"

"Of course. I can't see why it—"

"I'll take it."

"Jack, that's wonderful. I can't tell you how great that is."

Glenn couldn't think of anything to say, then he realized he didn't have to. The line was dead.

✦✦✦✦✦

It was second period before Glenn had gotten through enough of his paperwork to have noticed the note he had written himself the afternoon before. He would have to find out what the same old problem was. He glanced at the clock; classes would be changing in fifteen minutes. He could catch Jim Parks between periods. After quickly completing a memorandum to all teachers about year-end book collections, he left his office, glad to be away from his desk for a few moments. Giggling in the locker area ahead told him he had been spotted. Three girls could be seen dashing to safety in the restrooms. He decided to ignore it but would use this time to generally inspect one of the locker areas for damages and need of repairs. The bell sounded, filling the halls with noise and confusion. He had often thought of the sheer magnitude of the logistics of moving four hundred people from one place where they didn't want to be to another such place—all within four minutes! Looking at it that way, it was easier for him to live a few tardies, but he realized the tardies were invariably the same few people, and he couldn't help noticing the racial consistencies within that problem.

Jim was joking with a boy about his baseball game of last weekend, but the conversation dissolved as Glenn entered the room. Recognizing the student, Glenn asked, "You a pitcher like your brother?"

"He's a pitcher," Jim fired back. "But not like his brother."

They all laughed until the two men were alone in the room.

"I know you don't have much time, Jim," Glenn began. "But I was curious about something you said yesterday at the meeting."

"I probably said too much."

"No, no, and it wasn't about the drugs. Remember when there was a commotion before we got started?" With his head, he beckoned toward the hall and began to move in that direction for the privacy all its confusion might afford them.

"Yes, some Black girls were going at it. I don't remember who they were, but Don might."

"Well, somebody mentioned something about the heat or that tempers flared for some reason, and I *think* you said, 'Same old reason' or 'same old problem,' which I took to mean that you knew the reason and it was often the same reason. Did I get that correct, or am I reading in too much?"

"Oh, I see what you're after." Jim paused to choose his words carefully. "Put it his way—the Black girls around here are the first ones to get hurt. Normally you would expect these kids to pair off one-for-one. There are about as many White girls in an uproar and very jealous—even though they themselves may not like the particular boy or want to have anything to do with him. This is the way I interpret it, at least. They all feel threatened and, as they say, put down. There's friction. They seem to realize it's no longer one-for-one. The fight I've noticed, in other words, that is among girls, is over boys."

The sounding of the bell did not interrupt their conversation though Jim used it as an excuse to look down the hall. "Now how do you see it on the other side of the realm?"

"You mean the White boys?"

"If your theory were correct, wouldn't that explain any fights among White boys, and if so, why don't we have any?"

Jim smiled and looked down at the floor "They don't want to have anything to do with a girl after she has started following a Black. They probably didn't want to have anything to do with her before she did, and that's why she gets into it in the first place."

"Sounds like you've got it pretty well-thought-out."

"And you think it's an oversimplification. Are you going to try to find out what started that fight yesterday?"

Glenn grinned. "No, no, but I'll be watching. Thanks, Jim."

*****

It was noon recess before Tom had gotten to talk to Benjie. As usual, he was not hard to find and was by himself, leaning up against the wall by the door as if ready to return to the classroom as soon as the bell rang.

"Did you hear about the plane crash yesterday?"

Benjie was startled that Tom would even stop to talk to him. "No. Where?"

"Well, Jack's girlfriend is a stewardess…"

"Yeah, I know." His voice was eager.

"She was on it, and she's dead. I'm supposed to tell you, I guess, about not going out to the airport this afternoon. "Understand?"

Benjie nodded slowly and turned toward the door. Tom watched as he entered the building.

*****

The parking lot glistened as a light breeze made wavelets of the puddles which remained from the evening shower. The wet pavement made the traffic noise much more obtrusive as Jack leaned in the doorway. He wasn't certain why he had returned to his particular spot at this particular time, but he did find himself looking with anticipation for the young girl who had seemed so much at home here. Anyway, he himself could be unnoticed here yet maintain his contact with bustle of the rest of the world. Centerstage would come tomorrow at the funeral; for now, he was most comfortable in solitude. His thinking was brought into focus when a familiar cat rounded the corner, its fur damp but its steps deliberate.

Seeing it brought an instant excitement within him. If the cat would come, surely the girl would also. He was sure now that she was the reason for his lonely vigil. He scooped the cat up into his arms as if holding it there would make the girl come to him. Should he walk about the shopping center in hopes of finding her, or would that cause him to miss her here? He decided to wait. His thoughts again returned to tomorrow's ordeal. Janice's death was now a reality to him. The ceremony would not be a comfort, and he wanted it behind him.

It would be good to see both his brothers though the circumstances would not be ideal for a family reunion.

Jack knew his own life had found purpose and he would survive this blow. He had laughed within to realize that here he was waiting for some young schoolgirl because he was going to launch his own that he so quickly was able to occupy himself with a new diversion so as to dilute the grief he knew he felt.

He tried not to move when he saw a solitary figure approaching from the shadows across the parking lot. He could feel his excitement rising, and the satisfied confidence he got from finding himself able to anticipate another person's actions made him slouch even more deliberately against the doorway and give all his overt attentions to the cat. It was as if he were some spy having planned a rendezvous or sprung a trap into which his contact had unwittingly fallen. Long before he was able to recognize the girl's face, he was certain it was her floating toward him.

She greeted him exactly as she had before. "Hi."

He nodded but held on to the cat, which had squirmed to face her as she sat on the curb.

"It's a little wet, don't you think?"

"So I'll get wet too. No matter."

"Good enough for you, good enough for me," he said, sitting beside her. "Sorry, kind of walked out on you the other night."

She turned toward him and squinted slightly, examining him and questioning him at the same time.

He felt his confidence slip, and he hurried to bridge the gap in their communication. "Remember? I was sitting here when you got out of somebody's car the other night." He placed the cat in her lap, humbled that he had not created the impression on her that she had on him.

"Oh, yeah. Hi." All she could offer beyond that was a smile.

"Well, did you paint a picture of him yet? Of the cat?"

"You've got a good memory. No, I didn't, but I will. Do you live around here?"

"In the apartments. How about yourself?"

"Down on Gillette."

"What, that's pretty far especially this time of night. Are you waiting for somebody?"

"Waiting for somebody?"

That mimic—that repetition—and the forlorn expression almost made Jack hug her. It said so much, yet it said so little. He was fascinated and uncomfortable.

"I mean, you know, is somebody in your family coming to get you or anything?"

She had made him uncomfortable; she had made him feel sorry for her, and her look as she gazed at him said that she was sorry for having done both. Her ability to speak with her eyes held Jack captive. He knew no one was coming for her and that she didn't want anyone to. He wanted to hold her, as she was holding the cat, to comfort her.

Finally, she spoke. "Now you think I come from some kind of rotten family or no family at all. You're wrong. I have a mother and a father, and they both live at home. They both are artists, which is why I like art. My dad works for a living, and my mother is at home every day doing all the things your basic mother should be at home doing. There are seven of us kids." She turned toward him as if to give this last information special punctuation.

"Nothing like a big family, I suppose. Is that what you want to have when you're grown?"

"When I'm grown, I won't have a family. I don't even want to get married."

"Yeah, right." There was another long pause. "Well, anyway, I'm sorry the way I walked out on you the other night."

She shrugged, but he was not going to let it drop that easily.

"I guess we just weren't talking about the same thing, were we?" He was forcing an answer now and confident she would have to talk about drugs.

"I guess we weren't talking about the same thing."

His body slumped, then he started to chuckle softly. "You're too much."

"Because I don't talk about what you want to talk about?"

"Okay, okay, we'll talk about something else. Where do you go to school?"

"Yeah, that's pretty routine," she answered softly. They both looked at each other and burst out laughing.

"I go to West Junior High," she continued before fully stopping her laughter. "I'm in the eighth grade."

"West, huh? Ya hear a lot about that place. Tell me the truth."

"What you hear is the truth." She got up, and he took his cue. They began to walk. "It's true about the race troubles…if that's what you mean."

"What kind of troubles?"

"Race troubles are when people of two different races can't get along." They were laughing again.

Jack could see he was going to get nowhere into any deep conversation with this young spirit. "Where are we going?" he finally asked.

Home. I am, at least. Where are you going?"

"I might walk along with you part of the way. I know better than to ask you to my apartment!"

"I'm glad to hear it," she joked.

"Glad to hear what?"

"That you know better than to invite me to your apartment."

"Maybe some other time—since we're neighbors and all. Who is the principal over at West?"

She seemed a bit surprised at so sudden a change in the topic of conversation, but she answered matter-of-factly, "His name is Becker."

"Sounds like you don't care for him." He was baiting her, he realized, because it didn't sound at all like she didn't like him.

"No, he's okay. I really don't have too much to do with him…if you know what I mean. My brothers have, but they would probably say he's okay too."

"Do your brothers get into a lot of trouble or something?"

"Yeah, most trouble is handled by the assistant principal, but he's Black and not very well-liked. Anyway, the kind of trouble my brothers usually get into can't he handled too well by a Black."

"I'm supposed to ask what kind of trouble that is."

"If you want to, but I thought we were talking about the principal."

"Well, please tell me what kind of trouble it is and talk about the principal."

"They get into fights, and he's very calm. He never gets steamed."

"Are you saying he never gets mad or that he never shows his anger?"

"What's the difference?"

"There's a great deal of difference, but you've got to answer my question."

"I guess he has to get mad. There's plenty over there to get mad at, that's for sure."

Jack was pleased with himself at the way he could set her up to get more information out of her. Her reluctance to talk about his topics seemed to be slipping away.

"So why can't a Black assistant principal deal with drug problems?"

Now she was confused and registered it plainly. Jack saw that he had jumped to the wrong conclusion.

"What do you mean?'

"Didn't you say the assistant principal couldn't help with your brothers' troubles?"

"I think I said that they can't be handled by him very well."

"Okay, okay, so why can't he?"

"Oh, you think my brothers have drug problems. No, they just get into a lot of fights."

Jack laughed and turned toward her. "With Blacks."

"Right on," she kidded. "There's no way they are going to sit and listen to a Black assistant principal scold them either. Actually, it's not that they are all that anti-Black. It's just that they can't stand Mr. Bemis—nobody can—but one time when they did get into a fight with some Blacks, the principal dealt with it."

"So now they just paste a n——— every once in a while just so they won't ever have to talk to Mr. What's-his-name."

"I guess." Her answer was less than thoughtful, perhaps, Jack thought, because he had thrown her off guard with "n———."

"They're not so dumb. Seems like they could just go to the principal and say they can't stand the guy…"

"Mr. Bemis."

"Yeah, Mr. Bemis, and that they would rather have Dr. Becker deal with them whenever necessary. Of course, the obvious answer is to just stay out of trouble, and then nobody would deal with them."

"Dr. Becker?"

"Okay, okay, so I know him slightly. I just wanted to see what you had to say about him. Seems like your brothers could just stay clear of trouble if they are so against this Bemis guy."

"You don't know Jeff and Randy."

"True. See that window up there on the corner? That's my room. Bring 'em up some time, then you won't be able to say I don't know them."

"Do you work somewhere? I mean, what do you do?"

"Yeah, I have my little job, and then I come home and have nothing to do. I work at an electrical company, in their warehouse. Very important position," he added sarcastically.

"You married?"

"No, hey, I'm glad I got to talk to you. I'm interested in something you said about the principal having plenty to be mad at, but maybe you better get home now. Do you come by the shopping center often?"

"Every day."

"You mean every night."

"Every night."

"See ya."

"Later," she answered.

He turned toward the doorway and reached for his key but couldn't help glancing back toward her one last time. He was disappointed that she didn't do likewise, but her walk, her glide, so graceful and quiet, again caught his attention as she disappeared into the shadows.

3

The parlor was just about empty, and the late afternoon sun burned through the stained glass windows to fall softly across the casket. Jack had not had so much as a moment alone with Janice, and now the burden of his own sorrow hit him. Gazing into the casket at the face he would see no more, his mind raced back over so much time. He could not think of a time he had not known and loved her. What would life be without this companion, this part of him upon which he had come to rely, to enjoy, to want to share so much? He felt very weak as he turned toward his two brothers, the only people in the room. His expression must have told them that he would be alone now for a short time. They nodded and walked together toward the parking lot where he knew they would be waiting for him.

Now he didn't have to control himself or his emotions. What a relief it was to relax and let himself be carried by his grief. Tears came, and his vision of the face before him became clouded. He made no move to dry his face though he could feel tears rolling down his cheeks. *Why?* was his only thought—over and over? *Why to us? Everything was going to be so great.* The room became gradually darker with the sun's absence. *I love you—I always will. You were right. We could have married. We should have married.* With a resolve which *seemed* to strengthen him, Jack reached a decision which made him feel good within. *You'll always be the only one. I will always love you.*

Finally, he dried his eyes with the handkerchief he had been conscious of placing in his back pocket earlier that morning. He almost had to laugh at himself, remembering how he had thought then that he would never use it but how it would be the thing to have in case someone else did.

The heat and humidity jolted him as he swung the door open onto the nearly deserted parking lot. Sure enough, Ken and Jim were there waiting, the engine of Jim's car running. Neither noticed as he approached, so he jounced all his weight on the rear fender playfully before opening the rear door.

"What the hell…," Jim said, not looking back.

"Let's get something to eat," Jack said. "How about a hamburger or something."

"I don't know," his older brother, Ken, considered. "We're all three dressed up, which hasn't happened in quite a long time. Let's go someplace decent. I'll buy."

"I'll drive," Jim announced innocently.

"I'll eat," Jack chimed in.

The three rode in silence until Jim asked the logical question, "Where we going?"

"There's a steak house just past the shopping center up here. It's not bad. I ate there once with…" Jack's voice trailed off. "Yeah, right."

Neither brother could think of anything to say to fill the painful void, and they both jumped when Jack yelled, "Hey, pull over into the parking lot! Up there by the drugstore!"

The car lurched as Jim applied the brakes more than they should have been. The tires squealed, protesting the sharpness of the turn into the lot, and Jim gunned the engine with an urgency he felt but could not explain to himself. He saw a young girl—*not bad-looking*, he reflected—and two guys strolling between the parked cars, but he didn't see anything which had caused the excitement Jack had radiated. "Where to?"

"This is fine." Jack had the door open before the car stopped. "I'll be right back." Off he went toward the threesome, his coat flying in the breeze. He squeezed between two cars and emerged just in front of the three.

"Hey, what's up? Which one's Jeff, and which one's Randy?"

"Who's this?" The taller boy wanted to know. His question was not going to be answered though—not yet.

"Hi, that's Randy. That's Jeff." Jack thrust out his hand and heard himself announcing his own name, but he was listening to the girl's voice. "I thought you worked in a warehouse or something. You don't look like it. Looks like you been to a funeral or a wedding."

Jack relaxed his grip on Randy's hand, and Jean knew as soon as the words tumbled out that she had said the wrong thing.

Jack smiled the grin she loved, but she couldn't look at it long. "You're right on target," Jack assured her.

Seeing her discomfort, he placed his arm around her waist. "It's okay. I should have told you last night. I don't know why I didn't."

"Now, hang on," Randy began, sounding impatient. "Like, what's the deal?"

"No deal, no deal," Jean assured him. "He's okay. Later, all right?" Her raised eyebrows let everyone know that later would be all right and that for now, no explanations were needed nor forthcoming.

"Anyway, I got two brothers too and they're in that car and we're going to get something to eat before I have to return to sob duty. You got a pencil in there?" Jack asked, pointing to the purse slung across her shoulder.

"Yeah, sure. Why?"

"Well, it would be great if you would call me later tonight. No big deal, but it helped last night. I figure it couldn't do any harm tonight." The pencil was procured, and Jack made a deliberate show of looking back toward his brothers when he noticed Jeff moving between him and the opened purse. He scrawled his number on the edge of a piece of paper and handed the pencil back to her.

"Later. See you guys around." He nodded to each of them.

"Did I say I'll explain everything?" Jack said, cutting off any and all questions asked by his brothers. "The steak house is down in the next block, but just stay in the parking lot."

With orders placed, Jack began to recount the events of the last several days: the invitation to join the junior high faculty, his role in the drug attack, his chance meeting with the girl, and now his meeting the brothers who, he realized, were into drugs seriously—or at least he preferred to think so.

"What is it with this drug thing anyway?" he asked his older brother, expecting to get a medically sound answer.

"What do you want to know?" was the simple reply.

"Well, you're the doctor. I want to know everything from your point of view. I don't know anything, really."

Jim had lit up a cigarette and shot a plume of smoke ceiling-ward, which Ken watched as he began to speak slowly. "First of all, don't equate it to what you see there. If that little girl uses marijuana, it is not for the same reason that Jim uses cigarettes. He says he enjoys it or he says it relaxes him, but I submit it is the smoking, not the smoke. Therein lies the difference. The thing I think we have to keep in mind is simply this about drugs—it's fun—and you've got to say that to yourself over and over again. Try to conceive fun in its most elemental, its most basic way. All the choicest possible ingredients of fun can be found in that marijuana."

The conversation stopped as salads were placed before them, and Jim snubbed his cigarette; whether self-consciously or not, Jack was not certain.

"Okay, but is it harmful? Is it habit-forming? You know, what does it do? These are the things I want to know about."

"Sure, and you want to know them right now, and you want the answers in neat, foolproof packages of well-proven information." He smiled and dug into his salad.

"Whether it's habit-forming," Jim interjected, "seems to me to be up to the individual."

"Whether it's habit-forming depends upon whether you're talking about the physical or nonphysical." Ken was trying not to let the conversation interfere with his salad, but he rushed on with all the authority he could display. "Everybody is in the habit of having fun…particularly kids." His fork was pointed at Jack. "And don't forget these are kids. All this crap about drug education seems to forget that one basic fact. You can't stuff a kid's head full of factual information about anything and then expect him to use this information to make an adultlike decision. Our highway fatalities prove that. We all know that driving fast can kill you, but look at the numbers of kids who drive fast and get killed."

Jack's eyes dropped.

"Sorry," said Ken softly, thus beginning another difficult period of silence. At least the three of them had a salad to lavish attention upon.

Again, it was Jack who broke the silence. "All right, I buy all that, and it is a good point, a real good one. As I understand it, that won't be my role anyway though I probably would be more comfortable if I had those neat foolproof answers like you say…"

"I can send you all the medical journals you would ever want. They all say just about the same thing. We don't know for certain. Somebody finds brain-cell-structure change, somebody else finds this, and somebody else finds that. I figure it will be six or seven years, at least, before we know much for sure and longer than that in the area of chromosome damage. That will be a whole new ball game."

"Amen, but here's what is on my mind, at least one thing… should I try the stuff? Should I be able to speak from a point of experience with these kids? It seems to me they might respect that. It would all be that much more credible."

Jim spoke now. "The difference between humans and all other kinds of animals is that we don't have to experience something to learn about it. We don't have to experiment with everything. We can learn from other people or even animals who have learned firsthand. A dog has to experience something before he can learn it. We don't. They call it vicarious learning." He nodded and went back to his salad as if to show that there need be no more talk of drug usage for any reason.

"Oh, do they? Where are you whipping these words from anyway? What was that? Vicarious learning? Sounds great."

"It's a point well taken. I wouldn't suggest going the drug route for educational reasons because you would only be kidding yourself—or at least you'd never really know for sure. You could be just using that for an excuse, and in all your Army time, you're telling me you weren't…exposed…to drugs?"

"Well, sure it was there plenty. I just didn't get…I don't know. I wasn't interested, but now I just thought for the sake of learning…"

"That's called rationalizing," Jim threw in with a smile.

Both older brothers grinned as if to show they would patiently tolerate the younger. "Jesus Christ, I certainly don't want to be unvicariously rationalizing now, do I?"

"No, seriously," Ken began again. "You will be in a much stronger position if you are able to say you are have never used the stuff—even in the position you are in now—than if you have to say, 'Yes, I used it just to see what it was like.' That will come off as a weakness rather than a strength in my opinion."

"Should it be made legal?"

Simultaneously, both brothers answered him, but they disagreed and stared at each other in surprise.

"You can't legislate morality," Jim began. "It will never work and never has."

"There's your difference," Ken began, ignoring the waitress who was serving him. "You're thinking of it along moral lines, and I like to think I'm considering the physical ones. If it's dangerous, the public has to be protected."

"Follow that to its logical conclusion, and you have to eliminate automobiles, planes, and the works."

"Jack was looking down at his meal by the time Jim had realized the touchiness of the subject he had mentioned. "Man," he said. "You can't get away from it. I'm sorry."

"Yeah, right. It's going to happen, and maybe every plane wreck or even every plane I see is going to bring it back, but that will have to be dealt with as it happens. I agree with you, by the way, about legalization. It seems to me the government is stepping out of bounds when its starts telling people how and how not to mess themselves up."

"But let's back up one paragraph," Ken insisted. "Your bit about having to eliminate cars because people get hurt in them is not analogous. That results from misuse, not from the inherent properties of the car itself."

Jack waved all that aside with his hand as if to show that he had more pressing problems to worry about. "You guys aren't going to stick around tonight, are you? You're not expected to."

With that, the whole drug topic was dropped, and Jack's attentions were divided somewhere between his steak dinner and tomorrow's funeral plans and what to do afterward.

"Going to do any racing this year?" Jim wanted to know.

"Boy, I haven't even thought about that lately. I'd sure like to. God, I'm going to need something for a while. Could turn into a long summer."

"Take things as they come for a while."

"I'd love to get a car and really do it right this time. Who knows…?"

The subject of cars didn't come up again until the three had left and were walking toward Jim's car. "I never did drive this one," Jack hinted, whereupon Jim flipped him the keys.

"A car's a car," he said indifferently.

"Now there you go," Jack protested. "They're all different, and each has good points and bad ones. I'll show you what I mean."

This time Ken slid into the back seat. Jack accelerated to an open area of the parking lot and made several sharp turns, first one way then the other. The passengers swayed back and forth violently, Jim holding a cigarette up deliberately missing his mouth to amplify the motion. "What the hell does this prove?" he insisted.

The car straightened out. "That you need about four pounds in the right front tire."

"I'll have it checked right after my whiplash examination." He looked to the back seat, where Ken was shaking his head in bewilderment. Suddenly Jack got serious as they approached the funeral parlor.

"Thanks for the meal. You're going to be over at the folks' house?"

"Right."

"I'll probably drop by later."

It was after he had said this that he remembered the phone call he was expecting. *No matter*, he thought. *That's a long way off.*

The first hour or so of the evening brought on an entirely different feeling than Jack had experienced while alone that afternoon. A distance had developed, an unattached feeling which made him able to deal with people in an almost businesslike manner. It was as if he felt sorry for them rather than they for him. His resolve to never marry another girl became more ingrained and gave him strength, knowing that through this, he could show his devotion to Janice. It made the funeral nonessential and very temporal. The people coming to show their respects or pity had little effect upon Jack now, and he could deal with them comfortably.

Above the faces in the crowd, he saw Dr. Becker's and moved toward him to find that Mrs. Becker and Tom were with him. Beside Tom stood Benjie, bewildered looking but silent and serious. Glenn's large hand was outstretched, and the two shook silently.

Finally, Jack said, "Thanks for coming. Mrs. Becker, Tom, thanks for coming." He reached to shake Benjie's hand. "Hey, pal, I appreciate you coming. I hope you got a chance to sign the register. Tom, you met Janice, didn't you? Come here." He walked between the two boys, one hand on each of their shoulders. Helen gave a startled sigh, almost a protest, but Glenn gently squeezed her hand reassuringly.

They watched as the three approached the casket and kneeled briefly. The anxiety left Helen's face as the threesome stood and Jack began talking to first one boy then the other, seemingly answering questions, making gestures which are so much a part of everyday conversation.

"I like the way this guy operates," Glenn whispered.

"I'd like to know what they are saying," Helen finally answered.

The three stood close to the coffin for several minutes, and as if by prearrangement, everyone else in the room respected their privacy. No one moved until Jack led them away to a couch nearby where he sat between them. Glenn and Helen paid their respects and joined the others at the couch.

Benjie had been contemplating his shoes but was first to break the uneasy silence. "You were going to get married, weren't you?"

"Yep."

"Were you still going to be our baseball coach?"

"Well, I guess. Why not?"

"Would she still have been a stewardess after you got married?"

"Probably, for a while. You see, I'm looking for little better job right now, and if we were married, we probably would have needed to have her working too for a while."

Glenn interrupted at that point. "You're not looking for a job anymore, I hope. I talked to our superintendent, and it looks good. You haven't changed your mind, have you?"

"No, no. I just didn't know how final it all was." Thinking of the job offer reminded him of the phone call he hoped to get later that evening. He looked his watch involuntarily, which Helen took as a cue for them to leave.

"We must go now," she announced, rising, the others standing as if relieved of a great weight.

"Jack, we're sorry. You know you have our sympathy and support," Glenn said, extending his hand.

"Thanks, its means more than I can say. Thanks for coming, Tom. Thanks, Benjie, Mrs. Becker." The two nodded.

The phone startled Jack, but he pounced on it before the second ring. "Hello."

"Hi." The voice was soft and unmistakable.

"We've got a problem."

"We've got a problem?"

"Yeah, you call me up, and you don't even know what name to say hello to, and I don't know what name to say hello back to. That's a problem."

"Try Jean."

"And my name is Jack Flemming, and I'll bet you called more out of curiosity than anything else, right?"

"You left me a little surprised this afternoon, also Jeff and Randy. I didn't know what to say to them, but I did remember that your name is Jack."

"Well, I'm sorry for the confusion this afternoon. Things have been kind of rough for the last couple of days, and when I saw you this afternoon, I just wanted to stop and say hi. I didn't really think about what I was doing."

"You said you had to go to a funeral?"

"Well, the funeral parlor. The funeral is tomorrow."

"Whose?"

"It was a friend of mine." Jack reflected upon the way she had asked whose funeral it was—so softly yet so simply. Her voice, so innocent of deceit, made it clear she expected to be given a full answer; the silence on the other end of the line told him she knew she had not gotten one.

"It was my girlfriend," he blurted. "She was a stewardess on that plane."

"I know why you didn't tell me the other night and why you still didn't want to tell me now. It's because you don't want a lot of sympathy stuff. You don't like to show your emotions."

"I've been told that."

"Well, whether you like it or not, I'm sorry, and it makes me feel important to be asked to call you when things are going bad like this. I suppose you were going to get married soon."

"Yep."

"I told you how I feel. Now you tell me."

"You're too much. How do I feel?"

"I didn't know what time to call. I tried earlier, but you weren't home yet. That's when I figured the funeral was for somebody pretty close to you. I had it all figured out—at least I thought I did. I even knew what I wanted to say."

"It's always nice to be prepared. What were you going to say? I'll listen to anything."

"Oh, is that it?" laughed Jack.

"No, I mean, whenever I'm sad, I like to talk about it to some-body...even if it's just myself."

"You do have things pretty well figured out."

"So tell me how you feel."

"Hollow." The silence lasted seemingly for minutes until Jack continued. He could tell that his voice may have quivered, but he felt the same way he had when he was alone in the funeral parlor; it felt good to let his emotions carry him away. "Hollow and alone and mad." The last word came out as a whine, and he regretted it. "The trouble is there's really nothing to be mad at."

"Which is why you're mad."

"But most of all, I feel hollow, and I think that's bad because I have a hard time making anything else seem important."

"Why should things seem important?" she asked simply.

"Now that's you talking…for me it's different. For one thing, I'm older, and…"

"When you're older, things should seem important."

"I mean I'm not a kid. I can't just spend the rest of the time thinking about my own little problems."

"Big problems."

"Okay, they're big problems. I just wish I could get over this feeling. Maybe the funeral will help—sort of bring it all to an end, you know what I mean?"

"I read that that's what funerals are for according to some expert or something."

"Oh, now we have experts on funerals. Lovely."

"I know how you feel, and I'm sorry."

"Hey, I'm glad you called, don't get me wrong. I want to keep talking for a while. Well, now I say I know your brothers though I can't really say I remember which one is which."

"Jeff is the tall one."

"Jeff got a little uptight too. What, did he think I would bust you?"

"You've just got to understand Jeff, that's all."

"Well, maybe someday. Am I keeping you up too late?" Jack was almost apologetic.

"No, I'm always the last one to go to bed around here. It's still early anyway," she assured him.

"Suppose a person like me who has a real good reason for feeling sorry for himself wanted to take something just for the fun of it, what would you suggest?"

"Grass…for a person like you."

"Meaning what?"

"Grass doesn't do any harm. With a little practice, it can be great. The problem is people try it once and get nothing from it. It's not a fair judgment."

"Oh, I'd want to be fair, by all means," Jack teased.

"Why don't you try some?"

"Why don't you just tell me about it so I don't have to?"

"There's no way you are going anywhere out of listening to somebody tell you about a high."

"If there is such a thing as a high," Jack answered authoritatively. "And not just a matter of imagination. You should be able to describe it. I should be able to learn about marijuana from somebody else."

"No, you really should try it. You can't learn about something like this without the experience."

"Jean, that's the difference between man and all other animals. We can learn through others' experience. We don't have to experience things ourselves. It's called vicarious learning. Now a dog, that's different. A dog can't learn anything without first experiencing it."

"I had never thought about that, and I'm sure you know much more about things like this than I do, but there's no way I can tell you how to experiences grass. There's just no way!"

"So tell me why use it, then maybe I'll understand what it does and how it makes you feel. Why do you like to feel high?"

There was a long silence. She finally began. "Even that is hard to say. I guess it's partly because of everybody else who is doing it."

Jack almost interrupted but checked himself. At least she was talking. Silence, he was to discover, was the best way to learn anything. His patience was rewarded.

"I can't say it's all because of the group though. I can think right now about being high and I know I'd enjoy it just as much and I'm really by myself."

"Thanks a lot," Jack teased.

"You know what I mean."

"Yeah, right."

"It's like when you're high, you can be in any situation you want to be in. This might not be the right thing to say, but you could be with your girlfriend right now and everything would be real and just as…" She again paused.

"Realistic?"

"Well, yeah, but I mean pleasant. Just as pleasant as they ever were. Do you know what I mean?"

"I think so. It still wouldn't change anything though, would it?"

"Here comes the lecture."

Jack was amazed at himself, at her, at the course of the conversation. He was shocked at how readily she had picked up his motive. The challenge stimulated him.

"You want a lecture?"

"No thanks."

"That's good because I sure don't have one ready. I think all I said was that things wouldn't change."

"I didn't mean you could bring back the dead. It's you that would change—your feelings, your emotions, I guess."

"And what do you know about emotions?" Jack was satisfied with himself for putting her on the defensive. He realized he was smiling, and he felt the same thrill as if he were driving in a race. The feeling grew stronger with each second she remained silent. He would again wait her out.

Finally, she spoke. The softness of her voice was captivating. "So now we have experts on emotions. Lovely."

"You are too much. Aren't your parents after you to go to bed?"

"I'm not after them to get up. Why should they be after me to go to bed?"

"I see. All your homework done?"

"Yeah. I have a study hall."

"You know there's a song about you?"

"Song about me?"

"Well, a song named 'Jean.'"

"And you're going to sing it to me?"

"No, no. That's not my bag, but I'll go over the words after we hang up to see if they fit."

"Should I hope they do or not?"

"Well, I like the song. Anyway, some time I might be able to tell you a little better how much it means to me that you called. You're a neat person, but there's one little problem, maybe." Her silence compelled him to rush into an explanation. "You know, if we start bumping into each other regularly up at the shopping center then either of us doesn't show up for some reason, the other one might feel…?" He couldn't find a word.

"I understand, and I'm glad you said that 'cause sometimes I don't go up there. I feel so helpless. I know how bad you must feel, and I feel bad with you, but what can I say?"

"From you, every word helps."

"I'm sure you'll meet someone else. I guess that's kind of a dumb thing to say."

"Well, no. It's just that I feel like I don't want anyone else—ever. We had such a special…I just don't think anyone else will ever replace or even come close." He could feel that same wave of grief rushing over him but could say no more. He didn't want to break.

He had to strain to hear her voice, but her whispered words soothed him. "I think it's neat that you loved her so much that you don't even want to try to replace her. She must have been so special! I hope it helps you to know that I don't feel sorry just for you. I feel sorry myself because I'll never get to meet her and I wish I could and I hope the words of the song fit."

Jack wished he could simply nod in answer, but silence would have to suffice while he fought to control his emotions and his voice. He thought of how well this young girl expressed herself with her eyes and now with words; he wished he could do that himself now. Finally, he whispered back, "You're super."

"I wish I could do something to help."

Another long silence, almost painful.

"You can. We'll talk about it the next time we bump into each other…and thanks for your help tonight."

"Good night."

"Good night."

4

Jean lay in bed thinking—thinking about whether to use the phone again. There were several people whom she could call, and she realized it was difficult to make up her mind. The only thing that kept her fingers off the dial was the clock near her bed. Its hands showed one thirty, and it was always hard for her to call people that late. She held the receiver to her ear, listening aimlessly to the tone, wishing she were still talking to Jack Flemming and realizing he had dominated her thoughts for the last two hours. She became aware of a sound she had never heard and could not identify. She pressed her ear closer to the receiver then realized it was not coming from the phone. She hung up, and the roaring sound was now more distinct, but still she could not identify it nor tell whether it came from outside the house or not. Fear gripped her and made her decide to get up to investigate. She knew she was the only one awake and had been for an hour or more.

Opening the door to her room, she could smell smoke, and the roar was now clearly coming from somewhere straight below her. She pounded on the door across the hall, hoping to awaken her three younger brothers, and she heard her own voice screaming, "Fire, fire," as she raced toward her parents' bedroom. The stairwell was brightly lighted, but she saw no actual flames; the hall light switch did not work as she automatically hit it in passing. She flung her parents' door open and could see the form of her father stirring. "Fire. The whole house is on fire."

"Get the kids," came her father's firm reply. He pulled his wife across the bed and landed her on her feet. "Here we go."

Allen was crying as Jean led the three youngest into the hall. He raced to his mother's arms amid screams of confusion. Smoke was oppressive, and they all could see that by now there was no hope of using the stairs. Jean felt her father push the group back toward her own bedroom, and she joined in herding the family through the door. She watched as her father leaned out the window and felt the roof of the porch with his hand.

"Out you go, quick," he said to Jean. She was through in an instant, not caring about the knock she had taken on the forehead trying to duck through so quickly in the darkness. Smoke was billowing up from the rear side of the porch, and Jean's first reaction was to race toward the front and jump into the shrubbery.

"Keep 'em together," her father was saying as he handed the youngest through the window. Jean grabbed Allen by the hand, Timmy and Paul scampered through silently, and Jean was proud of her mother's gracefulness stepping swiftly through the opening. A crash could be heard somewhere below, and for some reason, Jean explained it to herself that the living room sofa had fallen through to the basement, but there wasn't much time to think about that. They edged along the wall toward the front of the house, then Jean saw her father take a running leap into the bushes below.

"Ouch 'em off," was his command heard above the roar of the fire and the screaming of all three young ones. "I'll get 'em." Feeling warmth under her bare feet made it easier to push them; it seemed the roof could hold up no longer. The three were handled nicely and were huddling on the lawn near the sidewalk.

"Come on, Mama. I've got to get the boys," came the next command, and Jean saw her mother jump, engulfed in her own nightgown. Jean heard, "Get off that roof," and felt herself land in the bushes. Her mother and father were picking themselves off the ground. "Go wake up the Nelsons. We'll get the boys."

Go wake up the Nelsons, thought Jean. *How could anybody be asleep?* But surely, as she raced up the walk of the house across the street, she could see there were no lights on, only the reflected glow of the fire. She pounded on the door and heard herself scream, "Help." It seemed years before the door opened, but in that time, she had had only enough time to turn and see her father racing around to the back door to the basement. The whole neighborhood was brightly lighted, and flames could be seen in the windows of all the upstairs bedrooms.

The door swung open, and Jean burst inside. Mr. Nelson, a man slightly older than her father, gasped, "Oh, God," then sprang into action, running to the phone in the kitchen.

"Jean, you're bleeding, are you all right?" Mrs. Nelson asked, coming down the stairs. She saw the fire across the street when Jean saw the blood down the front of her pajamas. Both stood transfixed until Mr. Nelson returned to grab a piece of his own pajamas and place it over the bleeding cut on Jean's forehead. "Hold this for her, honey. Is everybody out?" He was almost to the bottom of the steps.

"I don't know. I hope so." Jean felt weak, and Mrs. Nelson responded to her need for support. She was led to the kitchen where a clean towel replaced the torn pajama piece. Jean sobbed, tears and blood mixing and trickling into her mouth. "It was horrible. Jeff and Randy will never get out." She started to stand, wanting to get back to her family, but Mrs. Nelson firmly pushed her back into the chair without saying a word and began to mop the blood from around her mouth.

The front door opened, and the three brothers stood, staring wide-eyed but silent into the house.

"There will be plenty for you to do right here," said Mrs. Nelson. "Now hold this in place."

She hurried to the front door, arms outstretched, and scooped up Allen. "Come on with me," she said. "We need to help Jean."

★★★★★

Herb Gilmore had been in tough situations before. Turning back did not enter his mind, but the heat which drove him to the floor and seemed to be burning his lungs made him almost scamper across the basement floor to the room where he hoped to find his two eldest boys. Flame poured out of the door to the furnace room and extended halfway down the wall. The entire ceiling above him was a mass flame and smoke; the door through which he had just entered seemed to be pumping oxygen to the flames, increasing them and the thundering they made. The door handle to the boys' room burned his hand as he opened the door, and he slammed it shut as quickly as he felt the room's coolness. The only light came from beneath the door and through the small window almost at ceiling level. Herb could not adjust his eyes to the light but tore covers off the beds and yanked on the first pair of legs he could grab.

"Get the hell up," he yelled. "Wake up your brother."

Groggy replies greeted him, so he pried his way between the beds and grabbed an arm. Climbing across the other bed toward the window, he managed to awaken both boys. "The house is on fire." Neither boy said anything during their return to consciousness. "We're going out the window."

A rush of cool air greeted them as the window was jerked open, and a low moaning sound followed with the air rushing beneath the door to fan the inferno. Herb gave a jerk which tore the window off its hinges, and he flung it across the room where it shattered against the wall. If the boys were not aware of the seriousness before, they were by now. They were able to hoist themselves out handily and, each taking an arm, lifted their father through the opening and into the fresh air. The horror that was all around him seemed to vanish as Herb mentally accounted for his entire family. How successful the fire department would be did not matter anymore. The flames could have his house; he would have his family.

✶✶✶✶✶

Jack was roused from his sleep and cursed the noise of the sirens racing past his apartment. He sat up so as to see the flashing lights disappear down the hill then heard the definite roar of the fire engine and its wailing siren. A dull glow in the sky several blocks away quickened his pulse and woke him fully. Knowing that he could not sleep now and driven by curiosity, he got dressed and headed for his car.

The old house was alive with flame, each window a torch, both thrilling and frightening to Jack as he parked his car up the street.

Walking closer, he realized he was one of the few spectators and could lean against a tree in the next yard and watch the firemen in their swift efficiency. Several people were congregating on the front steps of the houses up and down the block. Jack's concern mirrored that of the firemen: is everyone out of that house? He saw a man talking with the fire chief and assumed it was the owner of the house.

The next sight hit Jack like a hammer. A shirtless kid, holding up baggy pants around his waist, moved from the porch to the chief's car and fell into a hug. Jack glanced around then moved closer for a better look.

Incredible, he thought as he recognized Jean's brother. "Randy," he called, coming alongside the car. "Do you remember me? Where's Jean? Is she all right?"

The boy turned from his mother's arms, perhaps embarrassed but unable to say anything. "Man, I'm sorry. Is there anything I can do?" Jack offered lamely.

"You know Jean?" the lady asked.

"Well, yes. We just met up at the—"

"She's across the street, cut her head somehow. Maybe you could take her to the hospital since you're out already," she added apologetically.

"Oh, certainly. Randy, why don't you go get her? My car is right up to the street. I'll turn my lights on."

When the boy had gone, he turned to the woman, seeing for the first time the resemblance to Jean, the softness, but oh, how forlorn and helpless! "You'll have to stay near a phone. Does Randy know their number? The hospital will need to contact you."

"Yes, one of us will be there."

With the streets deserted, Jack made good time, with Jean seated next to him. Finally, Randy spoke. "Who woke up first? How did we all get out of there?"

Jack could say nothing during the long silence before hearing Jean sob, "I was awake and heard it."

"You were awake?"

"I was on the telephone."

"Who the hell were you talking to at this time of day?"

It sounded to Jack as if Jean chuckled, but he could not be sure. "Guilty," he said.

The boy leaned forward, staring at Jack, waiting for an explanation. None came.

"Jesus," he said and sat back, resigned to remain confused. It was not until Jean had been escorted away, phone call made, and the two sat facing each other in a small waiting room that the subject was resumed. "So how often do you and my sister have these phone calls?"

Refreshingly blunt, thought Jack. He couldn't help liking the kid. "First time. She called me, actually, maybe an hour or so earlier 'cause I had a rough day."

"Join the club."

"Really! Does it make you uncomfortable or anything like that?"

Randy shrugged. "It's cool."

"I guess we'll be getting to know each other," Jack offered, feeling awkward again. "I'm Jack Flemming, and I'll be a teacher at West this year." It was the first time, he realized, he had described himself or even thought of himself as a teacher.

"Oh, yeah. I remember you from up at the shopping center, but I guess this changes everything."

"What do you mean?"

"Our house just burned down, remember?" The boy slumped. "We're sure not going to go to school there anymore?"

Jack let out a long breath, less sure that he liked the boy. I'm sorry. I just thought…"

"Do you realize what it's like to lose everything? I don't even have any clothing. Everything I own is on the bottom of a goddamn pile of ashes. You just don't understand. I lost everything."

Realizing the boy's anger and frustration, Jack was able to avoid taking it all personally. He stepped across the room and sat beside Randy on the couch.

"Randy, I could talk you under the table about losing if that's the way you want it, but maybe we ought about bouncing back." Hearing no interference, Jack pressed on as if afraid of silence. "Certain things can't be replaced. I know that, photographs mainly, and certain objects that have sentimental value—art, handicraft objects—but the majority of the stuff we humans say we need can be replaced, and often it comes back in better shape than what we lost. But you're right. I didn't think about where you'd be living, and that was my stupidity and my loss if you don't live in this school district."

Randy slouched further into the couch, staring absently into his lap.

"If your family can get out of this with one cut forehead, you're doing pretty well. I'm sure you neighbors will pitch in with a temporary place to stay tonight. Then I imagine it will be a motel until insurance adjusters have their say. I'm not saying it will be easy or fun because it won't be, but as long as you are able to sit here healthy and talk about it, you haven't really lost much." He wanted to throw in something about not feeling sorry for oneself but was saved by Jean being escorted through the door, bandaged but smiling.

Jack shot to his feet. "Should I pay for this now?" he asked a nurse.

"No, it's all been taken care of. You can go now."

Jack was driving more slowly—whether to prolong their time together or from lack of urgency, he was not sure. Then came the surprise.

"Remember what you said on the phone?" She said it not as a question so much as a reminder.

"Not really. What about?"

"You had something to talk about the next time we bump into each other."

"Sorry, it's not coming to me."

"I said," she began slowly. "I wish I could do something to help, and you said there was something and we'd talk about it the next time…"

"Oh yeah. Some other time, okay?"

"Some other time," she repeated.

"I think he means three's a crowd," Randy said as if to dismiss the whole topic.

"He's right," Jack said to Jean. "Some other time."

As they pulled to the curb, they could see that much of the fire had died down, people stood gazing, firemen more settled into the work routine, and that the house had been completely destroyed.

5

Jack got few enough callers at his door so that when his doorbell rang, it was surprise and anticipation which caused him to whack his shin on the coffee table in his haste to get to the door. "Sounds like you're having a fight."

Jack forgot the pain in his leg and beamed a smile upon Jean, who stood in his doorway.

"Hey," he finally laughed. "Come on in. What are you doing?"

"Just thought I'd see what you are doing about getting ready for school."

"Sit down. Hey, it's great to see you. I've missed you. Yeah, I'm getting ready for school, all right. I'm sure you could help me, but what about you? Have you figured out what you'll be doing?" Jack slowed down and smiled at her for a moment. "I haven't talked to you since you moved. You're on a farm somewhere?"

"We just own some land…maybe forty miles out." Jean looked to the floor. "We're pretty well settled out there now, and that's where I'll go to school. Dad had to come in today to settle some things, so I just came along. We start school earlier than you do here."

Jack nodded slowly. "Hey, it would have been great, wouldn't it? I mean, I'm sure you'll like it out there and all, but I don't know. It just would have been neat."

"I'm not so sure I'll like it, though, but I want to stay with my family."

"Does that sound like you have a choice?"

Jean smiled, then a laugh bounced out. "I guess you could say that I have been offered a place to stay here with a friend. Legally it can be done if my parents say so. I just don't think this is the time to ask about it."

"You got class, so you'll try it out there, in other words, then when you prove it to yourself that you don't like small-town living, you'll be able to move back in with someone in the district."

"Oh, it's not that simple…"

"I know, I know. I just had to hear, frankly, that you might, as they say, 'make the scene' at West—professionally speaking, of course." His wink caught her, and she laughed again.

"Can you stick around for a while? I'd love to talk to you. Like I said, I could use your help."

"I don't have anything to do, so talk."

"Well, let's see now…here I am jumping into something totally new. I'm anxious to get it going, and I have my own ideas of what to expect…you know what I mean? If I could somehow get the feel of what it's really like, what students are thinking, what's bugging them, it seems to me I'd be much better off and much more likely to be effective." There was a long pause. Jack slung a pillow into the corner of the sofa and stretched out, his head propped toward the girl who looked so ill at ease. "What is the biggest problem at West in your opinion? By that, I guess I mean the problem which is shared by the most people."

Now it was Jean's turn to relax. She settled back into her chair, gently shaking the hair out of her eyes. She finally spoke. "The problem is Black and White." That was that. There seemed no opening for questioning, and no amplification seemed forthcoming. Save for the *swish, swish* of the growing morning traffic outside, there was no sound until Jack ventured an answer.

"Okay, that's two problems. I asked for one."

"Two problems?"

"Black and White."

She nodded several times. "So…I'd have to say the problem is Black."

"You'd have to say the problem is Black." He liked using her technique of repeating an answer to probe for further explanation. He imagined that she didn't like having this used. Conversation was, to Jack, a stimulating combat, and he enjoyed this particular combatant.

"Well, they're the ones who are prejudiced," she continued. "I went to grade school with the same ones, and we got along fine. Something seems to happen at junior high. I don't know what it is."

"Something changes?"

"It had to…a bunch of us were talking once…"

"Us? You mean Whites?"

"Yeah, and we all felt the same way. The important thing is we all felt surprised at how they had changed."

"They—the Blacks. There you go. It's *we* and *they*. Can't you think of it as just we—Blacks and Whites?"

Jean sighed and turned to the window. She didn't need to say anything when she looked back at him.

"Okay, okay, I know, I'm an outsider," He sat up and kept up his attack. "So there is a change which the Whites notice in the Blacks upon entering junior high school. Now what are some differences between grade school and junior high that would cause this? First, what about the staff?"

"What do you mean?"

"The faculty—is it more Black in junior high? Less Black? Younger? Older? More men or more women? We're trying to find some variable which could cause the change you spoke of."

"I guess it's about the same. We had some Black teachers, a couple men. Agewise, it was about the same. I really don't think there was much difference—just that the one place is bigger."

"Okay, that brings up the next shot—size. Junior high is larger—more kids, more teachers, just plain bigger, but is the ratio the same? Are the Blacks more of a minority in the larger school?"

"Oh, no, not at all. If anything, the other way around." She cocked her head as if in serious thought. "No, it's about the same."

"No noticeable difference, in other words. So come on, what else could there be?"

"Who knows, but it sure happens, and I don't think it's our fault."

"'Our fault.' There you go again."

"You don't understand. You just…" She brought her hands together. Jack had not guessed she could become even this wrought up. "You wanted my advice. My advice is not to give sermons and not to hold Whites responsible for the friction. You will find out all about it, but if you want my advice, you'll side with the Whites because we aren't looking for trouble."

Jack lay down again as if to let this attack take special effect. Indeed, she did seem sincere. Then he began slowly and deliberately. "Or…I could go in there completely divorced from this 'us and them' concept. Take everybody where they are, show everyone equal respect, and I'm sure I'll get the same in return. Things may be different now, but when I was in junior high, the thing that I remember as being different from grade school was the relationships between boys and girls. Boyfriends and girlfriends, quote, going steady all became more important, so I'd like to hear from you if you think one group of Blacks is more, as you say, prejudiced than another. Who's worse, girls or boys?"

"This may surprise you, but I'd have to say the girls cause more trouble."

"I'll try to look surprised if you want me to."

"You mean you knew that's what I'd say?"

"I'm just asking questions, but your answer gives me an idea." He was sitting up now, facing her squarely. "Girls tend to mature more rapidly than boys—or so I've been told. Could it be that Black girls are further still ahead? Could it be that Black girls are more"—he looked to the ceiling as if searching for the right word—"threatened."

"Threatened?"

"Yes, with the worst kind of threat—being unwanted, unloved, ignored—that kind of threatened."

Again she looked down at the floor. This time she shrugged. "You've got it all figured out."

"No, not really. I'm just testing ideas on somebody who knows more about all this than I do, but it seems to me that compassion and concern, respect will correct the problem. These people need a chance."

"These people?"

Jack exhaled very slowly and very audibly. "Yeah, right." He stood and walked to the window. "I know it will work." He punctuated this announcement by slamming his fist into the palm of his hand. "Let's have some iced tea. How about it?"

★★★★★

Jack was feeling better and better with each day as the hot summer slipped by, bringing him toward opening day of school. An adolescent psychology course two evenings a week kept him busy, and his baseball team continued to be a diversion so that his thoughts of Janice, though frequent and melancholy, were not totally debilitating. He became conscious of a real feeling of optimism. He was confident and eager, and both were heightened when Glenn Becker stopped by to bring him copies of the textbooks he would be using.

"I think you'll be better off with fewer preparations," he said. "Some teachers prefer to teach several different courses, but for this year, maybe just the ninth-grade civics would be the best way to go. Of course, there is the possible problem of boredom. What do you think?" he asked, stretching his long legs out from the couch he occupied.

"No, I guess one course would be best. How many hours in a day? Six?"

"Seven. I've got your schedule here, I think." His attaché case was snapped open, and reams of computer printouts unfolded on the coffee table before him. "Okay, everybody gets one period free. We call it conference and planning. Yours is seventh hour. As it stands now, you'll have this civics class first, second, third, and fourth hours. That sounds like a long grind, but you will have lunch between third and fourth. Now as for fifth and sixth, I've been trying to come up with some way to get the kids to you. Force them at first." He smiled.

"Soon, maybe, you'll be able to zero in on a few that you want to work with, particularly in the drug area, but the problem is getting started, so…cutting, skipping, tardies—the whole attendance problem. In other words, we will hope to send to you kids who are notorious for skipping or being tardy. I've hand scheduled several candidates so that they have an art class or gym class fifth or sixth hour. We can pull them out of that kind of class with little harm. Your job will be one-on-one to try to correct the problem. You'll need to keep records, which we'll go over later. The main consideration is this. On the one hand, we're trying to establish rapport and penetrate the drug scene. On the other hand, we don't want to make tardies or skipping a crime which is rewarded by coming in and talking with Mr. Flemming. Do you see what I mean?"

"So maybe my fifth and sixth hours should be changed to eighth hour."

"That's something to consider, but I think as long as you keep it in mind, you'll be able to do something about the skipping and attack the drug problem. What do you think?"

"You're the boss. If you feel there is a need there for the attendance problem, I'll give it a try. I suppose the skippers are pretty much the druggers anyway, aren't they."

"I think so…though I'll admit I didn't know as much about our drug problem as I should have. I was talking with Jim Parks early last spring. He was pretty concerned about drugs, and his list was essentially the same as our most troublesome skippers. Most of those will be in ninth grade this year."

"Will I have any in civics?"

Glenn smiled. "Do you think you should? Would that be a problem?"

"I'm sure there will be problems, but having them in class shouldn't make any difference."

Good answer. Remember, I hand scheduled these kids. Between you and me, you'll have a full house."

Don't tell me who," Jack said. "I'd like to learn that as I go."

"Fair enough. Anyway, I thought you might want to look over the book. I'll be at school every day from now on. You're welcome to come over anytime if you want to get in your room. If I'm not there, just tell the secretary you're taking Jim Parks's room."

Oh? What happened to Jim Parks? He's the one who knew about the drugs, didn't you say?"

"Just got tired of teaching, I guess. He's joining his dad in the insurance business—kind of sudden. He had a way of getting kids to open up though—low-key, calm, and most important, nonjudgmental."

"I'll remember that, and I'll drop by someday soon. Thanks for everything."

✶✶✶✶✶

At first Jack thought he might be a bit too early, but he soon realized even the veteran teachers were in their rooms long before school was scheduled to start on this first day of the year. The gentleman in the room next to his was certainly a veteran. Jack saw only the man's back as he walked past his door, but moments later, Jack looked up from his computer printouts to find the man standing in his doorway.

"Good morning," they greeted each other.

"Jack Flemming."

"I'm Ralph Headley. Looks like we'll be neighbors."

"Good enough. I may be in need of help," Jack admitted shyly.

"Likewise!"

"Are you in social studies?" Jack asked.

"Right, mostly ninth grade. How about yourself?"

Yea, ninth-grade citizenship. I was just trying to figure out what the schedule is. I really can't make much of these printout sheets…a lot of names and numbers to me."

"Well, for now, all we need to know is whether you have a first hour-class. After that, everything will take care of itself. Here, I'll show you."

"I do have a first-hour class…that I remember," Jack offered.

"First through fourth."

Soon sheets ware spread across Jack's desk like so many road maps, with Ralph Headley pouring over them as if charting a course. Everything he said made Jack feel less easy, less sure of himself and the situation he had gotten into. The whole thing seemed impossibly unorganized, and Ralph's casual approach amazed Jack. There had been something about how he shouldn't worry about print-out sheets anyway. They never were accurate. Yes, Jack was right; he would have a first-hour class, but the kids would know where they were supposed to be. Use such and such a sheet to take attendance, but if anyone is not accounted for, don't worry about it. No kid is going to skip on the first day of school. There was talk about changed schedules, and Jack wondered how there could be schedule changes before school had even started, but Jack had a lot to learn.

"You've got some winners," the older man said, chewing on his glasses. "Where did you get your education?"

"Granada." Jack was surprised at himself and how easily this answer had come.

"Well then, you won't have much trouble around here." The older man was moving toward the door. "I'll come in after first hour and see if you need help figuring out which class comes next. I'll know a lot more by then. See you later, and good luck!"

"Yeah, right. Thanks."

Alone again, Jack found himself thinking back over the summer and how he had tried to prepare himself for this day and the many days to follow. He was confident of the subject matter by now and realized that he was more impatient than anything else. Anxious to get the day started, he had planned to take special note of exactly what happened when the eight o'clock bells sounded. He anticipated an orderly influx of eager students, and it would be interesting, he thought, to try to make some early judgments just for the fun of discovering later how correct he had been. All this was lost in a blended confusion of sloppily dressed young people who seemed to seep into the building unheralded if not unwanted.

Instead of the curiosity he somehow thought his presence would arouse, he was most shocked at how thoroughly he was ignored. A few times he would be bumped into as he leaned against the wall near his door, but even fewer times was anything said to him and, least of all, any apologies. A swirling sea of faces dominated by a few, a rising crescendo of noise punctuated by an occasional audible shout or greeting of one friend to another, and a constant ebb and flow of people chasing and being chased, pushing and being pushed caused the eight o'clock bell to go totally unnoticed and as ignored as he himself was. How was this mass of confusion to be gotten into classrooms—specific ones at that—at a predetermined time? Humbled, Jack chose to withdraw to his room and leave problems of that magnitude to other powers. He himself felt powerless beyond the sanctuary of his own room.

Soon it too offered little comfort, but at least there was a hint of territorial rights. It was as if kids knew it was his room. More than once, he was asked if his name was Flemming. That alone gave him some security. The rest he would have to build for himself. Another set of bells sounded, seemingly from everywhere, and surprisingly brought order within the room. Jack, for lack of anything better to do, walked to the door and closed it. He heard himself calling roll from the printout sheet, mild laughter being sparked by any mispronunciation of a last name.

Jack was more aware of the major pocket of resistance toward the back along the windows. Here sat a group of guys who might be able to get things started their way if not checked. They seemed to follow the lead of a sandy-haired boy who sat somewhat taller than the rest. He wore only a T-shirt and faded blue jeans which, even as he slouched on his chair, hid his shoes beneath what appeared to be a not-too-carefully sewn-on extension of the trouser legs.

Was he growing that fast, Jack wondered, *or is this part of the carefully cultured sloppiness so prevalent?* Jack worked his way down the list, hardly noticing others in the class and certainly not connecting names with faces until he came to one which had been entered by hand.

"Russell Carter."

"Here."

Now Jack knew his name. This would make handling the situation easier. Several more names were read before the star again stepped out of bounds. At least Jack considered his pig imitation as he called the name of a rather heavy Black girl steeping out of bounds.

"Russell Carter," Jack called in the same monotone voice.

"You called my name once," the boy responded.

"No…as a matter of fact, I called your name twice, and you do not want me to call it a third time."

"Oh, yeah. What happens then?"

Jack forced a smile and began walking toward the student. The room fell silent. When he reached the boy, he said, "Can you keep a secret?"

"Yep."

Jack bent toward Russel, who had not flinched, and in a stage whisper heard by all said, "So can I."

Returning to his desk, Jack could hear muffled chuckles, and someone murmured, "Cool," causing Jack to feel he had won that round.

The period was spent passing out books and then performing the myriad tasks necessary to getting a school year started, leaving Jack only a few moments to talk at all about what the course was to cover and how it would be presented and what his expectations were. He felt obliged to do all this but wondered, as he did so, whether he was accomplishing anything. He worked his way over to the door as he spoke, wanting to be there as the class filed out. Set off by the bell, the two dozen students erupted into noise and confusion again, but Jack managed to murmur, "Russell Carter, hmm…" as the boy passed him in the doorway.

"Jesus Christ, I don't know" was all Jack heard him say in leaving.

Faithful to his word, Mr. Headley was making his way through the hallway toward Jack, who wondered why he had not noticed the man's obvious limp earlier.

"One down." The older man smiled. "How did it go?"

"No problem…yet. How long does it take to remember their names? I only know one kid out of the whole bunch."

"I'll tell you one better learn fast." The old man put his hand on Jack's shoulder and smiled again. "Russell Carter."

"We've met."

"I'll tell you what I do. Get in there and block off a sheet of paper into five rows. As you call the roll, write the names in where they are sitting. You learn half of them by writing them, and you can keep referring to the chart."

"Good idea, but will they sit in the same seats tomorrow?"

"Almost invariably."

"Thanks."

It was not until last period that he had a chance to reflect upon his opening day. Having last period free seemed a good deal to him wondering, but for now, he was aware that he was very hungry and couldn't even remember what he had had for lunch. Dinner would be different, but his meal planning was interrupted by a cheerful "Hi," from the door. A striking Black woman carrying a bundle of folders came toward him, flopping her load on his desk. "I'm Harriet Jefferson."

Jack started to stand and noticed it brought surprise to the woman's face. "Hi, I'm Jack Flemming."

"I'm one of the counselors." She was leafing through a notepad. "Let's see. What did I need to ask you?" Jack was flattered and felt impressive.

"Oh, yeah. Jenny Sylvester. Was she here…let's see, fourth hour?"

To himself, Jack thanked Mr. Headley again as he reached for his pile of seating charts. Fourth hour was a blur to him, and the names on the chart didn't help much, but there was no Jenny Sylvester. He felt defensive and wondered what he had done wrong.

"Apparently not. Should I have reported that?"

"It's okay. I'm afraid we're going to have the same old problem we got started last spring. Jenny has to check up on her mom—or thinks she does."

"Check up on her mom?"

Harriet smiled, realizing she was not making sense to this young beginner. "This is all just kind of thrown together, you know? From what I've heard from her and from other kids—you know what I mean? And I can't really recall what the specifics were, but I think Jenny is afraid her mother is seeing somebody else while the father is at work. It seemed like every day she had some excuse to go home— like she was trying to surprise her mom."

"Fantastic. Unbelievable."

"Yeah, she never wanted me to call—which we have to do before we can send a kid home—so then she took to just skipping out at different periods on her own."

"That has to be rough. I can't wait to meet this one," Jack said, realizing that he had already assumed she was a Black girl.

"Well, let me know if you have any trouble with her in class, and I'll work on the out-of-class part—or try to," said Harriet, gathering her stack of folders. "Nice to meet you."

"Thank you." Jack was on his feet. "Nice to meet you, and thanks for telling me about the girl."

Alone again, Jack had time to analyze his thoughts. He realized he was genuinely flattered, even thrilled, to have been included in such personal information. Here the most elemental problems in the lives of perhaps several people had been simply dropped in his lap. His mind raced back through his own childhood. How would be have handled such a calamity? How many other similar problems—or worse ones—were being lived daily by the kids who had been in his class that day? How very much easier it is to tolerate the abuse he had had directed toward him in the last few hours! The rudeness, the insolence which had at first shocked then infuriated him now could be handled differently. He could at least try to put it into a class with clumsiness and acne.

His thoughts went back to Janice, to the funeral parlor. How secure it had all been! Even in death, there was complete and total loyalty, security, certainty. He had never, he realized, had to worry about his position or his relation to others—not at home as a youngster, not, thanks to Janice, in his college days or while in the service; and here was a school full of youngsters, each needing what he had found in the funeral parlor but many of them perhaps never having felt in.

Jack was to learn on days two and three what Mr. Headley had been talking about when he mentioned schedule changes. While the students did sit in basically the same seats as the preceding day, there were many news faces and names and many deletions. Noticing Russell Carter among these bought mixed feelings to Jack. First hour was more docile, he imagined, but Jack knew he would miss the boy, but not for long as he showed up in third hour.

"Glad you made it through the schedule change," Jack offered. "We give the same fine service here in third hour as in first. You can even keep the same book, if not the same seat." Russell's domain, rear, by the window, was third-hour occupied by a cluster of Black kids.

Glancing back, Russell mumbled, "I'll move out of the ghetto," and was relegated to a vacant seat near Jack's desk.

It would be a week before all schedule changing was complete and names could be safely entered into the grade book.

Jack duly noted Jenny Sylvester's return to fourth hour. She was attractive, mature, though somewhat larger than the other girls, and White. "Missed you yesterday," Jack probed but got nowhere.

With outstretched arms, she replied, "Here I am," with no show of malice or humor.

"I'm Mr. Flemming. Nice to see you're back." Learning closer, he whispered. "Also nice to see your front." That seemed to do the trick. She smiled warmly and again on leaving at the end of the period.

By the third day, Jack decided to see what he could learn about the tardies.

"Rose will have a list from each day," Glenn said. "You might see if there are any patterns developing this early. It's worth a try. If you want to talk to any, their schedules are on file out there on the counter. You can pull them out of class if you think you can do any good."

One name did distinguish itself by its frequency: Odell Tate. *Worth investigating*, thought Jack.

"Odell," Jack began once the two were alone in the hall. "Do we have a problem getting to class on time?"

"No, sir." Odell was looking at the floor.

"Well, wait a minute. Your name is on the tardy list five times, and this is only the third day of school."

Odell was playing it safe, saying nothing.

"Help me figure out why you are tardy to class so often."

More silence.

"Are you having trouble finding them?"

"Yes, sir."

"Well, here's my idea, Odell. We don't have time now, but if this continues to be a problem. I'll meet you right after seventh hour, then when the building is empty, you and I can practice going through your schedule—you know what I mean. We'll just walk through your whole day a few times so that you're sure where to go and how to get there."

So pleased was Jack on this first attempt that he decided to track down another noteworthy name. It produced a very fat but jolly—and that was the only word Jack could think of—Black boy. Very young looking, expensively dressed, the boy looked bright and friendly.

"Now, Roland," Jack began as soon as the classroom door closed behind him. "It seems you have been late to class several times already. Are you having trouble getting your locker open?"

"Yeah," the boy was quick to respond.

"I've got a solution. What we need to do next time it happens is spend some time, just you and me, after everybody else is on their way home and there are no distractions—you know what I mean?"

The boy's eyes were half-dollar size.

"And we can practice and practice on that lock until I'm sure—and you're sure—that you will be able to get to classes on time. Do you think that would help?"

"I don't know."

"It usually helps, but maybe you'd rather solve the problem yourself. We'll see. Thank you very much." Jack opened the door, ushering the boy back into the room. Returning to his own room, Jack wondered if he had already spotted an emerging pattern, and he began to think up all the possible reasons he could for being late to class and an appropriate after-school activity. It was certainly looking as if whatever reason he suggested, the student was quick to agree with. Messy lockers could be cleaned out after school. A locker too far from classrooms could be changed after school. Jack was beginning to enjoy the challenge.

The more important challenge, he felt, was to make his ninth-grade civics classes as interesting as possible. To this end, he had decided to start off with a unit on crime, studying criminal behavior, society's reaction to it, and including individual research projects on famous crimes and criminals. A mock trial was brewing in his mind. He found himself jotting down a series of questions which he kind of liked. He liked them very much the next morning, and by third hour, he had them well-rehearsed and refined. His timing would be perfect to end just as the bell rang.

"A man owns an old apartment building," he began. "It's losing money, so he decided to burn it down and collect the insurance. Now we know he is guilty of arson, but if someone dies in the fire, is he also a murderer?" He gave just enough time for hands to pop up. "And suppose he doesn't know anybody is in the building, but somebody is—a bum, vagrant, whatever—if that person dies in the fire, is the man also a murderer?" Another brief pause. "Now, suppose no one is in the building but a fireman is killed fighting the blaze, is the man also a murderer? Or let's say a fire truck is racing to the scene of the fire and hits a car, killing a little kid riding in the car. Is the arsonist now also a murderer?" He smiled. "Homework. Ask those questions to somebody tonight. Makes great conversation at the dinner table. Then we can talk about it tomorrow."

The bell sounded, and Jack began to think about Jenny Sylvester next hour, and conversations around a dinner table, but he didn't have long to ponder that paradox.

"You ask neat questions."

"Well, thank you, Russell. I'll bet you've got some neat answers." He put his hand on the boy's shoulder as they walked to the door. "If you need somebody to do your homework with, I'll be here this afternoon. Bring your gang from first hour. They have the same assignment. Later."

The boy was gone into the crowd on its way to the cafeteria, but the warm feeling stayed with Jack.

The warmth became absolute surprise seventh hour when Russell poked his head in the door. "What you doin'?"

"I work here," Jack joked. "Enter and be saved." The invitation was not necessary as Russell had already headed for his own desk. "What are you doin?"

"Oh, there will?" Jack smiled. "What, is this ninth-grade skip day or something?"

"No, I've got art this hour. So does Danny."

Danny Spinks, thought Jack, visualizing the tall blond who seemed to have not a care. Second hour is covered. "Anybody else?"

"Pam has a study hall, and Scott might get out of gym."

"I see," said Jack, wondering just what kinds of problems this was causing. "The various teachers don't care? Have you checked?"

"Sure—they're glad to get rid of us."

Sure enough, Pam and Scott entered as a couple, and Danny sailed through the door, sinking a candy wrapper in the wastebasket with a hook shot. He nodded to Jack, making the man feel he was one of the guys. "What's goin' on?"

Jack chuckled, "I think we just opened a ninth-grade lounge. You tell me what's goin' on, but sit down, make yourselves comfortable." He gestured to everyone, and before he knew it, he sat before a half circle of expectant faces.

There was a noticeable silence—finally broken by Jack. "It's your phone call. Am I supposed to say something?"

Russell rose to the occasion. "We just wanted to talk about what you said in class today…you know, the homework."

"You're kidding."

"If you kill somebody, you're a murderer. Let's start with that."

"Let's start with closing the door." Danny sprang to his feet. "You people are too much!"

The period flew by. Before the bell rang, ending the day, four students had discovered such concepts as premeditation, negligence, and the concepts of first- and second-degree murder versus manslaughter.

"Do me a favor." Jack summed up. "Tomorrow, don't be too quick to pump out the right answers…you know, the final say. Let people argue and thrash it out. I may ask you guys to lead discussions in each of your classes. Any problems with that?"

"That's cool," Danny agreed. Pam looked at Scott so that Jack knew whom to call on in fourth hour.

"Russell?"

The boy shrugged. "Sure."

"Well, I'd like to say come back anytime, but I don't know if this is a good idea."

"It's a great idea," said Scott, ending the afternoon with the bell. Jack was left alone with a very satisfied feeling but uncertain as to what he should do about what he could see as a light problem turn into a real problem. Talking about drugs, he realized, might not be too big a problem if he brought it about the right way in class. Whether to tie it in with the unit on crime he would have to consider very carefully, but for now, he was sure that at least four kids would grab the bait if it were properly cast.

6

The October winds whistled around the corner of the gym but could not create enough discomfort for Russell and Danny. They stood against the wall to avoid the wind and, presumably, any prying eyes. Jack had seen them leave the student center and knew they must be there. He also knew they wouldn't be smoking yet because of the absence of a lookout. This, he though, was the time to approach them.

"Hi, Mr. Flemming," said Danny, who first saw him come around the corner.

Russell turned and nodded, but he did not seem hostile.

"Howdy, men." Jack leaned up against the same wall. "Cold enough for you?" Without waiting for an answer, he continued, "Be warmer in the gym."

"You're telling me."

Jack sensed that Russell had something to say. "Oh, yeah?"

"You ever play basketball with 'em?"

"Them?"

"The Blacks. It's not much fun."

"They better than you?"

"The way they play."

"I'll check out the way they play. Anybody else out here?"

Russell playfully scanned the entire view. "I don't see any smoke."

"Don't let me see any," Jack chuckled, punching Russell on the shoulder. "Later."

The gym was warmer and beginning to smell like a gym. Jack edged along the wall toward the bleachers where he could observe. He found himself counting Whites as if trying to arm himself for an imaginary argument he was having with Russell. Soon he realized he was losing the argument. The thought, though, kept recurring to him that something—or someplace—had to be provided where those kids would want to be. and they would have to want it more than they would want to be out back smoking. A gym with basketball, trampoline—just plenty of space—all seemed enough to do the trick, but it certainly wasn't. Why not, and what would it take? He would work on the why not first. Later he could ask about what would it take. For the next fifteen minutes until the bell rang, Jack tried to forget about the activities out back and just observe as much as he could of what was happening before him. He could talk to Russell after school.

"Got a second?" Jack asked, poking his head into Glenn's office. Rose had gone home by now, and there seemed to be no one around.

"Sure, come in." Glenn pushed some papers aside and leaned back in his chair, hands clasped on top of his head. "What's up?"

"Well, I've just been thinking and talking and, you know, I can't get into the drug thing too quickly—maybe not at all, but anyway, I was wondering how we could attack this noontime thing. That's when they do a lot of it."

"Maybe they just really don't have anything better to do."

"They've got a gym."

"Right, that is what I'm wondering about. This is all just kind of spur-of-the-moment, you know. I really haven't thought it out. I was talking to Russell Carter, trying to find out why his group doesn't use the gym."

"And?"

"It's prejudice the way I see it."

Glenn was nodding and smiling. "You hit it."

"They don't want to associate at all."

"He seems totally unable to accept them, totally unwilling to try. Sure, he says there are some 'good ones,' as he calls them, but according to him, even the decent ones can't be that way at noon or else they get trouble from the others."

Scooting his chair up closer to his desk where he crossed his arms, Glenn shook his head. "Now wait a minute. You lost me there. Try that one again."

"Okay," Jack relaxed. "Russell was talking about David Thurmond. He's a Black."

"Yes, I know David."

"Yes, but wait a minute. He's seen as a Black, not a n———.″

The two men stared at each other until Jack smiled. "There is a difference. The word *n———* might be used carelessly by some people, but it has a specific meaning to these kids."

"I see."

"Now what I was saying about Dave Thurmond, according to Russell, and this is just kind of an example, I guess, he's a great guy, interested in making friends on both sides. He's apparently comfortable in their homes and them in his, but—and this is the important part—all that is done pretty much on the sly, out of school, even during the summer, from what I can figure. Around here, Dave and others pretty well isolate themselves and can't move either direction…if you know what I mean."

There was a long silence as Glenn stared out the window into the setting sun. "I know what you mean," he said absently. Suddenly his attention was back inside the office. "Last year, late last year, Thurmond had his bike stolen, and I remember how he kept saying there were other bikes much better than his. We had maybe fifty bikes locked in the auditorium. Somebody broke in during the day and stole his. It's as if they could have had their pick, but they stole his. He kept saying there were other better ones in there, but I didn't understand what it was all about. Maybe he knew what it meant. We have a problem I didn't know about. I'd like to know the names of others in the Dave Thurmond classification."

"Well, I guess it would include—"

"No, I don't want it from you. You can make a list if you want to because that's what I'm going to do, but I want it according to, say, Russell, or any of the others you can listen to. My list is going to be of Blacks who are having trouble with this kind of thing—lockers broken into, gym clothing missing. There has been quite a lot of it when you stop to think about it. I'll check with John to get his side of it, then we'll compare lists. I don't know what we'll do with it, but we'll see what we come up with."

"Right, sounds good. See you tomorrow."

Tomorrow meant a test in his four classes and football, Jack reminded himself as he saw Jim Leffington, the gym coach and coach of the football team, come out of the door at the far end of the gym. The two men really didn't know each other well. They had met once, but their respective schedules caused them never to cross paths during the day. Jack thought it strange that Jim was walking toward him on the teachers' parking lot. He thought he remembered seeing Jim Parks near the gymnasium.

"How's it going?" Jack greeted.

"As good as I can expect. We'll see tomorrow."

"I guess you had a light workout tonight."

"Yeah, most of 'em would like a light workout every night."

"Can I give you a lift?"

"No, no." Jim's answer was quick. "I was just going to catch the bus. Thanks anyway."

"Oh, yeah, do you always take the bus?"

"No, my car is in the shop."

"Well, listen, I can run you."

Jim shrugged. "Sure, if you don't mind."

The traffic inched along into the setting sun.

"This is your first year teaching, isn't it?" Jim began.

"Sure is."

"How do you like it at West?"

"We got some characters, don't we? Talk about gym class. I don't get over that way at all during the day."

"What do you mean?" Jim's eyes probed for insight.

"Well, White-Black, for starters."

A grin came over Jim's face as he flipped the sun visor down. "You hit it. It didn't take you very long."

"I'm not talking about individual problems necessarily. I'm wondering how the two groups—if that's the correct terminology—how the two groups get along. I can't really tell too much myself because in the classroom, there isn't all that much time for interaction. What I'm wondering about is in gym classes…is there much mixing…voluntarily?"

The two sat in silence long enough for Jack to think he was being ignored. He glanced over to see that Jim was deep in thought. Finally, he spoke. "I've noticed when I come into the gym to get a class started, the Blacks usually have a couple games of basketball going, and I can remember I used to try varying the number of balls I'd leave out on the floor. I remember I didn't want to use just two. You know what I mean? That would look too obvious. If I put three out, there were three games of what they call buckets."

Jack nodded. He knew the game.

"If I put out four, there were four games."

"You saying two White, two Black? All—"

"No, no, all Black. White kids just standing around, waiting for class to start. Now if I put five out, I'm out of baskets. There's still four games, one at each, and the White kids will be just screwing around but nowhere near the games under each basket.

"Wow," was all Jack could say.

"Now there's exceptions. It depends on the size of the class and the ratio, but that's pretty much the way it goes. During class, there's no real problem."

"Glenn and I were just talking about another kind of problem. What about the Black who might want to associate with the Whites?"

"There are some. I think they have it rough, if you ask me. You can just let me off here at the corner."

"You sure it will be ready?"

"Yeah, I called. Thanks a lot. See you tomorrow."

✶✶✶✶✶

Jack could still hear voices in the hall and an occasional slamming of a locker door as he sat at his desk, looking over the stack of quiz papers. His door opened, and Russell walked in.

"Looks like you changed your schedule…or did somebody change it for you?"

"Hedgepeth, the b———."

"Cool it," Jack chuckled. "The walls have ears, you know."

"To hell with the walls."

"She really got to you. What was it anyway?"

"God, I don't know." He ambled toward Jack and slouched on a front-row desk.

"Take off your hat," Jack said innocently.

"Not you too."

"So that was it. She didn't want you to wear that hat over your face." Jack was pretending interest in his stack of papers.

"She calls me in because I don't have my homework…"

"That's legitimate."

"Yeah, yeah. Fine. I'll have my homework for the rest of the year."

"Then it was not only legitimate but productive as well." Jack was still not looking at the boy.

"But what has my hat got to do with it? And what's my hair got to do with it?"

"Well, now we have a good question, but I can't answer it until I know what she said about it." He looked at the boy and stacked his papers neatly. "And remember, tell me what she said, not what you heard."

"That's just it, Mr. Flemming. She never says anything. Just 'take off the hat.'"

"I mean, she never gives a reason for taking off the hat. She just threw in the bit about the hair. 'You could at least wear a shawl to cover that awful hair!'" Russel's voice was an ugly falsetto, mocking the old lady. "For Chrissake, hasn't long hair been around long enough for her to get used to it?"

"Okay, be cool." Jack smiled. "Talk about the hat. Do you have to wear it? Do you wear it because it bothers her? Does the hat have some significance?"

"Some girl found it."

"And gave it to you."

"It was no big deal. We were playing softball—the whole gang. She found it and snuck up behind me and put it on me."

"So you sort of figured she liked you."

"Sort of…I guess that's what started it."

"She go to school here?"

"Not anymore. They moved."

"You still see her very often?"

"She comes into town once in a while, maybe for a weekend."

"What's her name?"

"Jean."

Jack's memory raced back to the girl floating across the parking lot that dark night of sadness. "What, did her father get transferred or something so they had to move?"

"No. Nothing like that."

"Nothing like that?"

A smile crossed Russell's face. He walked to the window. "That's exactly what she does."

"What's that?"

"She repeats a statement. It's like instead of asking a question, she just repeats what you just said to her. You know what I mean?" The boy was excited now, and Jack stayed deliberately calm though he thought he had an even greater reason to be excited.

"I guess I do."

"No, really. It's fantastic the way she can show you she doesn't believe you just by repeating what you say."

"You a good pool player?" Jack asked, certain he had the right girl in mind.

Russell's expression changed with the conversation. "I play… why?"

"I was told you are pretty good."

"Who told you that? I never talk about it."

There was a long silence.

"Jean told me."

"Jesus Christ. How do you know her?"

"Pretty well, but I didn't know she gave you a hat. I'll tell you how well I know her. I know she wouldn't want you getting into trouble over that hat. Now if Hedgepeth says, 'Kaibash,' then it's kaibash. You don't need to be told why. Just don't wear it. I'd rather talk about Jean."

"Right on."

"Oh my god." They both laughed. "Yeah, I had a little bad luck then a little good luck, you might say. The good luck was meeting Jean. It was late last spring. I admire your taste, by the way."

"What about her taste?"

"In hats?" They laughed again. "So what can I do for you, or did you really come in to find out how you did in the quiz?"

"No, it's just…yesterday, at noon, you know…"

Jack was lost. He shook his head and shrugged while struggling to remember anything about yesterday noon. "What do you mean?"

The boy shifted positions in the chair and looked down. Finally, he blurred out, "I never been punched in the shoulder by a teacher."

They looked at each other. Jack smiled. Russell turned to the window. Jack stood and walked to the front of his desk. "If you're talking teacher brutality, I'll deny everything."

"No, man. It's just like you're one of us and you're not so stuck-up like teachers are."

"Well, thanks for saying that, I'm sure it is hard to come in here and say all that…and I have something equally hard to say, which is that I think you're pretty special, and if you were my kid, I wouldn't just punch as meaning the same thing. Russell, I like you."

A half hour had passed before either one of them realized how late it was. Jack felt good about the closeness which had been established and had it confirmed when Russell accepted a ride to the football game. He was sure Russell would show up again if he stayed in his room after school the next day. He determined that drugs would be the topic of conversation, and he set about planning his strategy, most of which escaped him when the boy did enter the room.

Russell had called Jean, or so he had said before class, and there was all of that to get out of the way. "She's going to be up next weekend."

Jack saw his chance. "I'll bet she will be."

The boy's face contorted with surprise and confusion. "What?" he finally said.

"I suppose she gets up every weekend. That's what it's all about, isn't it?

Jack's stare pierced the boy. It was eye to eye. "Drugs."

The boy slumped and lowered his gaze.

"Not you too!"

"I didn't know I had to wait in line." *The words from last night's rehearsal are becoming useful after all,* Jack thought. "If someone else has you squared away already, I'll butt out."

"No, it's all right. I just meant—"

"No, it isn't all right." Jack stood and walked to the front of his desk. "It isn't all right because it is none of my damn business. The problem is I'm a hundred percent against it. I can't see you needing to be into it, and I'm too damn stubborn to give up. You're stuck with me now, and I imagine we'll do a lot of talking before we get over it."

The boy had been gazing down at the desk, but as Jack placed his hands squarely on it and leaned forward, Russell raised his head so as to peer through the long strands of hair into Jack's smile.

"And over it is what we're going to get. You'll learn, though I'm sure you don't believe it yet, that I intend to handle it alone. Whatever I learn stays with me. You don't need to worry about me telling anyone else 'cause there is no one more opposed to this crap for me to tell. When it comes to pot, I'm your worst enemy. What time is she getting here?"

"Uh, Saturday morning sometime. Why?"

Jack could see that Russell was uncomfortable and wanted to put him at ease. "Because you better bring her over, that's why."

"Where do you live?"

"She'll show you," Jack said with a smile, moving toward the closet.

"Jesus, I guess you do know her."

"Now, now, nothing like that, but I'll be honest with you—she's the first girl that ever offered me dope. Let's go. I'll tell you about it on the way home."

★★★★★

Jack's doorbell rang earlier than he thought it would, and he leaped up to answer it.

Jean's face radiated warmth and respect, but her mouth said nothing.

"Hey, it's good to see you. Come on in, Russell," Jack greeted the boy with a handshake then helped Jean with her coat. "Sit down. Sit down. Are you coffee swirlers? I was just having a cup."

"No," they both answered as they plopped themselves down on the couch.

Jack winked and tried to imitate Jean's gentle smile. He felt they could communicate forever without saying a word.

"Tell him the news," Russell finally said.

"Tell him the news," Jean repeated as if to say, "Already have told him the news"—and she had.

"You're moving back?"

"How'd you know?" Russell was incredulous. "Remember what we were saying the other day…she talks with her eyes."

She blushed and laughed uncomfortably.

"That's fantastic." Jack was not going to be stingy with his enthusiasm. "Are you going to rebuild your old house or what?"

"No, see, my family isn't moving back. The Griswolds said I could live with them, and my parents said it's all right."

"This intrigues me. First question, how close are the Griswolds to you, Russ? Geographically speaking?"

Jean took this up. "They live close to my old house down there. I don't know…five, six blocks."

"Five or six blocks." Jack was learning this technique.

"I just can't stand the country school, riding on buses, everyone nosy…"

"So you move back within six blocks of Russ where no one will be nosy." Jack was teasing. "Second question—when?"

"Well, our quarter is over next week, and yours is one week after that."

"So you're going to get a little vacation?"

"A little vacation?"

Russell and Jack exchanged glances each time Jean used this trick. He was proud to see her holding her own and glad too that she and his teacher got along so well. "I told her what you said the other day."

"Which was?" Jack hadn't even hoped it would be this easy to get the drugs dialogue into first gear.

"That she'll be up this weekend."

Jack forced a laugh then aimed his smile at Jean alone. "So now you're scared."

"Now I'm scared."

"Scared I'll win and you guys won't have any more fun. You know where I stand, but I've never heard what I'm up against. So talk…either of you." Jack poured himself a coffee refill.

"That's not too easy, you know," Russell finally said.

"What, do you think I'm after names? I could probably give you as many as you could give me." Jack bluffed.

"Surely you have something to say about…well, pot for instance."

"Why not? What does it hurt?"

"Here's the first rule." Jack slouched back in his chair. "We don't talk about the medical aspects. Maybe I could build a good case against the stuff on those grounds alone, but since I don't pretend to be a doctor, I don't talk about the medical." His pause let this sink into his two young listeners. "Unless, of course, you have some wisdom as to the medical advantages of marijuana which the rest of us are unaware of." His smile tempered his speech. "All I hear, though, is that it doesn't hurt. Living in the country doesn't hurt."

Jack watched Jean as she looked toward Russell, whom she hoped would speak next. Jack was too quick for him. "We'll let it go for now.

Next time you light up, though, maybe you'll be good enough to try to be able to explain why—what's in it for you, you know?"

Russell nodded while Jean looked at her feet.

"I've got something to show you," Jack said, breaking the tension. "I don't know whether you're into racing and cars and stuff, but I sure am." He opened a sketchbook. "I'm still just dreaming, but someday I'll out this rascal together." He dropped the notebook on Russell's lap, opened to a sketch he had drawn of a stock car. "Starts with a Mustang."

"Ends with a funeral," laughed Jean. Jack stiffened, and Jean caught the signal. "Sorry," she said, looking back at the drawing.

"It's okay," Jack said, returning to his chair. "I'm getting over it." A silence followed, then Jack said, "Poor Russell doesn't even know the problem. There's no problem. It's just that I got to know Jean about the time of a funeral. She'll clue you in."

"Now, wait a minute," Russell said. "You wanted us to talk about pot, and we did. You got to play by the same rules. So, whose funeral?"

A long stare turned into a smile, then Jack nodded. "I admire that, my boy. Don't ever lose that talent. You did that just right."

"Okay, that's good, but it doesn't answer the question, does it."

Jack chuckled. "You never miss a trick. My fiancée was a stewardess, and her flight crashed last spring—out on the coast. Maybe you heard about it. No one survived."

Russell walked over to the window. "How did Jean fit in?"

"I thought that's what you wanted to know."

"Damn straight."

"I was very…down as you might imagine. I was just sitting up at the shopping center, and she came along. We just talked for a while. I don't honestly remember whether I told her what my problem was. Did I?"

Jean shook her head but looked at Russell.

"I'm sure I wasn't hiding anything either. She probably figured it out. She usually does. Wait a minute. I met you and your brothers right after the funeral, remember?"

"That's when I found out," Jean answered.

"Hey, I'm glad to hear you're coming back to West. We'll have to get her into that third hour, won't we?"

"What time is it anyway?" Russell wanted to know.

"About quarter to ten."

"We got to go."

"Right, I know. Jean, it's great to see you and…well…thanks for coming by. This family you're going to stay with—they know your folks pretty well and all?"

"Oh, yes. We were neighbors. I practically lived over there, or else Diane was living at my house."

"We'll, that's fantastic. Let me get your coat. What about your brothers? Are they coming back?"

"I don't know." Jean dismissed the topic.

"Russell, Dr. Becker and I were talking the other day, and I said I'd follow through on something for him. Remember when we were talking about Dave Thurmond? Would you say there are others in his same…predicament?"

"Guys, yeah."

"No girls?"

"Well, that's not my area—if you know what I mean—but there are some guys. Yeah, I guess so."

"Like who?"

"What's all this for?"

"You got time. Stick around. I'll tell you."

A shrug from Jean and Russell's nod told Jack he had just bought more time. "After our conversation the other day when you told me about how Dave Thurmond would like to associate with Whites but has to hide this…"

Russell nodded again.

"I mentioned it to Doc—Dr. Becker—and he hit upon a theme that maybe the Dave Thurmonds at West are being…well…persecuted by the other Blacks. He would like to know which Blacks seem to be the least hostile, seem to be most comfortable around the Whites. His theory is that such a list will match—to some extent—his list of Blacks who have had things stolen, lockers broken into, you know."

"It will match," Jean said.

Jack swallowed the remaining cold coffee in his cup then looked at her. "That tells me that you already know about this whole problem."

"Sure, and you can be sure Thurmond knows," Russell added.

"My god, we're stupid. Could you prove it to me?"

"What do you mean?"

"Names."

"Monday, all right? I promise."

"What can I say?" Jack chuckled and stood up. "Jean, come back any time. Russell, likewise. I'm really looking forward to second quarter."

✶✶✶✶✶

On Monday, there was the usual staff meeting in the library. After the meeting, Jack handed Glenn Russell's list.

"Help me remember what this is." Glenn smiled. "Blacks friendly toward Whites."

"Oh, oh yes."

The two men moved down the hall together.

"Unbelievable," was all Glenn had to say, but he repeated it several times.

"I'll tell you something else. The kids already knew of the problem. It's like we're the last to find out and then kind of by accident."

"How do we overcome something like this? The whole aim, like whole objective, is being undermined."

Not since the night of the plane crash had Jack seen Glenn other than easygoing, almost jovial, but now he was deeply concerned.

"We'll keep pluggin'," Jack coaxed, wanting to break the silence.

"I don't know what we're going to do with this, but it sure proves something."

"See you tomorrow, Glenn."

"Right, thanks."

✶✶✶✶✶

Jack was taking the stairs two at a time. It was Friday, his classes over. He would check his mailbox to clear out the fan mail, as he called it, stacks of expensive ads for textbooks, audiovisual materials, and resource aids with which teachers are daily bombarded, then retire to his room to await the weekend.

"Hi." There was no smile. Jean looked down at the floor.

"Hey, I thought you were coming Monday. Great to see you. Wait right here while I get my fan mail, will you?"

Jack needed time to think. The girl was definitely upset about something, and Jack realized it was just plain curiosity on his part which would not let him overlook this situation. He remembered the parking lot meetings and felt the same excitement, the challenge of discovering and meeting other people's problems. The search for a way to help her without alienating her, without becoming an adult subordinating a child was a thrill, and already the hunt was on. There she stood, leaning against the banister. Jack overcame his desire to hug her.

"Come on downstairs. You got time?"

"Have I got time?"

Jack smiled. She hadn't changed. "So…are you moved in and settled?"

"I'm moved in."

"Yeah, I know what you mean. Is there plenty of room for you?"

"They got a big family, but I'm used to that. It'll be okay. I'll sleep in Diane's room."

"So what's the problem?" Jack was surprised at the bluntness of his own question but liked the forthright concern which it bespoke.

"Problem?"

Jack gazed ceilingward and let a long slow breath escape then returned his gaze to her eyes. "Jean, I love to talk with you, I love to be with you. I wish I had a kid like you. Already I have an awful lot of respect for you, but there are going to be times when I simply want to have you be forthright, honest, whatever. You can't always cover things up. People care. People want to know what's wrong. We'll share the good, so let's share the bad."

Jack could see that he had her and liked his dominant position. He charged on. "I know something is wrong. I could see that upstairs. I don't want to change you. It's great what you do, covering your emotions, like you don't want to be a burden to others, but damn it." Jack heard himself whisper for emphasis. "Let's say that once a month, for cryin' out loud, I get to have a straight answer. It's a red alert...you know what I mean? It's not going to make you a crybaby. You're not going to become a habitual complainer. It's just...I don't know." He was at the window. Another long slow breath seemed appropriate. "I'm sorry." He faced her. "I just don't like to see you—"

"I'm sorry."

No, don't be. Come on." He smiled. "Red alert. I've got a question that's buggin' me. You've got an answer." He sat back down at his desk but could not look at her.

Jean broke the silence. "Whiplet won't put me in you class."

Jack almost laughed. He felt that the reason the counselors were not giving him any more students was because they had already added so many who had been kicked out of other classes. "Now, let me see. That would be Ms. Whiplet?"

"Ms. Whiplet!"

"Okay," Jack spoke softly. "She's got her job to do. Before we do anything, let's make sure we know what we're getting into."

"What do you mean?"

"Well," Jack began. "Now it's kind of like friends, you know? If you came into my class, then I'm the teacher and you're the student. Who knows, you may not like me as a teacher. Everything changes a little bit. You know what I mean?"

"I thought about that, but I just don't think about you as a teacher, and you've got a lot of...neat people in that class."

"I figured that was it," Jack chuckled.

"No, that's not it. That's not anything."

"Well, we try to be selective." Jack loved teasing her. "That's probably why Ms. Whiplet wouldn't put you in here."

"You said red alert. You wanted to know. I told you."

Jack nodded then sank slightly into his chair. "Oh boy. I sure didn't mean to make fun of it. I guess I'm just used to humoring my way out of everything. I'm sorry…again."

"I really wanted to be in that class."

"Okay, let's go back one paragraph. I want you to think about the teacher-student bit. Think about whether you want to get into that situation. The friendship might be easier without being in the class, but it's going to be one hundred percent your decision. Decide quickly because I'm going down to the drinking fountain. When I get back, if you want it changed, I'll go talk to Whiplet.'

"That's Ms. Whiplet."

"You're catching on. Don't go away." He closed the door behind him and again found himself taking the steps two at a time.

✶✶✶✶✶

"Sue, can I talk to you a second?"

"Sure." The young counselor was locking her file cabinet as required by law. "Come on in."

"I don't know how to go about this, but I was talking to that new girl…"

"Jean? She's not new."

"Anyway, she'd like to be in my third hour, and what with all the losers you've been sending me, I'd like to have her. It might help with this drug thing."

"No problem. I just thought you were too full. I'll switch her English and civics. I don't know how I'll get that new schedule to her anymore today though."

"Put it in my mailbox. I'll give it to her Monday morning. Thanks." Jack started for the door.

"You know her pretty well, huh?"

"No, just a bunch of coincidences, I guess."

Sue looked across the top of her glasses.

"I'll give you a rundown sometime if you want. Interesting situation."

"Yeah, thanks again."

★★★★★

Jack was certain he had closed the door to his room.

Seeing it open, he was afraid Jean had left. He smiled, seeing her at his desk.

"Pretty long drink. May I see you pass?" she teased. "Pretty long hall and I never make a pass at my students—at least not that they can see." They both laughed. "What's your decision?"

"Well, since you weren't in the hall, that probably means you went upstairs. And since you went upstairs, you probably got it changed already. So I'll decide to go along with it."

Jack smiled. I'll never really know what your decision was, will I?"

"Nope."

"So…where do you want to sit?"

"Right here."

"No, that's mine." The bell rang, and the weekend was officially underway. Suddenly the door opened, and Scott Graham bounded in, carrying a small suitcase.

"Can I check out a book?"

"Jeez! By all means. Any particular one, or is this just for appearances?"

"What are you doin'? I thought you lived on some farm."

Jack could see the importance of the book had slipped as Scott discovered Jean sitting at the front desk.

"Here I am," she said softly.

"Really."

"I see you two know each other. Scott, my boy, what she means to say is that she's moving back and will start school here Monday. What have you got in the suitcase?"

"It's a trumpet case."

"Well, what have you got in the trumpet case?"

"Three guesses."

"Come on, let's see it."

"What?" The boy was surprised at this show of interest.

"I admire a man who can play a musical instrument. I didn't know you played. Show it to me, will you? Come on." Jack had hold of the case, and reluctantly Scott was snapping open the latches.

Jean slowly glided closer to them though pretending disinterest. "Holy mackerel, that's a beauty. Let's hear it."

"In here?"

"Hey, I'm impressed. Come on, wing out on it or just go up and down the scales. Come on, please."

Scott looked at Jean then back at Jack. "Why?"

"Why anything. I just think it's neat that you know how to play this thing. How come you have two of these?"

"They're mouthpieces."

"I realize that, but you only have one mouth."

Jack glanced to see that Jean had sat down again.

"It came with this one, but I like this one better. It's from my old trumpet."

"Great, that's all I needed to know." Jack was carefully lifting the instrument out of its resting place and inserting the correct mouthpiece. "Here, blast away."

The noise in hall was obscured as Scott's ascending notes filled the room. "What's so funny?" he demanded, seeing his teacher laughing.

"I don't know. I just think that's great that you can do that. I'd give anything to be able to play something like that."

The trumpet was being put away. "Here, don't forget your book. See you Monday—and thanks for the performance."

"See ya. See you around, Jean."

Through the door, Jack spied Mr. Headley peering this way and that. He decided the older man was looking for the source of the unusual noise but only had time to begin wondering if he had detected its source. He saw Jean shaking her head.

"What's wrong?" he asked.

"Did you see Headley out there? Just trying to get somebody in trouble. As if trumpet playing is going to hurt anything. I can't stand him."

"Well, I'm glad to hear that. For a while, I was afraid you didn't have any weaknesses."

Jean's gaze was outside the window, and she waited until Jack finished erasing the blackboard. "What did you expect to find?"

Jack's puzzled look told her he didn't understand. He was quiet and felt uncomfortable. The mood had changed, but he couldn't pick up any clues.

"In the case…what did you expect to find?"

Now he understood, but he felt even more uncomfortable.

An accusation was being made, and even his total innocence didn't help relieve the feeling within. He needed time to think. He began the daily ritual of closing windows and curtains.

"In the trumpet case?" he asked, half in humor.

Jean's nod was patient, and friendliness did show through.

"In the trumpet case, I expected to find a trumpet." With the curtains closed, the lighting in the room was softer, more subdued. He matched this with his voice as he walked toward her. "Your question says quite a lot, you know," He sat in a front-row desk. "It says quite a lot for sure. It says you think I was looking for something beside a trumpet, which could be a pretty heavy accusation, but it also says Scott is a drugger, doesn't it? If your first reaction, which is always the honest one, was that I was looking for drugs, you are as much as accusing Scott of having them in there—at least you're saying there is a possibility—and, Jean, we agreed to be student and teacher as well as friend and friend, and this is one of the problems we'll face. There will be things I'll find out about without even try-ing—that doesn't mean I'll do anything with the information or even that I want to find out. Do you see what I'm saying?"

"Yes?"

"About the other thing, the accusation itself, I have two points to make. First, I'm kind of ticked that you would accuse me of that, so it makes me defensive, you know?"

The door opened, and Russell announced, "I've been lookin' all over for you."

"You found me."

Jack couldn't tell whether it was her facial expression or the softness of her voice which seemed to say, "I'm sorry that I inconvenienced you. I didn't mean to, but I had no choice," and he wondered whether Russell caught it in the same way. "Sit down. We're into something heavy already. You don't play the trumpet, do you?"

Jean laughed, relieved.

"What?" Russell was lost and showed it.

"You're clean. Come on, sit down. What happened was this kid came in to get a book, okay? He had a trumpet case with him, and I asked to see its contents. With that much information, what would you say was my motivation…my reason?"

"Depends on who the kid is."

"Precisely, and Jean's first reaction was that I was looking for pot—which, in addition to being wrong, makes me mad and accuses the kid of being a drugger. That's where you came in." He again turned to Jean. "And I was saying it made me mad. That was the first point. Scott is a student of mine, and anytime I can find a talent or interest or hobby in a student of mine, I damn well better show an interest. In the area of music, specifically, I am in awe of anyone who can play any instrument. I can't myself—I wish I could. It takes a great amount of time and patience, I'm sure frustration, et cetera, et cetera. I simply admire anyone who can do it, and I think they deserve all the praise they can get. It was sincere."

"I know," Jean answered softly. "Here, you can have your desk back. You're better up here." She sat beside Russell before she continued, "As a matter of fact, that was the only thing I couldn't quite fit in."

"What do you mean?"

"I couldn't see how you could act so enthusiastic if you were searching for pot."

"It wasn't an act, okay?" He glanced at Russell and smiled. "The second point is the tough one, and I may as well say it to both of you. Jean, your accusation, your assumption is a classic example of paranoia, and I'm told that is common among the druggers. You are suspicious of everyone and everything. Do you guys remember when we were talking over in my apartment? I said I would never argue the medical aspects of this. I had other reasons. Well, this is one of them. You are so accustomed to living outside the law, your basic way of life, of enjoyment, is illegal. Its puts you on guard at all times. I enjoy being able to trust people. I don't know whether you can. Anyway, it's something to think about. Tell me what you dislike about Mr. Headley. Is it his limp or his age?" He thought he was talking to Jean.

"Oh god," Russell groaned. "All of the above. Between Hedgepeth and Headley, I've about had it. How can they let them keep teaching?"

"Do they know their stuff?"

"Yeah, but"

"That's all they need. That's why they are here. I'm not saying you have to like them, but if you're going to judge them, be sure the standards are fair. What other standards are there to judge a teacher by than whether he knows his stuff?"

"Knowing it is part of it, but being able to teach it is something else again…maybe more important." Jean's last words came out sounding like a question, and Jack realized he couldn't argue.

"Good point. I'm ready to go home. How about you two?"

"Home?" Jean repeated.

"That's right. Home is going to seem a little funny to you for a while. It will be interesting to see if it feels like home within the next few weeks." He watched Russell put his arm across her shoulder as they walked out of the room. Jack turned off the lights. "You never told me about Jeff and Randy," he continued.

"You've got a memory."

"For names, at least."

Raising both hands as if in triumph, Russell announced, "I get Randy."

Jack remained silent, and Jean answered the question. "Randy is moving in with Russell, and Jeff is going to stay at Griswolds with me."

"And come here to school?"

"Yep."

"That will be interesting," Jack said.

"School is never interesting."

"Ouch. Maybe it's just interesting to the teachers."

"There's what makes it interesting, right, Mr. Flemming?" Russell nodded toward Mary Lewis, who was well ahead of them on the walk.

"She teaches English or something."

"Speech, as if you didn't know," Jean laughed.

"Give a break." Jack noticed they were accompanying him to his car without an invitation. He moved to the passenger side and unlocked the door. The two scooted in.

"So…you have Lewis for speech?"

"That's Ms. Lewis."

"Oh, is it? Whom else do you have?"

"Try Headley and Hedgepeth."

"Whoopee," interjected Russell. "What hour?"

"I don't know. Whiplet has my schedule."

"That's…never mind," Jack chuckled. "Where does Flemming take Carter and Gilmore?"

I've got money," was Russell's answer.

"I'll bet you do. Friday is probably a pretty good day, isn't it?" Jack jabbed. The mood changed with his, but Jack decided to withdraw. Better to wait now until they were ready. "Sorry. So what shall we do with the money?"

"Caramel sundae," said Jean.

"Chocolate," said Russell.

"Make it two," said Jack. "So we hit the drive-in?"

"Yeah."

"Where?" asked Jack.

"Doesn't matter."

"Are you sure?"

"What do you mean?" Jean asked, sincerely interested.

"What I mean is I am not sure you two want to go into a drive-in down the street from your school—with you civics teacher!"

"Civics teacher will have to do," Russell said. "Until we can swing it with my speech teacher."

"Jeez. No, seriously. Is that a bad scene? It might be a problem?"

"No sweat. The problem now is I'm hungry. Did you check out the goddamn fish sticks today?"

"Pull in here, for cryin' out loud, and let's eat."

The order was placed for two chocolate and one caramel sundaes.

"So what's the game plan for the weekend?" Jack began.

"Hey." Russell fiddled with the sun visor then looked at Jack. "What about the money comment before? Seems like, well, I don't know."

"You want to get into all that now?"

"More like I want to get out of it."

"Clever…okay. Somebody brings the stuff into the school. There's money involved. Maybe there's several layers or stages. I don't know. I figure, Russell, my friend, that you may have interest in that kind of action."

The following silence told Jack he had scored. He moved on. "Let's try to make it easy. You may as well know again that my primary concern is to get kids away from drugs. If that had to start out as getting drugs away from kids, so be it. My interest—and this is the part you can't believe—is not in busting anybody. I gain nothing if kids get into trouble. I'm trying to keep people out of trouble. That's why I didn't know whether to come here or not, you know? It might cause a hassle for you. Anyway, I'd like to ask you a question, and, Russell, let's just say you either answer the question honestly or refuse to answer it at all."

They stared into each other's eyes, Jean looking tense between them.

"No problem," the boy assured him.

"We're just trying to get away from your need to lie. It's perfectly legitimate for you to just say you don't want to answer."

The sundaes were delivered, paid for, and distributed.

"So…what's the question?" Jean's voice was a whisper. Jack chuckled to think that it was Jean who was anxious.

"She's my spokesman," said Russell.

Jack patted her on the back of the head. "Well, maybe your spokesman can answer the question better than you can. Same rules apply." Jack now felt a surge of excitement within. He didn't want to scare either one of them. He took a big spoon of ice cream, swallowed deliberately, and turned slightly to look at them both. "The question is do you know the path, the system by which drugs enter our school? Notice I'm not saying tell me. I'm asking do you know it.

"Yeah."

"Thanks." His attention appeared to be on his drink, but Jack hoped for more interest. It was soon displayed.

"So?"

Jack looked up.

"Don't' you want to know anything else?"

"You better believe it, but I know better than to ask you. What I did ask you was what are you doing for the weekend?"

"It will be a lot of moving in, I guess," answered Russell.

He nodded to her before looking back at Jack with a smile, "And pool," he said reassuringly.

"Right." Jack beeped the horn to attract the waitress and gathered the dishes and napkins. "Should I just drop you down at the corner?

"Fine. Thanks a lot. See you Monday."

"Thanks for getting me in your class," Jean said as she slid across the seat.

"Thanks for getting in it. Have a weekend."

7

From Jack's door into the hallway, he could command a good view of the hall, the main stairs, a large portion of the locker area as well as keeping tabs on who came and went through the main entrance. All this pleased him, and he became conscious of this pleasure as two men—one White, one Black—strode purposefully through the door. They nodded but did not break stride. The Black man was, Jack noticed, considerably better dressed. *Just like the kids*, he thought to himself, turning to enter his room. He had hardly begun closing the windows for the day, reflecting upon how quickly the days were fleeing by, when he heard Russell behind him.

"So the juvies are here already." Russell's derisiveness was showing blatantly through.

"Say what?" Jack was pleased at how quickly he was adopting their way of talking.

"Salt and Pepper. They just marched right by here. Didn't you see them?"

Jack plunked himself into his chair. "I'm new here, okay?" He smiled.

"Excuse me! I was just observing," Russell teased. "That the juvenile officers have already made the scene for the school year."

Juvies? He thought for a moment. "Salt and Pepper juvies! Jesus. So tell me about 'em. I can't tell whether you like 'em or hate their guts.

"They're okay. They're cops, know what I mean. If you hear anybody refer to Steve and Edie"—he smiled—"it's them."

"Steve and Edie?" Jack began. "I'm with you at juvies, and I can handle Salt and Pepper, what with their racial composition, but I'm almost afraid to ask about Steve and Edie. Should I be?"

"The White guy is Steve Jarvis, so we call the other one Edie. I don't really know why."

"Terrific. What do you suppose they are here for?"

"I don't know…maybe to meet the principal or new teachers."

"There's always narcs to contact." Jack threw in. "So…would you say they're mainly into the drug scene?" Jack wanted to know.

"Since I know what your next question will be if I say yes, I'll say no."

Jack's smile showed he understood what his next question would be. Within he held great respect for the sharp intelligence sitting before him. Their eyes met for long moment. "Be careful not to say more than you mean to." With that, Jack got up and finished closing the windows. "Maybe I'll go meet the fuzz."

"See you tomorrow."

"See ya, and thanks for coming in and pointing them out to me. Always like to know when the law is around."

Walking down the hall, Jack had time to think. That he could associate comfortably with these kids was reassuring, no problem identifying whom to work on either. How to bring up the subject? "Well, maybe this will lead to something," he said to himself, pushing through the door to the office.

His reception there was a surprise. Glenn brushed past him. "Check your mailbox then go back to your room. I'll send for you."

Back at his desk, the shock still had not subsided; and as bewilderment was setting in, Glenn yanked the door open.

"I guess I need to explain. The heavies are here." He sat on a front-row desk, his long legs swinging. "I want you to meet the juvenile officers, but I just thought it would be best if the kids didn't see you guys together."

"I can understand that," Jack began thoughtfully. "You're saying the kids might not open up if they thought…or identified me with the police." He nodded as if agreeing with own thoughts. "Have you got a minute? Or did you want me to meet them? Whatever you think."

"Let's wait a few minutes. When the building has cleared out, come on down, and we can sit down for a few minutes."

"Sounds fine," Jack said.

"I think we can all be completely open. They're both, in my opinion, very professional," Glenn said. "And we can always allow you to be identified with them, if that's okay, but I was just afraid once you are identified with them, it would be impossible to undo… you know what I mean? That's why I didn't want you in the office right then. Sorry if I overreacted."

"That's okay. I'll be down in a few minutes."

The smell of cigar smoke hit Jack as he entered Glenn's conference room. Introductions were made. Russell had been right; Steve Jarvis was the White officer, the slightly younger of the two. Jack guessed twenty-eight or -nine. The Black man might have been ten years older. Jack couldn't decide if he was more taken by the man's outgoing friendliness or by his well-tailored look. He could tell that the whole image was carefully composed to have maximum impact. This man, Jack realized, could do a lot with kids. His name was Boles—Fred or Frank Boles. Jack hated to miss first names and determined to pick it up during the meeting.

"I was trying to explain what your role is," Glenn began, talking now to Jack. "How we're trying to give you some…avenue into the drug scene and at the same time eliminate the threat that the kids, at least, perceive in the juvenile officers."

The chair under Boles groaned as the big man shifted forward enough to snub out his cigar. A billowing puff of smoke was exhaled as they spoke. "And no way do we want to interfere with whatever you manage to get started." A ham-sized hand wave through the air, emphasizing the whatever. He then reached into his pocket, Jack hoped not for another cigar and continued, "And we don't want you to feel committed or obligated to us. You work for the school board, we work for the police department, but our goals are about the same. We want to keep kids out of trouble—not get them in trouble." With that, the gum was inserted, and Steve Jarvis took over.

"The only thing Fred and I are interested in"—Jack caught the name—"is the supply part. Do you want what I mean?"

"How it gets into the school in the first place," Jack said.

"Exactly. If there is some adult up the ladder someplace getting rich, we want him."

"But again"—Fred Boles was back in the conversation—"it's your decision what, if anything, to tell us about. We can only promise you discretion and confidentiality."

"This is all kind of hard to get started," Jack answered. "At least I'm finding it difficult, but I'm interested in the supply end of it also. Let me get your opinion. Would Russell Carter be the person to work with first?"

Both men shifted positions, relaxed. Glenn folded his arms across his chest. Officer Boles smiled and said, "You couldn't do better, in my opinion. Russell is a sharp boy. He can either do a lot of good or a lot of harm. If you can open him up a little bit, you might find something out, and if you think it's something we can use, that will help us get to the supplier…well, you decide."

"We don't want Russell to get hurt," Steve Jarvis added. "And he could."

"Or anybody else. These are kids," Boles said. "And we're not trying to bust any of them. It's just that they clean up when we're around."

"Let me ask another question," Jack said, his glance trying to include Glenn too.

"Shoot," said Jarvis.

"What about…" Jack hesitated. "How do you see it from a Black-White point of view?'

"You mean the supplier? asked Boles.

"Yes, do the White kids get it from the same source as the Blacks?"

"Probably not." Officer Boles was smiling, and Jack had the distinct feeling he knew it was definitely not, but he waited for amplification. "I personally don't see the two getting along that well under any circumstances…at least not the ones who use drugs." Jack respected the man's insight. "The ones who play on school teams with each other have learned to tolerate, if not respect, but the drug crowd kind of goes its own way, and outright hatred exits."

The meeting broke up with handshakes and assurance of cooperation both ways. Jack left with an uplifted feeling bullied by his own confidence that he could succeed in unraveling the supply line mystery where the juvenile officers could not.

With only his free period left in the day and remembering his meeting yesterday with Jarvis and Boles, Jack headed for the drinking fountain where he would be more in circulation. His attention was drawn from the bright-blue wad of bubble gum in the fountain to a growing knot of students outside Mr. Headley's room. Trouble. Jack knew a fight was brewing, but couldn't see who was involved. He began piercing the outer circle while saying, "Excuse me, excuse me," as he pushed young onlookers out of his way. Two students were faced off, but no action had started.

"All right, let's get to class," Jack announced to the crowd in general. The two antagonists stood chest to chest, looking equally coolly at each other. Jack recognized one of them as a seventh grader—Tyrone somebody.

"What you doin', Tyrone, giving dancing lessons?"

The crowd jeered, and Jack noticed the White boy relax, so he gently pulled Tyrone toward him, swatting him playfully on the rear and sent him on down the hall.

"No more of that," was all that was needed. The crowd was disappointed and let Jack know, but there would be no trouble.

It seemed the three o'clock bell had just sounded when Jack locked up to see the other boy standing before his desk.

"Hi, Rocky," Jack said, teasing. "What's your name?"

"Jim."

"What can I do for you?"

"I was going to say thanks for not turning us in today."

"You didn't do anything—but you're welcome. Thanks for breaking off so easily when I asked you to. What was all that about? You want to talk?"

Jim lifted himself up onto a desktop. Jack took it to mean it was going to be a long conversation. "How do you talk about it?"

"Honesty." Jack smiled. "My name is Mr. Flemming, by the way."

"I know. You teach social studies, don't you."

"Try not to hold that against me."

"Social studies is all right."

"Thanks…so what was it all about?"

The boy looked down at his feet dangling above the floor. "It was exactly what it looked like: Black against White." His muscles tensed. He looked up at Jack and continued, "I'd like to kick that n——'s ass.

"Could you?"

"Yeah. He know it too."

"So you started it?"

"No."

"Now wait a minute. He knows you can take him, so he starts a fight with you. That doesn't make much sense."

"He wouldn't finish it. Did you see the crowd?"

"I went through the crowd."

"What color was it?"

"Tell me. I was watching you."

"Mostly n——, all ready to kill me when I hit him."

"Maybe they just like to watch fights."

"They set up fights, but they don't like to fight by themselves."

"And you do?"

"No, I don't like to fight, if that's what you mean." There was a long silence. Jack knew there was more coming. "Well, I don't mind fighting, but I can't get suspended again."

"How many times has this happened?"

"What, fighting?"

"Okay."

"I don't know. All the time."

"So…here's the question. Does this involve you specifically—Jim whatever-your-name is—or is it anyone they go after?"

The boy slid down off his perch and started for the door.

"Come here, Jim."

"Thanks for not turning me in."

"Come here." Jack was on his feet, but the boy was out the door. He couldn't dwell on his loss for long.

Jean slid through the doorway and with one nod said, "Hello, hope you don't mind my interrupting your privacy. What's wrong, and can I help?"

Jack dropped into his chair while Jean sat before him on the same desk Jim had occupied. The two gazed at each other, Jack wishing he could communicate with her as easily as she could with him.

"Yeah, you can stay." Jack laughed. "Who was that kid who just left here?"

"Salsbury? That's the only one I saw."

"What's his first name?"

"Jim."

"Tell me about him."

"Tell you about him?"

"Hey, come on. I just want to know whatever there is to know about the kid. He came in to talk, and something happened. He just took off."

"I guess he'd be in the seventh grade. He's wild."

"Wild?"

"Fights a lot. That's kind of his thing, you know?"

"He has a reputation as a fighter?"

"I'd say so."

"How does he get along with Blacks?"

"I don't think he'd take much from them."

"You mean they wouldn't bother him?"

"He's like my brothers. He'd rather take his chances in a fight than be pushed around and insulted."

"Okay. How big a problem is this anyway? How much does it go on?"

She walked to the window and gazed outward across the lawn of blowing leaves. Finally, she said, "Not constantly, but almost."

"Almost constantly! Come on, I'd see it. Anybody would see it."

"What are you looking for?"

"I don't know…fights, pushing—"

"Who's fighting and pushing?" Russell bounced through the door.

"Well, the Minnesota Fats of West," greeted Jack.

Somehow Russell and Jean were seated on the same desk by now, but Russell pressed his question. "What's the fight? Did I miss anything?"

"Be cool. Jean and I were just talking about the problem around here." Jean smiled, knowing as Jack did that Russell would have to have more information now.

"And what, may I ask, is the problem around here?"

"Aha. Beautiful. Here is the key question, and Jean gets to answer it. Consider your words carefully, young lady. Just what is the problem?" It was Jack's turn to walk to the window. Somehow, he knew there would be a long delay then a short answer. He occupied himself trying to guess what she would say. Then he began to guess whether she would say anything.

"It's quarter to four," Russell said playfully.

Finally, Jean broke her silence. "Prejudice."

"Jesus Christ."

"No, prejudice."

Jack turned and looked at the two. "Jean, is Russell prejudiced?"

"No, I just hate n——."

"Hey." Jack approached his desk. "I'm serious."

"The problem is serious," Jean insisted.

"So answer my question. Is Russ prejudiced?"

"Is Russ prejudiced?" Her repetition meant to Jack it was not her question to answer. "Mr. Flemming, we're not talking about the same thing."

"Prejudice is prejudice, isn't it?" He collapsed into his chair, thinking he had won an argument. "You admitted the problem is prejudice."

Jean smiled. "We're not prejudiced."

"*We* meaning?"

"The Whites."

"She's right."

"You're telling me the Blacks are prejudiced?"

"Hell yes. I don't know of anybody who comes in here hating Blacks. We got along fine in grade school. I don't know what happens."

"Well, we were talking about this seventh grader—Jim what's-his-name. He seemed to be telling me that one Black will pick a fight, then when the action starts, they all jump in."

"Probably."

"Why him?"

"Mr. Flemming," Russell began. "I never can tell whether you are asking questions like in class where you already know the answer or if you don't know and really want to?

"I really want to know…your opinion," he added for emphasis.

"Well, we were talking about this once, and it kind of boiled down this way. Let's say there's three kinds of Whites—the ones that can take care of themselves either because they are big, athletic, whatever, or because they hang around a group that's pretty…you know…tight. The second kind is the weaklings who can't take care of themselves. The third group is the smallest. They are the, more or less, loners. Maybe they're smaller than average, but the important part is they don't take any crap from the Blacks."

Jean could see the confusion on Jack's face. "The Blacks expects everybody to be in either the first group or the second group."

"Sorry, I don't follow you."

The two looked at each other, then Russell tried again. "Okay, they don't bother me because I'm big and in a big group. They don't bother the second group because those kind of people do what the Blacks want them to do."

"Which is what?" Jack felt foolish under Russell's stare, but he endured, feeling that he was about to learn something.

"Like money?"

"If a Black asks you to loan him a dime, what do you do?'

"What do I do?" Jack said.

"Yeah."

"I ask if he's got change for a twenty."

"Terrific, but your basic group two coughs up a dime or quarter or whatever."

"Does he get it back?"

"Not hardly."

"It's polite robbery," Jean added.

"Not so polite," Russell corrected.

"Now, see if I have this right. I understand group one. The hard guys, or burnouts." Jack smiled. "Group two is totally…submissive. They knuckle under. Is that what you're saying?" He pressed on. "It's the group three I'm having trouble with. Are you saying the Blacks expect everyone not in group one to knuckle under and they can't stand anyone who stands up for himself—by himself?" He stood up, delighted with his newfound inspiration. "So that's what you mean when you said they want people to be in either group one or two."

"You got it."

"I got to get going," Jack said as he gathered papers from his desk and began loading his briefcase. "Tell you what I'd like to have you do. See if you can come to an agreement as to how many students are in this group three. That's something I'd really like to know."

He locked his door and headed for the office, leaving the two to stroll down the hall together. He was now alone to wonder why his question had driven Jim Salsbury from the room so quickly.

*****

As usual, Jack stayed in his room before school the next morning, but he made it a point to be in the halls between periods. He wasn't sure what he was looking for, but there was plenty to see. He tried to look beyond the running and the surface commotion. He deliberately ignored conversations which normally would have attracted his attention. He didn't even look at those who spoke to him. What he did see appalled him. Had it been there all along? he wondered. It was subtle, but the defiance was there. The intimidation was smooth but very much present. Group twos were everywhere, their paths through the halls erratic and complex while straight and slowly the Blacks ambled with studied nonchalance and labored swagger. Occasionally shoulders would hit, and threatening glances were exchanged. While no actual threats were audible, there were snarls.

He was looking for actual talking between races. Expecting to see extortion unfolding before him, he was disappointed. The traffic began to thin, but Jack held his position. He had never really watched a period start from anywhere but inside his own room. It was a revelation; as the traffic decreased, the speed increased. Stragglers began to hurry. Lockers slammed. Teachers down the line began to close their doors. The bell sounded, and a few students broke into actual running. Within seconds, the hall was empty except for Black students who seemed unhurried, continued to converse and move as if having not heard a bell. Feeling resentment toward these and realizing he was at this point no better than they, Jack moved into his room. His mind stayed in the hall.

He had noticed the same pattern throughout the day but especially wanted to observe Jim Salsbury. Now he waited knowing Jim would be in the area as he had been yesterday, though, Jack hoped, less pugnacious. It wasn't long until Jack spotted him and felt a rewarding thrill to see how nonchalantly the boy moved. Jean had been right. He wasn't daunted by others' movement. He was aloof. It was almost as if he didn't notice others, but that was not true. When he spied Jack, he beamed.

"Hi, Mr. Flemming."

"Hey, Rocky. How's it goin'?"

The title may have thrown him, but he was not shy at the teacher's attention. "It'll be better after social studies." He pulled up alongside Jack as if willing to continue a conversation.

"I hope you mean because it's the last period of the day—not because of social studies itself."

"Whatever," the boy laughed.

"Do you ride the bus home?" Jack asked.

"No, why?"

"Drop in after school, will you?"

"Later."

✶✶✶✶✶

The bell ending the day had scarcely stopped echoing through the halls when Jim bounded through the door.

"My lord, did you even go to social studies?" Jack teased.

"It was a drag."

"What kind of grades do you make?"

"Okay."

"I didn't know we had an okay on the grade system."

"I can get Bs."

"Super, let me tell you why I asked you to come in—through you're welcome to come in anytime, asked or not." Jack moved toward the door, which he pulled shut to cut out some of the noise. "I'm closing that to keep the noise out, not to keep you in." Jack smiled at the boy, but Jim dropped his head as if ashamed.

"Okay, so you took off in kind of a hurry yesterday. I figure I said something wrong or asked something that wasn't much of my business. The reason I asked you in was to give me a chance to try to set things straight. Can you talk about it today?"

The boy shrugged and looked up. "I'll talk."

"Well, let's see…backing up twenty-four hours…asked you if it was you, specifically, that they want to fight, they being the Blacks."

"I don't know about anybody else, but somebody has it in for me and spreads rumors to make me look bad."

Not totally believing the boy, Jack groped for perspective. "Do you know why? Do you know who?"

"Yeah."

"Do I get to find out, or is that the hard part?"

"There's this Black chick. She wants to go with me."

"Go with you?" There was a long silence.

"You heard me."

"Yes, but I don't understand the problem. Either you do or don't want to go with her. It seems like—"

"I don't want to go with her, so she tells guys that I say stuff about them or that I'm prejudiced."

"Now I see the problem. That's a tough one to crack, isn't it?"

"You said it," the boy agreed.

"How has she let you know?"

"You know, notes, showing off." The door opened. It was Russell.

"I hope I won't interrupt anything."

"I hope not either." Jack smiled.

"Sorry, I'll be back, okay?"

"Good, see you in a few minutes. Thanks." Jack looked at his watch then back at his boy on the desk before him. "So, Jim, you're sure this is not your imagination. There's no way you could be making something that doesn't really exist?"

Expressionless, the boy filled through his math book and extracted a folded piece of paper. He tossed it on Jack's desk. "Read it whenever. Sorry I took so much of your time. See you later."

He was almost to the door when Jack managed to say, "Remember, I asked you in. I'm taking your time."

The boy didn't stop, and almost as if on cue, Russell came in as Jim left. Jack stuffed the note into his shirt pocket. "So…what's up? Where's Jean?"

"She should be here. She has gym last hour today."

"You need a ride?"

"No, no, I just kind of wanted to get your opinion on something."

"Shoot."

"Randy's taking my dad's car for joyrides."

The two stared at each other in silence. "You lost me," Jack said matter-of-factly.

"Joyride, you know? Hop in a car and go."

"I know that. Who's this Randy?"

"Jean's brother. He's staying at my house."

Jack let out a long, slow whistle.

"I don't know what to do."

"When does this happen? At night?"

"Yeah. He'll get up at one or two and go for a spin."

"Does he ask you to go along?"

"He doesn't think I know about it, I guess."

"And the keys?"

"He doesn't need 'em."

"He hot-wires your dad's car and drives it around town? Terrific." Jack walked to the window. "I'll tell you what I'd like to do…" The door opened, and Jean floated in. She pushed a desk closer to the one Russell was on and sat down. Jack nodded and began closing the blinds.

"Whenever I walk into a room," Jean began. "And everyone stops talking, I figure they were talking about something I'm not supposed to hear."

Jack chuckled, "Or else they're talking about you."

"Where you been?" Russell was quick to take it up.

"I told you I'd be in the gym."

"That's cool. Let's go. You ready?"

"Okay, but I just got here."

"Got to play some pool. Come on, let's go."

Jean rolled her eyes condescendingly. "Pool!"

"See you tomorrow, Mr. Flemming."

"Good luck in your game."

8

Jack had never seen so forced a smile on Jean's face, but then he realized he had never seen her in the morning. Perhaps she always looked this way, he thought, wondering if beauty can be confined to the postprandial. She looked awful as she wended her way toward him, and he could tell she was purposefully coming his way.

"Good morning," he greeted.

"Can I talk to you after school?"

He forced a chuckle. "Don't you talk to me every day after school?"

Her eyes looked floorward across the armload of books she carried. The growing noise in the hall and her downcast stance almost prevented his hearing her utter, "Red alert."

"Oh, uh." He wanted to touch her but heard himself say, "Meet me inside the counselor's office. We'll find a place in there."

Preoccupied as he was during his morning classes, Jack gave the rendezvous little thought but realized he was deliberately avoiding any confrontation which would need to be resolved after school. His anxiety heightened at noon when he was unable to find her anywhere. Just a nod or smile or wink, he thought, was all he needed—to either give or receive. That would be enough to assure her and him that whatever the problem, they could work it out.

Fourth hour arrived, and so did Jean, but nothing seemed the same—no sparkle, no talk, no participation. An open book lay on her desk, and she was writing during the few occasions Jack glanced her way. A hopeless, desperate feeling left him unable to do anything but assign some questions at the end of the chapter. How could all that rapport, that warmth and understanding have vanished? The more he pondered, the more he internalized it, and the more he blamed himself. He had stood by her while her home lay in ashes, and she had not looked this totally alien. Then it hit him: *She must be on drugs, guilty, and hating me—right here in my classroom, for Chrissake, and I can't even pick up on it until the period is over.* He tried to sort out the terrible feelings within him. Was it fear, resentment, jealousy? He hoped not.

Saved by the bell. "I probably didn't give you enough time for all of that," he was announcing. "Let's plan to finish them up the first part of class tomorrow. See you then." His attention was attracted to a tightly folded piece of paper so smoothly deposited on his desk as Jean passed in front.

"Gotcha," he acknowledged. Not picking it up until the room was empty, he unfolded it with trembling hands.

Dear Mr. Flemming,

I would rather meet you in front of the hardware store where we first met. It will be much safer than the counselor office. I'll be there soon after school and will wait. But don't feel sorry if you can't come for some reason.

It you do come, stay in your car. Okay?

Jean

That felt good. He has time to reflect back to his education course. The professor had emphasized, "If you're going to survive in education, you'll have to learn to leave all the problems behind you when the bell rings at the end of the day."

"No way," Jack said to himself and vowed that Jean would not have to wait for him. This was what he was waiting for: a kid on drugs wanting to talk with him about it. *Hmm! This*, he thought, *is better than winning a baseball game. This is total victory.*

Jack had little time to think about their first chance meeting in this very spot, and he had determined to play this one by ear. No prepared lines, no practiced speeches; he didn't even know whether he would show anger or hurt or indifference. That she was going to talk to him superseded all else, making him shun even slight preparation. *He* could not have prepared himself for what was to come anyway. She didn't even come from the direction he had been expecting and watching in anticipation. Suddenly the door opened, and she was on the seat beside him, her books randomly settling between them.

"I feel like a doughnut. How about you?" he started.

"You don't look like a doughnut."

Well, the ice was broken, and how quickly she had changed from her somberness of fourth hour!

"There's a doughnut shop over in Parkwood. Let's hit that since you didn't have any lunch."

"Since I didn't have any lunch."

Jack wasn't going to answer that one. He was just glad she was herself again. He was on familiar territory.

"What do you know about dogfights?" she blurted.

"Depends on whether you're talking World War I or II or Vietnam. Why?" He was instantly aware that he wasn't on familiar ground at all. He didn't even look at her until he had pulled into the parking lot, yet she had managed to convey to him an inundation of failure. As he stopped the car, he looked at her, enabling her to accuse him of joking about something very serious, of noticing about the problem she had borne all day—all this before she spoke. When she did speak, doughnuts didn't matter anymore.

"I'm talking dogfight dogfights…for money, you know?"

"Oh… What do I know about it? Nothing. Somehow, when I think of dogfights, I think of Arkansas…for what that's worth."

"Better think again"

"Well, help me. What's brought all this up?"

"I think Randy is making money at it."

"Your brother? Go on."

"He finds dogs—or steals 'em—and sells them to some man who holds dogfights."

"Terrific. Without telling me how you found out, try to tell me all you know."

"That's about it. It is some man around here. He gives twenty-five dollars for each one. I know Randy made seventy-five dollars last week sometime. What I don't know is how he gets the dogs to this guy."

Through the window, Jack saw what looked like a cinnamon roll being served along with a cup of coffee. "I think I do," he said absently.

"What do you know about all this?" surprise, for once, clearly in her tone.

Jack cleared his throat before taking time to explain. "You didn't want to talk to me in my room. You didn't even want to talk about this anywhere near school. I assume that's because you don't deserves that same protection. If I told you what somebody else shared with me, you'd assume I would tell other people anything you tell me. Make sense?"

"Gotcha."

"There are some things I will tell you, though, like how I felt today and what I thought, but maybe we ought to solve this dogfight thing first."

"Solve it?"

"Well, what did you have in mind when you decided to tell me about it?"

"I don't know."

"If we started listing all the things we could try, what would they be?"

"You could talk to him about it."

"Or you could."

"No, I don't think—"

"Jean, we're just listing all the ideas we can. One is for me to talk to him. One is for you to. Another one is for both of us to…get what I mean? We're not yet deciding anything, just listing options."

She nodded thoughtfully but said nothing.

"We could tell the police," Jack continued and saw her start to say no, but she held back. "Or we could do nothing or you could tell your parents. See what I mean? We need to consider all the ideas and then try to decide which ones is best."

Her silence frightened him, and he sought to get her involved again. "Let's say we take your first idea. I talk to him about it, and by the way, there are several things we have to consider like he's going to know how I found out, and once I say anything, I'm sure as heck can't unsay it. So from then on, if he chooses to continue, you and I sure aren't going to find out about it. But back to what I started to say, here's what I want you to think about—while I go in and have a doughnut." He saw a momentary smile. "If I were to talk to him about it, what angle would I take? The cruelty part, the stealing part, or does it come out, 'Hey, kid, you need to stay in bed at night 'cause you need your sleep.'"

"The cruelty part."

"Damn."

"What's the matter?" Her voice was almost a whisper.

"You were supposed to think about it while I went in to get a doughnut, and, hey, I'm not making light of this at all. I know how you feel about it, and I share those feelings, plus, I feel for the little kids who cry themselves to sleep and can't think straight when they're awake because they don't know what happened to their pet."

"I know."

"But, Jean, we have to take out time and handle this carefully.

There is something more important than extracting Randy from this mess. That won't save any dogs nor enable any more kids to sleep at night. How about a doughnut?"

"I'll come in with you."

"Good."

With two cinnamon rolls and coffee on the way, Jack continued, "I'm glad you told me about this. I wonder if you'll be willing to wait maybe a few days or even a week before we do anything. In the meantime, you might hear something important. There are two things important to us. One is getting randy to see the light, but the other is to break up the ring, if that's what it is, and it certainly sounds like it."

"Just think about it. What kind of people could sit and watch those poor dogs? I don't want to wait, but I don't know what else we can do. But I'll try to find out more."

"Just don't appear to be too interested, you know?"

"Okay." She was picking at her cinnamon roll. "So…tell me what you were going to tell me."

He gazed at her for a long time, thinking, *She doesn't miss a thing*, feeling almost relief that it hadn't been a drug problem. He chuckled, "I was really worried. I couldn't find you at noon, and during fourth hour, I hate to say it, but I thought maybe you were stoned."

"I was."

Jack's mind went blank. He put his roll back on its plate, swallowed his coffee, and swiveled his tool so that he faced her directly.

"Why?"

Her look showed absolute surprise as if she could not understand his concern. "I was bummed out," she said matter-of-factly. "And I was down at the bridge at noon."

"The bridge?"

"That's where everybody goes."

"What are you talking about?"

She smiled. "It's the most beautiful place around. You know where the walkway crosses over the creek? It's right down from the home ec room."

"I'll have to check it out."

"Well…it's neat down there, and we can sit around and not be bothered."

"And…"

"What are you thinking?" She challenged.

"The pot burns, the pills roll, and the booze flows." They both burst into laughter.

"So you were stoned in my class." Jack was now serious and sounded hurt.

"Yes," she whispered. "But I am…often."

"Jesus, I just don't understand."

"See, you need an explanation all the time. Is there some explanation for eating a cinnamon roll or drinking coffee? Can't we just do dope or whatever without some super explanation?"

"Let's not talk about drinking coffee and doing dope in the same paragraph."

"Why not? There are enough similarities and not many differences."

"One's illegal." Jack plunked some coins on the counter. "Let's go."

The late afternoon traffic was picking up, and progress was slow. Jack asked, "What would happen if I'd come down to the bridge someday at noon?"

Her silence was so long he thought she was ignoring him. "Hello?"

"I don't know. There's no danger of catching anyone, so that wouldn't be a problem. It would be all right, I guess." She looked over at him when the car stopped for a light. "Just don't tell anybody I invited you."

"I'm sure. When you said, 'Everybody is there,' what did you mean? Who're we talking about?"

"Why don't you come down and see?"

"No, I don't mean names. I mean, you know, what kind of people?"

"What kind of people?"

He knew that was coming. "I know, I know." He gunned the engine and swerved around a truck. "But you know what I mean. I can't help it if you don't want to admit there is a certain kind."

"We're all friends."

"I should hope so. Be a shame if there were some narcs down there in the middle of it."

"Mr. Flemming, I'm trying to answer your question."

"Maybe I can help. Are there any athletes down there, people on any of the school teams?"

"No."

"Any students? And you know what I mean by that."

"No."

"Would anybody down there wear anything but blue jeans?"

"Not really."

"Anybody in the band?"

"No…well, Scott is."

"How many cheerleaders?"

"None."

"French club? Spanish club? I'll tell you what. Some time when the conversation lags, try to find out if anybody down there knows what he wants to be doing ten years from now." He glanced her way before pressing it further. "Jean, we've got our hands full with this dogfight business. We need to work together on it, but getting stoned just because we're disappointed or bummed out by it isn't going to help. Where should I drop?"

"I can walk from your apartment."

Nothing more was said until the engine had been shut off, and Jean began to gather up her books.

"I hate it," Jack began. "When we're in opposition to each other, and I think we are right now. The part of the problem I didn't tell you about is…jealousy."

"What?"

"Strange, isn't it? I've thought about it since noon, and I have to admit that's what it is."

"I don't understand."

"It's like I want you to be a certain way, you know? My way, straight, and feel like if Russell can get you high, then he's winning you away from my ideas. You know what I mean?"

She stared straight ahead for a long moment. Finally, she whispered, "I didn't know it mattered that much."

"You think teachers just like to get kids in trouble? Here we go again. Maybe we should talk about all this some other time. I just wanted to admit that I was…I don't know…hurt, mad, jealous, whatever, that you'd get high instead of—"

"I understand," she interrupted. "And I'm sorry."

"I'm glad you told me about this dog business. Let me know what you find out. Okay?"

"Thanks for the doughnut. See you Monday."

As she disappeared around the building, Jack began his preparations. His only hope was that the school was still unlocked. There would, he knew, be too many Carters in the phone book, and all his plans hinged upon locating Russell's house.

By the time he returned to his apartment, he had become surprisingly familiar with the Carters. He had learned, to his comfort, that their front yard and driveway were clearly visible from the rear lot of the shopping center. He knew what kind of car Mr. Carter drove (complete with license number). He had familiarized himself with the entire subdivision which at first had seemed a maze of winding streets but which only offered three routes of exit, two of which would be eliminated if one turned right coming from the Carters' driveway. Either direction the boy chose to go, Jack would not have to follow him through the deserted streets of the subdivision but could contact and follow from the point where he pulled onto the busier streets.

With a small foam cooler, some cookies, oranges, and two sandwiches, Jack felt ready for what he knew would be a long night—a long night of failure he had not bargained for, but the anticipation had kept him alert. All he had learned from his efforts was what time the boys came home.

Halfway through the second night, he began to have feelings of doubt. Maybe Russell had laid down the law; maybe Jean had said something or made some threat. At any rate, he had to force himself to return on Sunday night; 2:00 a.m. was the limit which he had established for himself, and even then, he wasn't sure about making it through the day at school.

Shortly before his own deadline, a flash of light reflected off an opening storm door. Jack was wide awake and forced himself to watch calmly as a dark figure moved across the lawn. The interior light of a car glared momentarily then went out. He heard no door slam. The car sat still for so long that Jack began to think no one had gotten in it, but then it started top roll down the drive to street where it turned right. Jack started his engine and glanced back to see that the headlights had been turned on.

It was then that he noticed what he could not have known Friday afternoon, and it would make his task infinitely simpler. One of the two left-hand taillights was burned out. Following that car at quite a distance would be no trouble at all. He drove to where he knew Randy would pull out of the subdivision and drove slowly enough so that the boy would have plenty of time to pull out ahead of him. He stayed nearly a block behind but held back even father when Randy turned down a dark side street and pulled to the curb. It was a few moments before Jack realized where he was. Randy would be, Jack guessed, parked right in front of his old burned-out home. Another interminable wait, during which Jack's imagination covered dozens of possible explanations for this particular stop, ranging from a pitiable desire to relive happier days to sex to drug dealing finally ended with the headlights routinely turning on and the lopsided taillight pattern slowly climbing the hill beyond.

"Careful now," Jack told himself. "Not too close. Better to lose him than scare him." Jack had to acknowledge that the kid wasn't bad as a driver—nothing erratic, no overbraking, and, he was glad, signals given before every turn. Jack was even able to turn one block early and parallel the boy for a few blocks. Never had his own headlights seemed so bright, so piercing as they did while following that one burned-out taillight. Once as an oncoming car's headlights played across the windshield, Jack thought he saw a second person in the car. His own curiosity and desire to keep this kid out of trouble almost caused him to pull him over and send him back home, but the memory of Jean's anguish kept him intent upon his original plan. Up ahead, a red stoplight shook off all thoughts of Jean. Rather than pull up behind or alongside the boy, Jack turned onto a side street and made his way around the stop. He was now committed to a gamble that the boy would turn onto the highway. Jack pulled into a service station and hoped the boy would turn this way.

A light rain began to fall, and Jack flipped on his wipers. Glancing in the mirror, he saw headlights pull up to a pump behind him. He sat frozen as he saw the driver get out and pump gas but was unable to identify him. Inside the car, though, there was enough action to catch Jack's attention. Against the wet windshield could be seen the silhouette of a large dog pacing back and forth along the seat. Jack calculated that no more than five gallons could have been pumped before the hose was replaced, and the driver entered the shop to pay. *At least he's got some overhead,* Jack thought, cautiously turning to look at the boy in the well-lit station. Now he was sure and decided to drive off slowly and let the boy pass him so as not to attract attention to himself following.

He crept along until he saw the headlights pull out of the service station and gain rapidly on him then slow, signal for a right turn, and disappear down a side road. Jack wheeled around, trying to concentrate on just where the boy had disappeared. It was almost too easy; there was the familiar lopsided pattern of lights going over a hill. Jack turned in and drove slowly now by only the light of his parking lights, and as he crested the hill, he turned them off also. Brake lights glared far ahead, and the boy pulled into a clearing on the left.

Jack stopped and rolled down his window in time to hear a door slam. Within a surprisingly short time, the lights went back on and began to back out onto the roadway. Jack sank down in the seat and listened as the boy roared back over the hill. Jack now had what he wanted and slowly drove past the clearing, able to see a small house set well back from the road. Deciding to drive by again after school, he returned home for some sleep but couldn't help driving past Russell's house to see that the car was safely returned. Somehow, he found himself in awe of that kid. A kind of respect was due for a kid who could pull that off not once but several times.

This feeling was renewed in the morning when Jack scoured the absence and tardy list. Randy had made it on time. It would be interesting, Jack thought, to see how he holds up through the day. By fourth period, he had doubts about his own ability to hold up and was content to just sit at his desk rather than stand in the halls between periods, and after school, when the usual crowd began dropping in, he had to force himself to stay. Jean came in without Russell.

"Sorry I didn't get down to the bridge," Jack joked.

"I was expecting you."

"Maybe tomorrow. Any news?"

"I think he went last night. I don't know what to do. Maybe you should talk to him."

"Well, let's see. If he went last night, we probably have a few days before we have to do anything. I'll think about a way to talk with him, though, and still keep you covered."

"Sometimes I could just kill him."

"Right. That doesn't sound like you. Need a ride?" He was closing the curtains and locking the windows.

"No, Russell is over in the gym. We'll walk home."

"See you tomorrow. Don't give up."

She smiled and turned away.

✸✸✸✸✸

Jack could see that the place was deserted and decided to risk walking around. Not a desirable place to live, he thought, but a good location for things clandestine. A few scrubby-looking kennels were lined behind the main house. A shed beyond showed neglect. A large pulley hanging from a high branch caught Jack's eye. A thick rope ran through it with a knot at one end. Some dogs lay in the various cages; most seemed indifferent to the visitor. Interestingly, all the cages were locked. Other observations of note were the absence of a space to turn a car around and the absence of a doorbell. Jack was glad to notice that the dilapidated porch light fixture held no bulb. He was careful to notice any obstructions between the house and the road, the most potentially dangerous of which was a drainage ditch; but if he stayed on the gravel, there would be no danger of tripping of falling. It was just a question of when, and tonight, he thought, would be as good as any. His only worry while driving home was that he might be too excited to fall asleep.

That proved to be no problem, and by nine that evening, he awoke hungry and ready for a shower. He was pleased at how businesslike he was behaving. With a frozen dinner in the oven, he dug through the closet in his bedroom until he came upon the shoebox he knew was there. Briskly he took out the Luger and two shells. Passing the bathroom, he grabbed a towel then returned to the kitchen. A paring knife was all he needed to slit the soft tops of the bullets. Accuracy would not be important, but the four-quartered bullets would do unbelievable damage to flesh and sinew as they hit and spread. It would be painless, he rationalized, more than could be said for the dogs which died agonizingly. The buzzer on his oven startled him, and he had to laugh at himself for being so jumpy. He preferred to look upon this whole undertaking as something which was being done for someone else—a person whose scruples were so low, whose motivation was so self-serving, and whose joys were so perverse that he simply had to be eliminated–and why not be businesslike about it? He was not doing this for himself; it was a business, a service.

By ten, he was on his way. The Luger, towel wrapped, sat heavily in the right pocket of his old coat. He drove past the familiar house and could see a car parked there. He turned around and pulled up in front of the house. He felt the hood of the parked car. It was cold.

His knocking seemed painfully loud; a dog barked from behind the house. He knocked again and heard someone approaching the door. It opened, and a small man stepped out into the darkness.

"Yeah," was his only greeting.

"I hear you might want to buy a dog," Jack said flatly.

"That depends."

Those were his last words. Jack squeezed, and a muffled blast tore upward through the body before him, sending it up and back before it crashed heavily on the wooden porch. There was no need for the second bullet.

Jack walked to his car, noticing that no lights went on in the house. He wished he could free the dogs from their pens but knew that was impossible. They would be taken care of. He had done his part.

He could think only of Jean going to bed about now. What would be her reaction, he wondered. How long until this hit the newspapers? A twinge of excitement raced through him as he anticipated reactions among the various participants in this whole drama. For now, he could content himself in the realization that it had been clean. Authorities would assume a gambling feud had been played out or some other nefarious underworld strife had led to retribution.

9

He had awakened with a conscious feeling of confidence. He could—and would—solve any and all problems. Teaching was almost secondary to problem-solving this morning, and in Jack's mind, he was the one to do solving.

Jenny Sylvester arrived a good ten minutes late, and he decided now was the time to wade into a mother's extramarital activities or whatever goings-on warranted the early morning watchfulness of his habitually tardy student.

"What do you have second hour?" he asked as he signed her tardy slip.

"Home ec," she answered, not looking at him.

"Would you stick around after the bell rings? I want to talk with you a few minutes. I'll give you a pass to home ec."

"Sure." She returned to her seat; the tardy slip lay on the desk, giving Jack a moment to ponder its contained non sequitur. Under "Reason for Tardy," it said, "Late." They always just said "late." How could late be a reason for being tardy? Don't they mean the same thing? As the class before him considered questions about TR's foreign policy, Jack reflected absently upon the irritation he felt over this whole tardy mess. The problem was massive. Tardy slips were given out wholesale, with someone's illegible initials on them. He felt guilty that he himself had contributed nothing toward solving the problem. *Who, besides me, is keeping records?* Jack wondered. *Is anybody?* The laxity of the system—if, indeed, there was a system—allowed kids to walk in anytime they wanted to, but Jack had little time to think about what exactly should be done about it before the bell rang. *That's another thing*, Jack thought. *I don't dismiss my classes. The bell does.* Teachers wanting to give last-minute instructions or words of encouragement had to time them to the second because if caught in midsentence by the bell, no one was left to talk to. But he had someone to talk to now.

"Jenny," he started with a smile. "I've never really had a chance to talk with you before this, so I don't know whether we will be able to solve anything or not. You've probably already figured out that the subject is tardies." Jack's smile was met with a shrug. "I need help in deciding whether these tardies could be eliminated, or is there a problem beyond your control?"

The girl simply looked down at her desk. Jack waited then pressed on. "We don't know each other well enough, maybe, to talk very much yet, but let me guess. It's not just a case of your being too lazy or too slow moving to get to my class on time. I think you're too smart to just let that happen." Still there was nothing volunteered. This was the hard part, he realized—getting her started without showing that he knew about the home situation. "So…if I follow my own reasoning, if you're too smart to let it just happen, then there must be something, some problem which is to you more important than getting to school."

"I like your class."

"Thank you. That's not the question, is it?"

A very long sigh encouraged Jack.

"Jenny, am I right? We do have some problem here that's keeping you from getting to school on time?"

She nodded.

"Do you want to talk about it sometime?" The last word came out like some kind of safety valve. It kept things open if they became closed now.

"There's nothing you can do about it."

"Well," Jack said. "I have two things to say about that. One is if it's been going on this long, whatever you're trying to do sure isn't working, and the other thing is sometimes we just feel a little better if we can share our problems with someone else, and it doesn't have to be me necessarily." Another safety valve, he realized.

"What would you do if you thought somebody in your family was doing something wrong?"

"That depends," Jack began, somewhat surprised at his success. "It would depend upon whether wrong means illegal or harmful or self-destructive."

"Let's say the last two."

"Harmful and self-destructive?" He waited for an affirmation. "By harmful, I mean hurting other people."

She thought for a moment. "I've noticed there's always a bunch of people in here after school."

"We're not exclusive."

"They're mostly ninth graders, aren't they?"

"Mostly. You'd fit right in. Okay. If you don't want to talk about this now, fine. You let me know when. I'll find a place. Now let's get you into home ec." He scrawled a note, signing his first and last name.

"I'll try not to be late tomorrow." She cast back to him as she headed for the door.

"Thanks for staying. See you tomorrow."

By noon, Jack was ready to confront the gang at the bridge. So as not to catch any drugs users, he wanted to be there early before the crowd arrived. He took a sandwich from an a la carte line, forgoing fried chicken, and ate as he ambled across the courtyard and down the slope toward a bridge. It truly was a beautiful spot if looked at benevolently. One had to edit the nearby drainage pipe running under the road and substitute natural outcroppings of rock for the globs of hardened concrete which lined the bank in no particular rhyme or pattern. The gold and red of the leaves overhead certainly could not be faulted, and then already dropped leaves were doing their best to cover the candy wrappers and ice cream cups. The bridge itself was well occupied already, and Jack could see that his presence had been detected and the alarm sounded. Like flocks of birds in flight which respond in unison to some undetectable signal, everyone on the bridge responded subtly to Jack's presence; and he hated that, but he was committed now and wanted to be admitted. He felt like he was walking into a crowd with his zipper down. There were cigarette butts and twisted remnant of joints being carried away by the brownish water of the little creek. Jack chose to ignore them for the moment. "You've got the best place on the campus. How do you rate?" He leaned back against the rail.

"There's no nigs down here. We like it." Scott broke the silence. He was stretched out on the warm concrete as if trying to absorb all of what probably would be the last warmth late fall had to offer.

"Are you guys going to drive them away if they want to take over? I can just see the headlines." This brought good-natured laughter throughout the group. "Or did they drive you down here from somewhere else?"

Russell could always be convincing. "We feel it's our choice."

"Well, as long as everybody's happy."

"We're happy."

Jack smiled. "I'll bet you are."

The general silence gave Jack time to realize how difficult it was to talk about drugs with this group. Easier, he thought, to deal furtively with a lowlife as he had done last night—eliminate the problem once and for all. That he had taken a man's life didn't really bother him—at least he didn't feel it as a bother. It was a solution to a problem, probably many problems, and involved no real fanfare. Why couldn't this be as straightforward?

"I wish we could talk about a problem openly and in a trusting way, not a threatening way."

"What's the problem?" Jean asked softly.

"The problem seems to be drifting away in the creek," Jack answered.

"Openly, Mr. Flemming," said Russell. "I'll talk openly if you will. Why can't you say it openly?"

Their eyes met, and once again, Jack felt unbounded respect for this youngster. Jack nodded thoughtfully. "The problem is drug."

Now a voice was heard which Jack had never reckoned with. A muscular, mature-looking kid on the far end of the bridge looked out from under his long yellow bangs and said, "Who says it's a problem?"

Jack took time to lean back, cross his arms, and scratch his chin. "I take it you have a point of view. I'd like to hear it. Do we have time now?"

"Yeah, we have time. I just don't think it's anybody's business."

"What exactly is it that's nobody's business?" Jack pressed.

"You're trying to keep us from using, right?"

"Nope." Now he had everyone's attention. "When can we continue this? Anybody doing anything after school?" There was another uncomfortably long silence before Russell spoke, Jack hoped, for the whole group.

"I think we're coming to your room for a lecture on drugs."

"I can't promise a lecture, but I'll take the dare if you will—that's if you can stand me two times in the same day," Jack added as a reminder that many of them would be together next hour. He managed to conduct that class with deliberate routine, devoid of allusion to the meeting he had provoked. He was consciously aware that he had not felt this good, this buoyed up by events in general since before a plane crash, which now seemed so far away. "Flemming," he said to himself. "You're on a roll." He did intercept Jean and Russell in the hall. "See you later?" he asked.

A smile and a nod told Jack they would be there. He had all seventh hour to prepare himself, and he would be ready. He was not, and there was no way he could have been. Counseling, he would learn, meant winging it—not that he could not have a plan, maybe even several objectives, but no prepared speeches. The turnout was to be encouraging, obviously the word had spread, and the male/female ratio was now about even. Maybe this would become a social event.

Jack was careful to notice that Russell was more reserved than when he and Jean alone came in after school. A nod was his only greeting as he sat at a desk in Jack's previously arranged circle. The desk next to him was left vacant for Jean but didn't stay vacant for long. Jack was consciously waiting for the blond bangs to enter and had almost given up when the door swung open and there he was; he even brought a girl with him.

"Posen, you guys going to the show tonight?" somebody asked. That was all Jack needed. He had heard the name Greg Posen before. Now he could speak on a first-name basis.

Moving from his desk to one in the circle brought everyone to attention.

"I appreciate your being here," Jack began. "And one way to show that appreciation is to start promptly. As for ground rules, I hope you can each realize that I want a feeling of equality. It's hard, I guess, to be students and feel absolutely equal with a teacher. It's kind of a stacked deck in favor of the teacher, but let's try not to have this become a classroom setting. I want to hear and be heard, and I hope each of you feels the same. And likewise, when you feel you want to leave or have to, you are free to go. In other words, this isn't my meeting. Let's just see what happens.

"We left off when Greg said I wanted to keep you from using drugs, and I denied the charge. Let's start from there." Jack knew the silence would not last long.

"So…what's your angle?"

"Okay," Jack replied to everyone. "Greg wants to know what my point of view is. Is there anything else someone wants to talk about?"

"Does the school check lockers at night?" Here was a surprise from Pam, sitting noticeably close to Scott.

"Good…good question. Pam wants to know about her right to privacy. Anything else?"

Russell asked, "What would happen if somebody got caught? Let's say smoking grass."

"Okay, the penalty, right? Anything else?" Silence told him they were with him. "Let's start with the lockers. This is strike one for me, Pam. Have you seen any evidence or know anyone who has of lockers being searched?"

"No, not really," she said with a shrug.

"Her locker is too much of a mess anyway," Scott chided. "Good luck finding anything in there."

"Has anybody suspected that their locker has been entered or searched?" Jack asked, not wanting to lose the momentum. "Let me put it this way. Would any of you search lockers to try to find drugs?

Would you store drugs in your own locker? With all the vacant lockers around here, even a large-scale dealer, a wholesaler, would have no trouble stashing stuff in a locker and avoid detection. You know where it is kept, and I know, so we can assume that the administration is as smart as we are. But maybe Pam was asking more about the right to search and her right, if any, not to be searched, and to be honest, I really don't know. If you want me to follow up on that, I'll ask, but not unless I hear from you later. Okay?

"Now let's talk about Russell's concern. You tell me. What's the policy around here? Let's say I walk into a restroom and somebody is expelling smoke and holding a lighted joint. Take it from there."

Russell began with a laugh. "The kid needs help, but let's say that actually happened. You'd take him to the office, right?"

"Why?" Jack interjected.

"'Cause it's against the rules."

"Well, come on, anybody, what would be my reason for taking the kid to the office?"

There was a long uncomfortable silence finally broken by a stage whisper, "Busted."

"See," Jack insisted. "You can only think from the kid's point of view. Think about it from the school's point of view. What is the message if I do nothing in this scenario?"

"I see what you mean," Russell answered. "You've got to do something, or else it looks like it's all right to do pot in the restrooms."

"Good. Now go on—I take him to the office. What next?"

Russell smiled, seeing the path he was being led down.

"For the same reason, Doc has to do something, so he suspends him."

"Right, and he's suspended until the parents come in for a conference, and I imagine the juvenile officers would be at the conference."

"Ouch."

"No, there is no punishment, is there? The school has simply reacted to a circumstance. To me at least, *punishment* is the wrong word. It is against the policy of the school to do pot at school. Somebody does pot. He is out of school. To get back in school, parents have to give assurance that pot will not be smoked here. Where's the punishment? Now for Greg's question. What's my angle? Let's go back to lunch again. Somebody said I was trying to keep you from using drugs. If I keep you from using drugs, I have failed. The trick is to get you to keep yourselves from using drugs. In my view, you probably will not be using them, say, ten years from now. You won't want your own kids to use them. Something has to bring about that change before the pattern has done too much harm, and I'm sure Greg would say, 'Just leave us alone, and we'll grow out of it,' but there are some problems. Now I don't know whether you want to stay here and talk about this further right now or if we could get together again tomorrow." Jack realized he was gambling here. Hoping to have even more in attendance, he risked losing those he already had. "What do you say? Will you come back tomorrow? We can talk about the problems as I see them, then we'll all know where we stand on this. Is that okay, Greg?"

"Fine."

"Great. Bring anybody else you want to bring, each of you, and thanks for coming. See you tomorrow."

*****

Tomorrow brought the morning newspaper, and Jack was up fighting a raw wind which drove a misty early morning rain. He found a newsstand and could tell before he had deposited his coins that the story had broken. Two photos, one of the little cabin, one of the row of pens, highlighted the article under its headline: Man Found Slain. He felt watched as he read the article and realized that guilt was less a problem than fear of being caught. He was relieved to learn that the police had no suspect. He was impressed at how accurately the time of death had been established. He decided to play dumb and let the repercussions follow their own courses. Satisfied, he tossed the paper on the back seat and headed for breakfast.

The steady rain and gusty winds had convinced Jack throughout the day that kids would not be willing to stay after school, and as the day dragged on, he became more and more certain that all his careful planning late into the previous night had been in vain. Feeling that his drug discussions should not be tied in with class work and not wanting to have his own students feel coerced, Jack resisted the urge to ask Jean or Russell if they were planning to come in after school. Better to have them come of their own volition. *But would they*, he wondered.

Jenny had been on time to class, accompanied by a see-I-told-you-so smile. From then on, the day had been a blur of wondering how the police had discovered the killing, wondering if the dogs would find their rightful owners, and cursing the weather, which he was sure would squelch his planned meeting.

To his surprise, though, the final bell brought a large turnout, and the circle of desks had to be expanded.

Finally, Jack took his place and began. "For those of you who weren't here yesterday, we spent that time talking briefly about two questions. One was whether the school searches through any lockers, and the other one was what would happen to someone caught with drugs.

"But Greg asked what business all of this is of mine, or in his words, what's my angle? And I guess this will sound like a speech or lecture as you said, Russ, but it is important to me that each of you understands exactly what I am up to so that nobody feels threatened. Someone asked me yesterday if I was trying to make you stop using drugs, and I'll stand with my answer then—no, I'm not. What I do want is for you to make yourselves stop, and I have several reasons. I'm not a doctor, so I won't dwell upon the health reasons, but there are some. The literature on chromosome damage is not complete because the research is not complete, but what is known is frightening especially if you plan to be a parent and a grandparent. So I have to put those two important reasons aside simply because of ignorance on my part.

"Let's consider the crutch effect. Remember your first experience with, let's say, grass? You were the center of attention with your friend or friends catering to your every emotional need, and it was a good feeling. There was good human warmth, there was camaraderie, there was approval. In short, all the emotional needs you could ever imagine were satisfied with your first group experience with grass. Whether there were any physical effects or not was unimportant. They have simply become reminders to your subconscious of that totally wonderful first experience. So one has to wonder how much of your so-called high is really a subconscious relieving of that utopian experience.

"Nonetheless, it becomes a crutch. You rely upon it to get you through any of a huge assortment of problems in your lives. One of the most important of life's skills, though, is learning to survive indeed—thrive—on difficulties. Every day presents frustrations, setbacks, worry, problems which must be dealt with intelligently, and learning to do this takes place when we are young, not after we have grown up. Now what happens if we raise a whole generation that has not learned how to cope? So that is one valid reason why you should want to stop using drugs—at least as a crutch. With me so far?

"*Now* the other reason. It acts like a wedge. It drives itself between people setting them apart. For instance, yesterday when I came down to your bridge, everything changed because I was there. You were uncomfortable—or at least indignant—and I was uncomfortable. As long as drugs are important to you, you will see me or anyone in my position as an enemy, as someone who is trying to bust you. People call this paranoia, but it is more than that. It becomes this insurmountable wedge that prevents honest communication, honest respect, and mutual concern, so anytime I want to talk with one of you or tell you a joke or shoot the breeze at the bridge, this wedge will be there. You'll suspect me of me. Therefore, Greg, it's my business.

"It's my business because I suspect there are several people in here who hold the same preferences as I do for, let's say, music. Somebody else might like racing as I do, and there are a lot in here that I could learn from and would enjoy being around with, but as long as that wedge is there, it ain't goin' to happen, and that too is my loss.

"End of lecture," he said with a nod to Russell.

"I never thought about it that way."

Jack smiled. "Now that's one of those statements that doesn't say anything." He saw puzzlement. "If Jean bakes you a cake and you say, 'I never tasted a cake like this,' she doesn't know whether it's good or bad."

"If she ever bakes me a cake, I won't complain," got him slapped on the arm. "See what I mean, not the domestic type. Mud wrestling, maybe, but not cake baking."

Russell could always break the tension, and Jack admired that. "That's really all I have to say unless anybody has any arguments. I had thought you might want to talk about this among yourselves and that it would be best for me to just leave, but with the weather like this, I don't know. How do you get home?"

"Are you giving rides?" Russell was smiling.

"So that's why you come in here…and I thought you wanted to hear what I had to say. Well, who needs a ride? I'll see what I can do." He was glad to see Russell, Jean, and Randy raise their hands. He was orchestrating Randy into the back seat where he might see the morning newspaper.

"Anybody else? I'm going out toward the shopping center."

Scott thrust his hand forward, and Pam nodded. "Okay, we can pack 'em in, and I really do appreciate your coming in, rain or no rain. Come in any day, by the way. You don't need a special invitation. Thanks again." With that, the meeting broke up, no desks were slid back into place in their rows, but the departure was orderly.

Jack felt a sense of relief; the day had gone as well as he had hoped. Whatever followed would be icing on the cake. Still it was going to be exciting, and he felt the excitement growing within him.

It has turned colder, and a fierce wind battered them as they shoved the door open. "Unlock it," Jack said as he flipped his key case to Russell. The group scurried on ahead, Jack somehow deciding that if Russell opened the door, he and Jean would get the front seat and the others including Randy would be relegated to the back. Jack got there as Jean reached over to unlock his door for him with Russell handing him the keys.

He adjusted the rearview mirror down slightly and tried to watch Randy without being noticed and still concentrate on his driving. He could see that Randy too was concentrating. The idle chatter, comments ranging from the weather to other students did not draw his attention away from whatever he was reading in his lap.

"Randy," Jack pressed. "Where can I drop you? Shopping center okay?"

"Sure," the boy answered, looking out the window as if to see where they were.

Switching the conversation to Russell, Jack asked, "Now can you guys walk home from there?"

"Oh, yeah. I live right behind it…just across the back parking lot."

"Okay," Jack said, pulling into the shopping center. "I'll drop you up by the mall." He was looking for a parking space where he could stop long enough to clinch their earlier conversation. Finding none, he slowed and began to speak, addressing the group generally. "I really do appreciate you coming in this afternoon, and I hope I didn't offend anyone. You didn't have much of a chance for rebuttal, but you know where I live or else drop in after school. Okay?"

Randy was quiet, but the others thanked Jack for the ride as they climbed out and raced for shelter.

10

Jack sat waiting for the newscast, looking at a photo of Janet and thinking what a help she would have been and how some of these kids would have liked her.

The phone rang. "Hi." Jean's voice was a soft whisper.

"Well, hello. You made it home from the shopping center?"

"I've got news for you."

"You and CBS."

"Are you busy or something?"

Jack could imagine her apologetic look to match her voice. "No, no. I'd rather hear your news anyway. What's up?"

"I think our problem has been solved."

"Our problem? Do we have a problem?"

"The dogfight problem."

"Oh, that problem." Jack was enjoying teasing her, knowing that her concerns were erased.

"Have you read the paper today?"

"I can't even find it. I bought one this—"

"Randy took yours."

"Well, better than that stealing dogs. What'd he do, swipe one that needs paper training?" It was good to hear her laughter. "So what's the news anyway?"

"The guy Randy was dealing with got killed."

"Killed?"

"Murdered."

"Sounds like the big leagues. How did you find this out?"

"It was in the newspaper. Randy saw it in your car. Somebody just went to his house and shot him."

"What was Randy's reaction to all of this?"

"Kind of shocked."

"Well," Jack said. "What I mean is was he mostly concerned about his loss of income or the horror of a murder? Is he scared or mad or what?"

"He was talking to Russell mainly, and I guess he realizes he was, as you say, in the big leagues."

"Did Russell know about this?"

"I don't think so."

"But Randy is a scared cookie."

"Slightly, yes."

"Well," Jack continued. "Let's take advantage of this. He doesn't know that I know about this, right?"

"I don't think he does."

"Then you've got to carry on alone. In order to make an impression on him, call him up and ask him whether anybody in the ring or dogfight business knows his name or where he lives. Then drop some hints about, quote, gangland killings."

"Gangland killings?"

"Well, just tell him that you heard that when the newspapers imply that criminals kill each other off, it is often the police who do the killing just to get rid of a problem. It is always easy than for them to allow the public to feel that the underworld is fighting it out."

"Does that actually happen?"

"Probably not, but let's let him run scared for a while. How about the dogs? Did the paper say anything about getting them back to their owners?"

"Their owners?"

"Oops, I said something wrong, I can tell. What was it this time?"

"Dogs aren't owned…just like people aren't owned."

"Okay, but somebody assumes the responsibility for feeding them, giving them a place to live. So did the paper say anything about getting them back to the people who assume the responsibility for feeding them and giving them a place to live?"

"Very funny."

"Well, now I know dogs aren't owned. I hope you never say that to somebody who spent twelve hundred bucks for a purebred Dalmatian, but I appreciate your calling me to tell me the news. What I need to know is what do you feel about all of this? Do you think our problem is solved?"

"I think I will call him. Whether I can scare him or not, I don't know, but I'll find out more about it. Are you going to be home? Can I call you right back?"

"I'd like that, thanks."

"Bye."

The phone startled him. Too quick to be Jean, he thought, unless she had had a change of mind. He let it ring a second time before answering. "Hello."

"Hello, Mr. Flemming? This is Jenny."

"Well, hi. What's up?"

"Do you have some time now, or should I call back later?"

"Both." There was a long silence. "Jenny?"

"Yes." Jack could hear traffic noises over the phone. "That was a neat answer…kind of surprised me."

"How so?"

"I never thought anybody wanted to talk to me, but you made it sound like we could talk right now and…in the future."

"We can. First let me listen to you. What's goin' on?"

"This is not the kind of thing I can talk about in your room after school…you know what I mean?"

"Surely."

"But you remember our conversation…it's just so hard to talk about."

Time for a long shot, Jack thought, sure that the counselor's information had been correct. "When are you allowed to go back home?" he asked.

"Not 'til ten o'clock," she wailed. Tears were coming in a torrent, Jack could hear. Frighteningly short bursts of breath then long sobs and moans warned Jack of a girl who was about to lose it, but at least it sounded as if the girl was still holding the phone to her ear, so he tried to keep up the conversation.

"Jenny, I'm still here, and I'm sorry. I didn't mean to say anything to upset you. When you can tell me where you are right now, I'll be able to come and pick you up. Then we can talk about all of this. Of course, if you hang up on me, I'll have to check every phone booth in town—at least every one on a busy street—to try to find you."

"I'm by the city hall."

"Ten minutes. See ya." He hung up, torn between the desire to help this poor kid and that of staying for Jean's call. Priorities were easily set. Jean was in no imminent trouble whereas Jenny really did sound desperate.

Traffic was a snarl; his ten minutes stretched to twelve then fifteen, but at least it gave Jack an opening line. "Sorry I'm late. Thanks for waiting for me."

The girl had regained control and dropped into the seat to begin combing her hair.

"That's all right. I'm sorry to bother you."

"No bother. Maidens in distress is my specialty. Besides, I hate to eat alone. Let's go split a chicken dinner."

Jack tried to resist making comparisons but could not help it. Hard and soft were the two words which recurred to him as they moved through the traffic. Jean was so soft, so unobtrusive. He imagined her about now, trying to phone, wouldn't even ask him where he had been. Now that the tears were gone, his newest challenge seemed much more callous, harder, but Jack knew she was vulnerable, and after all, maybe Jean would be a little callous if she were regularly locked out of the house so her mom could do tricks.

Jack knew also that he would have trouble starting the conversation, but he wanted to while they were still in the restaurant booth. There would be no tears in public, he was sure, and he was ready for tears. With a box of chicken in front of each of them, he was ready.

"So…let's talk. Picking up from our conversation the other day, I remember you saying there was some kind of problem, but you didn't want to talk about it because I couldn't do anything about it.

Maybe there has been a change now, and you just want to talk about it, but it's kind of hard for me to do without being more nosy than I should be."

"How did you know I was…locked out?" She was picking at her mashed potatoes, not looking at him.

"You were crying, and I heard traffic over the phone," he said simply. "From that I guessed."

"Did you guess anything else?"

"I could but gets a little dangerous. You want to fill me in?"

A sigh told Jack he was going to hear the whole story. "My mom is only twenty-eight."

"And you're thirteen?"

She nodded.

"I see. We're starting with a young bride," Jack said with a smile but was unable to elicit one in return.

Jenny continued, "And I guess she never could really settle on one guy. It seems like every day it's someone else. She's either never home or else she won't let me come home."

"Do you ever talk to her about this? Tell her how you feel?"

"She says it's her life."

"I suppose you thought this through pretty well yourself, so I won't be saying anything new. When your mom was your age, she was probably pretty much on her own. May not have been her fault, so she feels little responsibility toward you. The trick is, pardon the pun, to break the cycle. In other words, what can we do to enable you to experience a more"—he paused for a moment—"conventional lifestyle so that your children won't be having the same problems you're having." Jack was relieved that the conversation had been, so far, unemotional.

"I just don't know what to do. You probably think I don't care about school 'cause I'm always late, but I'd like to get there and do well."

"Let's just dream for a minute…suppose you could do anything you wanted to about this problem, what would you do? How would you like it solved?"

"The best would be for her to marry some guy that I could like and respect so Danny and I could have a normal family. I've heard kids complain about having to go home to dinner—"

"Wait a minute. Who's this Danny?"

"My little brother. He's staying with my grandmother."

"Your unmarried grandmother."

Finally a smile and a nod.

"Your unmarried forty-three-year-old grandmother."

"You're probably close."

"Okay, from what you've told me, that probably won't happen, will it, but I understand that's the ideal. By the way, why don't you move in with you grandmother?"

Her eyes dropped to the table. "She says there's no room, no money, you know."

"Easy to see where this cycle began, Jack realized. "Now how does this actually work? How are you kept out of the house?"

"If the front door is locked, I can't go in. Simple, huh?"

"Very." Jack was about finished and eyeing the girl's untouched piece of chicken. "You have certain rights. If there are no other facts, going on just what you've said, this would be a clear case of child neglect. The morals thing just ices the cake. Another part of the problem is that legally, technically, I have to report this, but then it could get out of our hands. It brings up the possibility of foster homes, etcetera, so I need to know from you just what you are willing to do."

"Are you going to…report this?"

"I can wait. You've told me what would be ideal. Let me say what I think would be. Suppose we found someone or maybe a couple or even a family, where you could go any time you need a place… you know, somebody you'd like and would like having you. I'm just thinking out loud now, but what if we found such a person and you could even spend the night there if necessary…kind of a home away from home. You know what I mean?"

"I'd pay for it."

"Yeah, what about your finances? Does your mom support you that way?"

"Sure, I can pretty well have what I want…except a place to live." Bitterness crept into this last sentence, and she slid the box of chicken away from her, signifying she was finished.

Playfully, Jack pounced on the remaining piece, and they both laughed. "I thought you'd never ask," he teased. "Now for the immediate problem. What do we do from here? There's no way I'm just going to dump you off somewhere at 7:15 to roam around 'til Lord knows when."

"Ten o'clock, remember?"

"That's just automatic, you mean?"

"Well, yeah, kind of."

"Now, what would happen if you didn't come home at all?"

"She wouldn't care."

"You guess she wouldn't or you know she wouldn't?"

"She doesn't know whether I do or not. I don't see her."

"How about in the morning?"

"Rarely."

"This is too much. You want me to believe that two people live in the same house and never see each other? How about weekends?"

"Saturdays I spend at my grandmother's."

"And Sunday?"

Jenny looked directly at Jack for the first time and answered in a strange clipped staccato, emphasizing each word as if to heighten the paradox of it all. "My mother takes me and Danny to church."

It had been a long night, having driven fifty or sixty miles from one shopping center to another, waiting for the hours to pass, but Jack had been determined to take the girl home so he could know where she lived. By ten thirty, he was ready for sleep, but he knew Jean's phone call was imminent.

When the phone rang, he felt a smile cross his face and admitted to himself that this kid was something very special.

"Sorry I was out for a while there…just—"

"You were?" Was she teasing? "I was about to apologize for calling so late."

"Nobody tells you when to go to bed, as I recall. Anyway, what happened with Randy?"

"Panic city. I have never known him to be worked up."

"Now are you sure it is fear or maybe just concern over loss of income."

"No, no. His imagination is running wild, or maybe he has a real reason to worry, I don't know…but he thinks somebody is doing 'em in maybe for squealing or something. He wants to move back out with my parent."

"And how do you feel about it?"

"How do I feel about it?"

"Jean, you don't have to ask the question. Just answer it."

"Well, naturally I don't want him to get killed. I'm sure he won't be in that business anymore, but he ought to stay here in school."

"Yeah, I suppose if he just lays low for a few days, everything will blow over. All we can do is see what happens next. As for the original problem, I guess it has been solved. Let me know if I do anything with Randy, okay?"

"Okay, I'll see you tomorrow."

"Good night, and thanks for calling."

An icy glaze glistened on the lawn as Jack pulled into his parking place, hoping to get his lessons organized before students began to show up. Pulling his curtains open, he did not hear Jim enter and sit on the desk in front of his own, exactly where he had been two days before. Jack was startled when he turned around but tried not to show surprise.

"Do you always get up this early, or did I lock you in here last night?"

"Quite an affair you had last night."

Jack was inclined to ask which one but hoped the boy was referring to the group meeting after school. "You were more than welcome. Is yours an idle curiosity or a genuine need? We take all comers."

"What exactly are you trying to do?" The boy was so matter-of-fact, so unthreatening and nonjudgmental that Jack gambled that this might be worth his time.

He slid the textbook away from him with a sigh and finally looked straight into Jim's eyes. "It's hard for me to know where you're coming from, but I admire your direct approach. I'm going to assume you had some reason for coming here, and I'm going to trust you to continue to shoot straight like that. The answer to your question is drug prevention."

"Never," Jim said simply.

"Does that mean you don't think I'll succeed or you don't want me to try?"

The boy looked down, watching his feet swinging above the floor. The delay was long enough to cause Jack to say, "Direct answer…now."

"I don't think you'll have much success with them."

"Meaning they're too far gone?"

Jim nodded but was unable to look up.

"I can't play God, my friend. It's like you're saying, 'Write them off.' I have to try, and you just might be wrong about how hopeless it is anyway. You're welcome to stick around, but for a minute here, I need to get organized for the day. My homework…if you know what I mean."

Jim slid off the desk. "See you around, Mr. Flemming."

"Thanks for coming in. See you later."

It was later—much later, and at home—that Jack realized what had happened, but what could he do now? He cursed himself and vowed to be more heads-up tomorrow. He had missed it, but it had been a cry for help, loud and clear. He felt foolish, ignorant, but most of all a burning anger at himself. Could he salvage this? Would Jim be there early tomorrow? Jack would be there to find out.

Someone was at the bike rack, Jack noticed, as he swung into the lot, and he hoped it was Jim. All his regular chores, his morning routine of curtain opening, window adjusting, and desk straightening seemed unimportant, but he did then deliberately as if trying to keep busy—or look like it. The door opened.

"Hey," Jack laughed. "The night shift is still here. How you doin'?"

Jim entered, smiled, but did not venture to say anything. Jack felt his own excitement pumping as he slouched into his own chair. Jim was again perched atop the desk in front of him, legs swinging.

"I've been thinking a lot about what you said yesterday," Jack began.

"It's true," Jim injected.

"It's also true," Jack said, walking around to the front of the desk. "That I have all kinds of time." They were now so close Jack could have reached out and put his hand on the boy's shoulder. "All kinds of time." Jim looked up when Jack did touch his shoulder. "So my time is yours, even though you're not in my class."

"I already quit."

"Then you're the kind of person I need. Tell me how you quit and why. Also, what exactly did you quit?"

"You name it…grass mostly."

"So why did you quit, and how did you do it?"

"I guess the way and the how were the same. My mom said she'd turn me in to the cops if I kept it up."

"It meant that much to her, did it?"

"Yeah, so now I'm into weight lifting, you know."

"Sounds good. Is there a problem I'm missing?"

"Friends," the boy said simply.

"That's always the problem," Jack said almost to himself as he again moved toward the boy. "Try to explain to me something. Is it your old friend trying to keep you in the drug scene, or is the problem one disassociating yourself and being accepted in the straight world?"

Jim looked up thoughtfully and smiled. "How do you know so much about all this?"

"I was young once."

"Well, everybody was, but I mean…I don't know. It's easy to talk to you."

"I'm glad you said that, but what you're really saying is that it's easy for you to talk to me. Some would find it impossible to talk to me, and as a matter of fact, it is easy for me too. If you want to know the whole truth, I was hoping you'd be here this morning. But some kids are really hard for me to talk to. Now answer the question… time's running out."

"If I had to pick one or the other…" He thought for a moment. "What was that word you used?"

"Disassociate."

"That's the hard part. I can still hang around with the burns and not use the stuff, but the problem is everybody else still thinks I do still use it."

"Jim, think about what you just said. There is a cause and effect there."

"What do you mean?"

"If you still hang around with the burnouts, how can you expect the straights to think anything else?" The door swung open, signaling the end of their talk. Jack had only time to say, "Think about it 'til tomorrow morning. Talk to you then."

Jack was preoccupied as the room began to fill up. He could still carry on needed conversations—enthusiasm over a boy's victory in basketball, concern for a girl who said she was getting a cold, and he was even able to referee a minor dispute over the ownership of a pencil. His mind, however, was plagued by an overriding concern. He couldn't help wondering how many of these kids were at this moment under the influence of some mind-altering drug. It would be a challenge, he thought, for kids to get totally stoned and then come to a meeting with a teacher trying to get them to stop doing drugs. *Like coming to the school dances drunk*, he reflected. Certainly there had been some of that in this own past.

What he needed, he realized, was an accurate decision scheme. Observation simply was not enough and very unreliable, even mis-leading. To simply observe thirteen-year-olds and be able to detect which ones were on drugs would be impossible. The age group is marked by sudden mood swings anyway. From giddy effervescence to quiet seriousness to intense hatred or apathy is a spectrum of emo-tions not uncommon to a teenager within a very short time span. They simply defy all the usual characteristics, and Jack knew it. A plan had developed before the tardy bell rang, bringing him to his more immediate concerns.

It was not until his free period, weaving his way through scurry-ing students, that he spotted Jim apparently in another standoff. Jack got there before any action had started and playfully graded him by the back of the neck. "No dancing in the halls, remember. Let's go down to my room."

"I've got social studies," the boy protested.

"Oh, we don't want to miss that. Is this going to turn into anything?"

"No. He just wouldn't let me get to my locker. I'll tell you about it after school, okay?"

Jack let go of the boy's neck. "You know how I'll look if this turns into a fight," he cautioned. "Keep a lid on. See you later."

"Later."

Not until Jack bade goodbye to the usual crowd and started for his car did he see Jim leaning against his front fender. "You should have told me you'd be here. I wouldn't have kept you waiting so long. Aren't you cold?"

"No problem."

"Hop in." Jack motioned, swinging the door open. "Getting right to the point," he continued. "Who did you come to school with more or less all the time before you began staying all night?"

"It was always the same general group, you know…"

"And you don't want to talk names."

"Right."

"See, that's the way it works. You guys say a lot more than you think you do by just clamming up. If I had asked you who you walked to school with and you said Tom, Dick, and Harry—or whoever—then that's all I would know, that you walk to school with whoever. But now you have effectively told me that grass smoking is common on the way to school." Then Jack found himself in the middle of a tirade. "And that's one of my big complaints against the whole drug scene. It forces you to be sneaky. Dishonestly becomes second nature—even desirable. The whole thing stinks."

"Hey, what did I say? I quit, remember?"

Jack excused his long silence by looking at his watch. "Yeah, sorry." He looked directly at the boy and continued, "I really like the way you're put together, and I think all the pieces fit."

"Meaning what?" Jack assumed the boy was fishing for compliments, but he deserved a few.

"Well, I guess it takes a certain kind to quit. You mentioned you're into weight lifting. That's self-motivating activity, if there ever was one. You have to have enough pride, courage, guts, stick-to-itiveness to make yourself adhere to some weight lifting schedule without any outside control. Also, I've noticed you have certain rigid ideals of what people can do. Certain bounds, like today I guess somebody stepped over your boundary, and you were willing to sacrifice it all to uphold your own integrity. I daresay it will never be a question of doing drugs again. It will only be a question of how to deal with the problems caused by quitting. I don't know…it just seems like you're awfully strong, but my problem is how to help—if that's the right word—the kids who don't have that kind of strength. They get their strength from the outside, and that's what we call peer pressure."

"Thanks for what you said, Mr. Flemming."

"Thanks for being what you are and for being here where I can say it to you."

"You're right. Kevin is all upset because I quit. It's like he doesn't know whether to do it or not. I think he started more because I was doing it."

"Kevin?"

"Think first hour. He likes you, by the way."

"And he's you protégé?"

"Whatever."

"Now…does he still smoke around you?"

"Some."

"But you feel he wants you to smoke too."

"He makes the offers."

"So you come to school early to avoid walking with him?"

"More or less."

"Jim, in your opinion, in a class of, say, twenty-five, like my first hour, how many would be stoned on any given day?"

"I don't know…not many."

"How about a number," Jack pressed.

"Out of twenty-five? Maybe five or six."

"See, my problem is I can't tell just by observing who is and who isn't."

"Nobody can."

The conversation seemed to come to a halt right when Jack least wanted it to. Then the boy said, "Why do you want to know who is?"

"Well, it is just seems that it's something I ought to be able to do with reasonable accuracy. Maybe with practice I could determine just by observing…like a doctor, who ought to be able to observe the difference between epilepsy and coronary arrest. Get what I mean?"

"You could probably get enough practice to be able to tell about a certain person, but…"

"I understand that, and you're probably right, but it's a start."

"Are you goin' to bust him?"

"What do I gain by that? No." Jack smiled. "This is purely in the interests of science."

"So…I'll walk to school with him and let you know."

"I'll have to know before class starts, not after school, you realize."

"I can't just walk in and tell you that David is doing grass on the way to school."

"Are you willing to walk with him and somehow reveal to me whether he has or has not?"

"As long as nobody finds out…ever."

"Okay. If you were to walk in my room with David, all we need is a signal. Say, 'Hi, Mr. Flemming,' if he's high and 'Good morning,' or nothing if he isn't."

"Sounds simple. I'm trusting you to not let anybody know I'm doing this."

"And I'm trusting you to be accurate, also sober." He punched the boy on the shoulder.

Jim flexed his muscles playfully. "I'm a weight lifter, remember."

"Can I give you a ride?"

"No, thanks, see you tomorrow but not quite as early."

"Thanks, Jim."

★★★★★

Jack realized that when alone, his thoughts always returned to Jenny wandering the streets, drifting, frustrated, and angry. The solution came to him easily. The mother couldn't be eliminated—that would be more harmful to the children than beneficial—but kill a customer right on her doorstep, that would stop the business cold. Attention would be focused and questions raised. Once the decision had been made, the rest seemed easy. He would park anywhere along the quiet street and just keep slowly walking back and forth until his victim emerged. The only danger would be if Jenny happened to see him, then the idea of a disguise crept into his plans. Dressed as an older man, he could walk slowly and not be seen as a threat. A thin wire loop pulled tightly from behind the neck would suffice. Jack was sure there would be no commotion. That would come later.

And it did. Though there was no mention in the morning paper, news got to Jack through its logical channel. It was almost exactly as he had predicted.

Jenny scurried in before school. "You won't believe this." She had gasped.

"Try me...and good morning."

"Yeah." She smiled then lowered her voice. "Some guy was killed on our street last night."

"You mean a wreck?" Jack asked."

"No, murdered—strangled."

Jack looked at her as if incredulous then questioningly.

"Is there some significance to this? What I mean is what does this have to do with you?"

"It was one of my mom's guys. You know?"

"Oh, boy. You're right, I don't believe it."

They were silent as the door opened.

With other students arriving, Jack said, "Stick around after class. Home ec can wait...again." He smiled. "Do you think you can concentrate today?"

"Make it interesting," she whispered.

"Always."

✶✶✶✶✶

Alone with her again after class, Jack sat in a desk pulled up close to Jenny. He began. "The obvious question is does this have any direct effect upon you, either good or bad?"

"I don't know," she said hopelessly.

"Okay, start at the beginning. When did you find out about this?"

"Last night. There were police cars all over the place, lights flashing, the whole bit. My mom was hysterical."

"So you've had, what, ten hours to think about this. Are you glad it happened or sad and bothered by it?"

"I don't know. It's hard to say. I'm not glad that somebody got murdered..."

"But..."

"But, yeah, I'm glad it happened. I think she'll stop...for a while at least."

A flood of relief swept over Jack. *Mission accomplished*, he thought, reaching for a pass to fill out for Jenny as students and their commotion began to fill his room.

11

The first snow of the season always brought excitement Jack remembered from his own days in school. No matter how light a fall, someone was sure to notice and make an appropriate, if not overenthusiastic, announcement. Excitement grew as the wet heavy blanket began to build up and peaked halfway through seventh hour when Glenn came on the intercom to dismiss students immediately and ask teachers to report to the library for a brief meeting.

"I want to let you get out of here as soon as possible, but we need to check signals for tomorrow." He started the meeting. "The decision to close will probably be made tonight, but it will be late. We will be glad to call you if school is cancelled either tonight or early in the morning. If you want to be notified tonight, before midnight, sign here with your phone number," he added, placing a sheet of paper on a table to his right. "Your other choice is to be called in the morning or listen to the radio, which means you may not find out until after some of you would have to leave home. If you want to be called after six tomorrow morning, put your name and number here." He placed another sheet on a table to his left. "If you don't sign either one, we won't call you. Take it easy on the way home." His nod seemed to adjourn the meeting, and Jack was at the table, signing up for notification that night.

Jean and Russell were waiting for him by his car. "Are we going to have school tomorrow?" Jean wanted to know.

"I'd say have your homework ready."

"So what was the big meeting all about?" asked Russell.

Jack stuck a snow brush in his hand and pointed to the windshield. "We had to take a vote."

"A vote?"

"Yeah, on whether to have school or not tomorrow."

"I can about imagine how that turned out," he said. Jack had the engine running. "Get the back window then hop in. I may need you to push."

"We may need you to push," Jean corrected as she slid to the center of the front seat. Jack smiled, and Russell shook his head.

Once underway, Russell pressed for an answer. "No, really, are we going to have school tomorrow?"

Jack began. "Whoever makes the decision won't until late tonight. Then I guess they call the radio stations and the word gets out."

"For that you have a meeting?"

"What do you think we did?"

"I think you know whether we're having school tomorrow."

"And just what would you do if you didn't?"

"We'd think of something."

"I bet you would."

"Hey," Jean whispered, almost moaned.

"Hey what?"

"Every time you say something like that, it sounds like a criticism or something."

Jack heard himself say he was sorry, but he knew he really wasn't.

"Well, what did you mean by it?" She pressed on.

"What did you think I meant by it?"

"I don't know, but I assume you were referring to drugs. Then you'd say I was paranoid and fit into some kind of a mold."

"Are you angry?"

"A little."

"Me too," Jack responded.

"What about?"

"Same general subject—drugs. People say I'm wasting my time that you guys will never change. I don't know. Maybe I want the impossible."

For once Jack liked the silence that followed. He relished it, knowing his audience was thinking. "Whether we like it or not," he continued. "People have certain preconceived ideas…you know what I mean? If I say the word *alcoholic*, a certain idea pops into your mind, and you apply it to any and all alcoholics. So I fall into the same trap."

"Okay," Russell joined in. "Tell us what your stereotyped view of us is. I'd really like to know."

"Good word, but before I can give you my stereotypical thinking, I need a label. What word are you asking me to respond to?" Now he had them. He would wait for their answer even if it meant sliding into a ditch.

"What do you mean?" Russell asked.

"Are you an alcoholic? No. What are you? If you are going to get my stereotyped answer, I need to know what I'm answering."

"So we have to put a label on ourselves."

Jack smiled and glanced toward them both. "Right on."

Again the silence was delicious.

Finally, Jean spoke. "Is it slippery?"

"The road isn't, but I think you guys are trying to be."

"Listen to him," Russell said.

"Well, come on. Give me word."

"Well, sometimes one hears the term *airhead*."

"Airhead," Jack began. He had his response ready. "Synonymous with burnout? My stereotypical view of a burnout, alias airhead, is someone who is nearly constantly under the influence of something… or wishes he was. Who is comfortable socially only when under the influence and whose recreational pursuits are"—he paused—"dominated by drug usage?"

"But it's not that way," Jean protested. "We don't do it all the time. We can have fun without it."

"I see."

Her voice was again soft, pleading. "I just wish you didn't think of us as druggers instead of just people."

"Me too," was Jack's whispered answer. They drove on in silence until well into the shopping center. "As for the meeting, if school is cancelled, I'll know by late tonight—late tonight." Jack didn't want to let them out of the car and out of contact for perhaps an extended time without at least achieving a positive note. "I'll try to remember what you said," he began. "It's hard to look past the drugs…if you know what I mean. I wonder if you think of me as a teacher or as a person, a friend who just happens to be a teacher. In that regard, I'd have to see you as friends who just happen to be…and there comes the problem. What's the word I should use? There's no neutral label. They all sound negative."

Russell had his hand on the door latch as they slowed to a stop. "So…take your pick. You don't need a label when you talk to us, only when you talk about us. Thanks a lot for the ride." And the door was open.

"You got class—both of you. See ya."

Glenn's call had been welcome even at eleven thirty, and Jack looked forward to sleeping late the next morning. The snow was deep by now and still falling.

The phone disturbed him, though, at eight thirty.

"Hi."

Jack smiled. Jean's voice always brought a mile, he realized. "Good morning."

"We wanted to know if you want to play softball this afternoon."

Jack cleared his throat purposefully, trying to sound unfazed by this strange invitation. "I'm sure glad you said this afternoon 'cause I was planning to work in the garden this morning." He loved to hear her laugh. "Who is supplying the equipment?"

"Don't worry, we have all the equipment."

"I see," he teased. "And I supply the tickets to Miami."

"If you want to play, come on down to the park at one."

"I'll see if I'm done in the garden by then."

"Is that a yes?"

"I'll be there," Jack said. "But what kind of gloves does one wear for this game?"

"Gloves?"

"Never mind. See ya."

★★★★★

Jack flopped back into his pillow. There it was. It all came to him as he started at the ceiling, trying to imagine who would be there. His thoughts returned to the bridge, and he tried to review each face in his mind. The whole group, no doubt, would be involved.

The Bridge Committee, he thought. *Playing softball in thirteen inches of snow.* It figures. The committee would surely all be there for a clear demonstration that they didn't have to use drugs. Softball, for Chrissake! Why not sleigh riding? Softball? Maybe they would all be stoned, act of defiance. He hated to think that. He wanted to think they were coming around and putting in a bid for his approval, but the haunting notion of an act of defiance kept him from returning to sleep. The TV was dominated by news of the thirteen inches of snow. How to prepare for a softball game in thirteen inches of snow? He had to laugh. "Think young," he told himself.

By one o'clock, the streets were cleared enough to convince Jack to drive rather than walk to the park. He carelessly plowed his way into the parking lot until his car could go no farther in the virgin snow. Sure enough, there were the makings of a softball game.

"You're out in field," Russell shouted to him, and it didn't take Jack long to learn that the rules of the game were marginal at best. In that first inning, the three outs were a flyball caught, a batter nailed by a snowball on his way to first, and another mauled and practically buried just after she bunted the ball to the it pitcher—but they were having fun, and the loose game was really only an excuse to frolic in the snow. It turned out there were some reasonable rules. If a fielder could not find the ball, he had the option of hitting the batter with a snowball made near the spot of the ball's disappearance. It was a hitter's game, and the score was high then disaster. Cold hands, wet bat, too many kids standing nearby; it was bound to happen.

As Jean swung the bat, it slipped from her hands and caught Scott squarely in the forehead, knocking him back onto the snow. A bright-red flow of blood coursed down into his eyes and ear, mixing with the moisture already in his hair, making a common scalp cut look like a wound of considerable seriousness. Jean's shock and grief were understandable, but Jack knew he would have time to deal with that later. When he arrived at Scott's side, the boy was trying to sit up but seemed confused. The swelling had already started.

"I need a pocketknife," Jack announced as he took off his own coat, laying it in the boy. Heroically, Randy produced a knife, and Jack instructed him to cut into his sweatshirt sleeve so that the entire sleeve could be ripped off.

"I always wanted to make a cutoff out of his," he joked as he wadded the cloth and told Scott to hold it firmly over the cut.

"Now we'll do the same thing with the other sleeve." He gave the next piece of cloth to Pam and said, "Clean him up enough so he can see. Jean, stay with her. Keep him lying down. Everybody else, let's get my car out of the snow."

He saw that Pam was squeamishly unable to daub into the fresh blood. "Pam, he has to be able to see. You can handle it." He motioned to Jean. "Maybe a couple of those coats. Let's keep him warm."

Freeing the car was no problem, and with it on dry pavement, he called them all to him. "I'm sure you all will want to know as soon as possible how Scott is doing and how all of this is going to turn out. I don't care who goes with me, but I'd like to have two people besides Scott and Pam. If you know where the rest of you will be, I'll call from the hospital as soon as I know anything. I think it might be best if we carry him over here though he probably could walk. Can some of you guys do that? Russell?" He motioned to the boy to come closer, and when they were alone, Jack put his hand on the boy's shoulder. "Jean feels pretty bad, so stay with her, you know? Now here's what I want. Can you get hold of Scott's parents and let them know what's happened and tell them the hospital will call them? It's important that they stay where the hospital will be able to reach them. Now what's your number?" He reached in on his dashboard for a pen and scribbled the boy's number on a dollar bill. "I'll call you as soon as I know anything."

Scott was being carried toward the car, leaving Pam bringing the bloody sleeve. The boy was conscious but frightened.

"Good thing you aren't any taller," Jack said. "You'd have caught that sucker right in the mouth. Could have ended you trumpet career." Scott smiled and scooted into the front seat, Pam beside him.

To Jack's great surprise, it was Greg Posen who was wedging himself into the back seat followed by Jean's brother, Randy. "I appreciate your coming along just in case we get stuck somewhere, but we might be a while as Randy will agree."

"No problem. Let's go."

To the group in general, he said, "They'll probably want to keep him overnight for observations. I'll let you know as soon as I find anything out." He winked at Jean. "Don't worry. Happens all the time."

✶✶✶✶✶

With Scott wheeled away to an examination room and the clean efficiency of the hospital functioning around them, Jack took the three to a nearby waiting room.

"Well, Pam, it's going to be fun trying to explain this to everybody. Hit with a baseball bat! Right."

"Thanks for bringing him over here and taking care of everything."

"Well, what the heck. It just seemed like the right thing to do, me being the only one who drives." He glanced at Randy but got no particular reaction. The reaction came from Greg and took Jack by surprise.

"You knew right what to do. How did you know what to do without even thinking about it? When I saw all that blood, I just went blank."

Jack chuckled and looked into the boy's eyes beneath the long wet bangs. "Next time you won't go blank. I guess a little first aid training would help, but if it's something like that, you only have to think of one thing: direct pressure. Just push something straight onto the cut to try to slow the bleeding. If you know you have to do that, it will cause you think of shirt sleeves or towels or whatever."

"Will he have a scar there?" Pam wanted to know.

"Sure, but if they do a good job, with small enough stitches, you won't be able to see it."

"But I still think it's neat the way you knew what to do, and I wonder what would have happened if you hadn't been there."

"It's not like I always know what to do, you understand…like right now, I feel terrible, as you might imagine, and I don't know what the hell to do or say." Jack saw an opportunity here and was going to get the most out of it.

"About what?" Randy wanted to know.

Jack walked to a window and stood for a minute before returning to his silent audience. "Here's how it goes down in my book. I start with a bunch of people I really admire. I then invade their private lives to tell them they're doing something I don't approve of and that they ought to do something else…anything else…so they do. They play softball in thirteen damn inches of snow, and they even have enough…class…to invite me along. Then one of them practically gets his head torn off. It seems to me like they'd soon start to think about what they were doing right now, and I can't even do anything about it or say how sorry I am."

Greg looked at Randy. "Got a quarter? I can do something about it. Come on."

Jack followed the three to a public phone down the hall.

"Hey," Jack heard him say. "What's goin on?" A brief pause while Greg turned his back to the others. "No grass, no nothin', and we're going to kick some butt otherwise…yeah, they're workin' on him now, but there better not be anything missing when I get back." The phone was cradled emphatically.

Jack's eyes clouded, but he silently reached out to shake Greg's hand before pulling him into an embrace while tousling Randy's hair and hugging him. He buried his face between the two boys, resting his arms around their shoulders. "God, you guys have got class." He could feel their arms around him also, and he could hear someone say, "Thanks, Mr. Flemming."

"Can you remember where a soda machine is?" Jack asked Randy as they released their hug. "I feel awful good except the softball game made me thirsty."

"You buyin?"

"I'm buyin'?"

"We'll find a machine," Greg said.

*****

Snow, soda, softball, and stitches—it all went down pretty well as Jack lay in his bed, hoping that school would not be cancelled tomorrow. The phone rang. Jack chuckled at its predictability. He could hear her nearly whispered "Hi." He let it ring again, thinking of what to say.

"Hi, slugger."

"How did you know it was me?"

"It sounded like your ring. How you doing?"

"How's Scott?" Her voice was a whisper now.

"Probably asleep like we should be."

"Were you asleep?"

"No, just waiting for your call. I'm glad you called, Jean."

"Is Scott going to have a scar?"

"You mean a noticeable one? Probably, but he'll love it, I assure you."

"Will he be at school tomorrow?"

"Nope, and he'll love that also,"

"I guess you know how I feel."

"Are you accusing me of having hit somebody in the head with a baseball bat?"

"Mr. Flemming." She was whining, and it startled him.

"Sure, I know how you feel. So does Scott. Think how I feel, and thanks for inviting me to play."

"I'm sorry it turned out that way."

"How did it turn out?"

"Greg said you felt pretty bad, but I don't know quite why."

"You can figure it out. I feel good now though."

"You feel good now?"

"Yep. I don't have to think of you as just druggers instead of people."

"Well," she whispered. "We'd all like to come in and talk to you tomorrow…after school."

"You really don't need an appointment."

"It's important."

"I understand. I'll be looking forward to it. Any agenda I should know about?"

"You can figure it out." She laughed.

He felt the usual excitement that came with trying to glean guarded information then decided he had met his match. "I'll work on it. Don't worry about Scott. He's a hero."

"See you tomorrow."

"Good night."

★★★★★

An unusual showing, Jack thought. This was the whole committee, and their arrival had made it doubly unusual en masse, no straggling. It was as if they had congregated elsewhere, checked signals, and then descended upon him. If ever there was to be a chance to talk to the whole group, this was it. The walking, however, was not to be his job.

"We kinda got together yesterday," Russell started off. He, along with several others, was standing against the back wall. Some had taken seats but wore their coats. Jack knew the meeting would be short. "And we decided to try what you've been talking about. No more drugs." There was an uneasy silence. "We just wanted you to know."

Jack took deliberate time to look at each one—positive eye contact, a smile, a nod. He wished he could talk with his eyes as Jean could. Feet started to shuffle; the silence was becoming uncomfortable as he began to answer, to say something.

"Well, I guess…" Then he dropped his chin to his hands on the desk as if in thought. Then he blurred out, "If I said anything like 'thank you,' it would mean I thought you were doing this for me, and that wouldn't be quite right. I can't tell you how good I feel right now, and I hope you feel as good. What it boils down to is this. I respect you, and that's with a capital R. You've all got a lot of class. We'll remember this day." He got up and began shaking hands, hugging, mumbling, "Thanks for coming." Then they were all gone.

The snow glistened as the scudding clouds opened briefly to reveal a golden sun low in the sky. Jack had just closed the drapes, plunging the room into artificial light, when his door opened and David Thurmond came in.

"Can I talk to you a second?"

Jack didn't answer but smiled and pulled the drapes open. "Sit down…up here, David. What's up?"

"Quite a gang you had in here. I figured I'd better wait."

"That was probably a good decision, under the circumstances." He felt that David might well be curious about the circumstances. "I'm sorry you had to wait."

"I know you've got a lot of things going on in here," the boy began. "And maybe this won't work out at all, but anyway, we want to print a sort of underground newspaper, and we need somebody to help."

Jack cleared his throat purposefully then smiled. "What was you pronoun?"

"Uh?"

"Who is we?"

"Oh, there's really just a few of us—ninth graders, you know."

"David, is this a Black newspaper?"

"Oh, no. No, man, nothing like that."

"Whew," Jack exaggerated his relief, and the boy relaxed. "Now, my second worry—what do you mean by 'underground'?"

"That's probably not the right term, but have you read the school paper? Its corny jokes, puzzles, who loves who, and maybe an article about last September's football game and always a list of people with birthdays during the month. I mean, who cares?"

"I understand. How is yours—ours—going to be different, hopefully better?"

"That sounded good. We want articles about school problems, drug problems, racial problems—things more important than what somebody's favorite color is and whether they like pizza."

"Okay, now, is this going to be a statement of protest? Are people going to be hurt or offended?"

"I don't think so. You'd have the final say, Mr. Flemming."

"I'm comfortable so far," Jack said. "I'm just trying to ask all the questions now that are going to bother me tonight if I don't. Are you going to sell this, or is it a freebie?"

"Dime a copy. I figure that will pay for the paper. We need you so we can use the school mimeograph."

"You've got it all figured. What's the name?"

"That's the first problem. We don't have one."

"When do you want to get started?"

The boy was cautious. "Here I go sounding like a boss. I thought if we could all meet someday after school, we could decide on who's going to do what and set a date when everything should be turned in, then maybe you and I can edit them and lay the thing out."

"And the typing?" Jack asked.

David smiled. "That's our other problem."

"But not an insurmountable one," Jack assured him. "I think I can take that responsibility. Now there's one more question. Do you mind if I check signals with Doc Becker? You know, tell him what's going on…even let him read it if he wants to?"

"That's fine. Mr. Flemming, you've got a neat way of answering my question. You just sort of got into it without ever saying yes."

Jack stood up to close the drapes again. "If you'll remember, you didn't ask me a question. You just came in and announced that you needed somebody to help, but if you are asking me, how could I say no to a project like this?"

Jack locked his door while balancing his grade book and a stack of papers and turned to David. "We got an artist?"

"Gwenn can draw anything."

"Oh, can she. Woman of many talents. Just an idea—we could have her draw the head of a bull…big, long horns, you know, maybe winking one eye. Surround him with a wreath of clover or something for our title page and in big letters call our newspaper *The Bull Sheet*." There was only a moment's shocked delay, then they both broke out laughing.

"Do you think we could?" The boy's enthusiasm was unbounded. "That's great. We'll sell a million."

"As long as you don't tell anybody where you got it."

"You're on. Thanks, Mr. Flemming."

"Thanks for, uh, asking me. See you tomorrow."

Jack had doubly good reason to feel elated, buoyed up by his successes. He thought of calling Scott in the hospital, then he saw someone sitting on his car, waiting for him. *Good old Jim*, thought Jack. "Howdy, you keep strange hours. You guarding my car?"

The boy slid off the fender. "You did it." He smiled.

"I did?" Jack was again balancing books and fumbling for keys. "Here"—he tossed the boy his key case—"do something intelligent with this. What is it I did?"

Jim swung the door open. "They quit. I didn't think you could do it."

"News travels fast. Hop in. Now…just how did you find out about this—before I did?"

"Just hangin' around. Everything was different at noon."

"A foot of snow will do that." Jack pulled out of the lot. "How about a doughnut? Got time?"

"Sure."

"So…noon is the time to find out what's goin' on," Jack began.

"It was the big news of the day. Congratulations, by the way."

"I got lucky," Jack said. "Couldn't have planned it if I tried. Now I need you…" And then it hit Jack. This kid was way ahead of him. "You knew I'd ask you, didn't you."

The boy shrugged and smiled.

"Will you be able to tell me what I want to know?"

"I'll tell you whatever I know. I'm not sure it will be what you want to know."

"Very good…" They drove on in silence before Jack spoke again. "Do you know Dave Thurmond?"

"Yeah. He's okay."

"He seems like a pretty good guy to me."

"He's not a n———…if you know what I mean."

"How do I tell the difference?"

There was a long silence. Jim was grinning. "Have you heard of the 'Duane or a train' rule?" he asked.

"You lost me. Let's eat," he said, pulling to a stop.

Stirring his coffee, Jack continued, "Now what's this about trains? And what were we talking about anyway?"

"There are certain names that are Black. *Duane* is one of them. *Lionell* is another one, you know? If a person is a n——, he fits the 'Duane or a train rule'."

Jack burst out laughing, causing him to choke and sputter on the coffee he had sipped. He grabbed a napkin quickly and glanced at Jim as he tried to stifle his choking and coughing. The boy's smug smile only heightened Jack's reaction. His elbow bumped the saucer, splashing coffee onto the counter. The more he felt himself losing control, the more he laughed, and the deadpan expression on Jim's face was not helping. "Too much!" he finally said. "Duane or a train…who thought of that?"

Jim shrugged. "It's true," he mumbled, his mouth full of doughnut.

"Well, if you've got one for the female side, please don't tell me it now." He absently stirred what was left of his coffee. "You know, that might be the most important thing I've heard all day…especially if it is true."

"There are exceptions."

"Always. I'll have to give it some more thought. By the way, does it work on the female side?"

"Even better."

"Jim, what about this drug thing? I know it sounds sneaky and all, but I really want to know if we're getting anywhere. Sure, it's spying, plain and simple, but no one is going to get into trouble. I could just talk with them or even give them a better chance to tell me themselves if I already knew what was going on."

"I said I'd let you know."

It was as simple as that. Jack wanted to know how he would get the information but decided to trust Jim's resourcefulness. "Well, that's good enough for me…if you're comfortable with it."

"No problem. Thanks for the doughnut. Next time I'll bring a mop."

Jack was laughing again.

12

The *Bull Sheet* was selling briskly. David was beaming from behind a table in the lunchroom where a line of customers had formed. Jack could see others reading them as they ate their lunch.

It had been a three-week ordeal, but David had certainly performed as promised, and the writers had turned in their contributions on time. The lead article was about rock concerts written by David himself and was, interestingly enough, based upon an interview of sorts with Russell. Jack realized it was dynamite—cleverly, if not discreetly, distorted. Russell's reaction, Jack felt, would be at least as interesting as the article itself. He moved toward David's table.

"Teachers get a copy free," David joked, handing Jack a copy.

"Just what I need." He leaned against the wall and flipped to the article, wanting to read it again as he knew what Russell and other members of the committee were doing.

The title did tend to jump off the page, Jack admitted to himself.

Where There Is Smoke…

A noticeable increase in big-name rock concerts
has prompted this writer to interview a frequent
patron of these events. It seems like it is understood that everyone comes stoned or prepared
to get that way. A haze settles over the audience,
and drugs, according to the eyewitness, are every-

wherefreely and openly traded and used. Drugs
are so prevalent that the witness could not even
estimate which specific drugs were most popular.
Perhaps the type is unimportant as long as the
amount is sufficient, and apparently the amount
is not at all lacking.
Second in importance to drugs must come
volume. Conversation, we are told, is impossible
due to the intense, throbbing sounds. Of course,
all of this is accompanied by splashes of light in
varying colors which, we are told, flash so as to
lights shine upon the musicians, but again our
interviewee was not certain about that seemingly
noticeable point.
Costumes and other staging are often out-
landish, but again, concertgoers are not able
to relate much about what they actually saw.
Questions about the cost of a concert brought a
chuckle and "That depends…" Can we assume
it?
depends upon how much and what kind of drugs
are necessary to enjoy the music?
Oh, yes, the music. Again, not much was
said about the music. Volume is important, but
music? Well, our interview wasn't able to talk
much about music, not really understanding
what the words like *mellow or smooth* mean.
So what is the attraction? Do these druggers
find strength in numbers? Are they looking for?
the rest of us to approve of their illegal acts? Do
they think that a concert lends a touch of class to
they think that a concert lends a touch of class to
their weakness?

Jack couldn't help looking at Russell, wondering if he was
reading the same article so intently. Nothing was said of it in class;

the eruption came after school. Russell was first in the door. The usual pleasantries and formalities, of seeing that Jack was not busy, were waved.

"Did you read this?" Russell cried, flopping the rumpled paper on Jack's desk.

"I typed it."

"Well, what are you trying to do, for Chrissake? I said I quit. What more do you want?"

"I really don't see any relationship." Jack remained calm but did not flinch from the boy's angry stare.

"He's making me out as some kind of…I don't know."

Jean came in along with others, but Jack's attention stayed with Russell. He had never seen the boy this worked up.

"Are there any lies in the article? Is there anything in the article that you didn't say?"

"It's just the way he says everything to make me seem like I'm completely out of it and stupid or something."

"The pen is mightier than the sword." Jack smiled.

"Hey, I'm serious."

"I can see that you are, my friend, and I don't like your attitude toward me. You came in here saying you quit as if that totally wipes out the past. That's like a bank robber saying he's no longer a criminal after he walks out of the bank. You're going to have to live with your past, Russell, just as the rest of us do."

"Why didn't you let him read the article before you printed it?" Jean asked.

Jack leaned back in his chair, hopeful that he had blunted Russell's attack. "Well, he wasn't on the staff. He had nothing to do with it, and it didn't mention him by name."

"It's pretty obvious though."

"Is it? What does that mean? Do you want to bring Dave in here tomorrow and talk it over with him?"

Russell jumped back into the fray. "I sure as hell don't want to talk to him. He's all yours now…and if you're still going to think of me as a burnout, then I might as well be one. Let's get out of here."

"The article has nothing to do with how I think."

But the room was fast emptying, only Jean offering an apologetic-sounding "Goodbye." Jack tried to remember back three weeks or thereabouts to how good he had felt that day when these same people had made what seemed like a firm commitment. The bad feeling of failure, he now realized, had far more impact than the good feeling of success.

He could not help reflecting back over that three-week period, trying to reconstruct, relive, see where he had gone wrong.

There had been a clue in something Russell had said, and Jack tried to piece it together. He realized most of his time had been spent with Dave and his newspaper. Not much reinforcement for the committee there. He had been so anxious to get favorable reports from Jim that he had again not left much time for Russell and the others. He would have time now, he mused, but probably no contact, and how could he rebuild the old feelings? Why did this have to happen on a Friday?

He was glad Jim was not waiting for him. At least he could be depressed alone. He went back into the building and headed for the office.

"Glenn, you got a minute?"

"Sure, come on in. How's it going?"

"Hills and valleys," Jack said simply. "But I just wanted to talk about something that came up recently. The kids have a theory about the Blacks that goes something like this. If a Black has a standard White type of name, he's okay, but if he has a name more typically Black, if you know what I mean, he's likely to be a troublemaker.

"So…anyway, the other night I went through my grade book and marked the ones whose first names sounded like they'd be Black. Being as objective as I could be, I had to say that for the most part, they were my lowest students. It was interesting."

"Also dangerous," Glenn said with a friendly smile. "Your theory runs like this, I'll bet. Low-mentality Black parents choose ethnic names for their children." He was still smiling.

"What else could it be?"

"I'm not saying it isn't that, but there were some interesting studies, I think, in California. In one, half of the new elementary teachers in a school district were told they were being given below-average students. The other half were told their students were advanced, very bright. By the end of the year, the students whose teachers thought the students were bright had higher achievement test scores than those whose teachers thought they were teaching slow learners. You see there is something there about expectations."

"Yeah."

"Wait, there's more. A class of college psychology students was secretly divided into two groups. They were training rats to go through a maze. Each student was given one rat. Half the students were told that their rat came from an exceptionally good strain of rats with good learning characteristics. The other half was told its rats were from strain that had always been hard to train.

"I suppose you can guess the outcome," Glenn continued. "Frighteningly enough, the rats which were taught by students with high expectations did much better than those whose teachers didn't think the rats were very bright."

"Wow," said Jack. "So what you're saying is that we don't expect as much from the Lionells and the Reggies and the whatever, therefore, they don't do as well."

"I'm not in a position to say that, and if it is true, I think it starts well before junior high…like maybe kindergarten. It's the same thing with physically attractive children. If we eliminate really gross learning disorders or environmental factors, if all other things are equal, the cute or handsome kids do much better. They're more appealing."

"Okay, then if what you're saying is valid, we should check the grade books of Black teachers or Black teachers with ethnic names and see if those students do better in their classes."

"No, you're missing my point. I am suggesting that due to lower expectations all along, they actually are lower achievers now. It's not something we can just turn on or off."

Jack sat silently for a moment. "Okay, what you say helps explain the exceptions. An Odell who does well in school may have had a battery of teachers early on who didn't fall into this trap for whatever reason."

"Possibly."

"But how about the kid's theory?"

"What's that?"

"You know, n———, a certain type of behavior, aggressive, whatever."

"Well," Glenn began. "We've always noticed White or Black, a correlation between what we call low achievers and high disrupters. If you are put down, so to speak, by the academic demands of school, you tend to compensate somewhere else. Often, particularly at this age, they compensate through aggression, tough-act kinds of behavior. We had a Black speaker in here last year talking about this at a staff meeting. I remember one thing he said in particular. 'Black kids swagger when they are scared.' He explained the word *scared* as being threatened. They come to a predominately White school, with predominately White teachers, predominately White expectations and White values. It's tough. They're…threatened."

"So if you're a minority," Jack said, showing deference to the man he respected. "Your name could be a ticket to success or failure. You're right. It is frightening."

"Well, if it means anything to you, it's not just minorities. Care to hear another experiment? Get this now. Two sets of college-theme papers were prepared—identical. Half were given names like Bill, Jean, Susie, etc., and the other half were given names like Bertha, Elmer, and Marvin. What kind of grades do you suppose they got from college professors? Believe it or not, identical papers got better grades if they bore a name like Jim or Sue than Elmer or Bertha, so it cuts all ways."

"Well, for what it's worth, I think all teachers should be reminded of this often."

"Oh, I agree. The kids pick up on the slightest cues. We give approval or disapproval in thousands of ways, most of which we don't even realize ourselves. A smile or nod, tone of voice, sharing a secret, a joke, a pat, or punch…it's not all just A, B, C, D, or F, and that's the hardest job the counselors have—trying to decide when a change from one teacher to another would be productive or not. Often kids want to change teachers because a friend is in a different class or it changes their lunch hour, but sometimes a kid has a real good feeling about some teacher or a bad feeling toward a teacher he already has, and maybe a change would be to the better for all concerned."

With the conversation thus off the original topic, Jack decided to go. "I guess I better get the weekend started," he said absently. "I just hope I can keep all this foremost in my mind come Monday."

"Thanks for sharing with me. You're right, we all need constant reminders…and by the way, good job on that newspaper. I know you put in a lot of extra work. See you Monday."

The word *Monday* brought back the reality of the situation and how miserably long the weekend would be. He turned to see Glenn pulling his office door closed, overcoat draped over his arm. His long strides brought him to Jack's side quickly, and without any prefacing remarks, Jack began to unload.

As the two men neared the main entrance, he began. "The trouble with this drug thing is that once you get somebody squared away, you can't devote enough attention elsewhere without losing the first ones. They need constant reinforcement or something."

Glenn stopped. "I need to do a little of that myself. You've done well, I think. I was looking at attendance and tardies among you… target group…is that's the right word? It's really improved within the last couple weeks."

"Well"—Jack looked down—"I lost them today, I'm sure. The target group is called the Bridge Committee, that being where they hang out regularly."

Glenn said something totally surprisingly to Jack. "I want to talk about this," he began. "But I don't want you to be seen standing here talking to me. You're better off if we maintain a distance in the kids' eyes. Do you have plans tomorrow? Why don't you come over for supper? Tom would love to see you, and we can talk all of this over."

"Well, sure, I'll—"

"Say six?"

"Super. I'll look forward to it. Thanks."

"See you then."

As he drove home, Jack realized how much he needed—craved—adult conversation. That would get him through the weekend.

The phone startled him; he let it ring a second time, giving himself a chance to decide whom he hoped it would be.

"Hi," the familiar voice said. It was whom he hoped.

"Hello. I thought you'd be mad."

"I can still call, can't I?"

"What's up? I blew it, didn't I?"

"I don't know."

"I feel terrible," he admitted. "So I must have blown it. Where are you?"

I'm at home, and nothing's changed."

"Where's Russ, and more important, what's he doing?"

"What's he doing?"

"Jean, don't always make me feel stupid that way. You know what I'm asking."

"They're partying."

"I'm glad you're not." Jack waited for confirmation until he was sure none was forthcoming. "What's he like when he's high?"

"What do you mean?"

"Well, you know. I've seen him happy and now mad. I just wondered how he acts when he's stoned."

"Do you want to talk to him?" She caught Jack off guard.

"What do you mean?"

"We could go over to his house. I'll bring him outside, and you can see what he's like."

"Do you think I should? Do you want me to? It's ten o'clock."

"It's a Friday," she said simply.

"I'll be on the back parking lot, behind the shopping center," he said. "In, like, fifteen, twenty minutes."

"Bye."

All Jack knew was that Jean would be there. What would happen beyond that, he had no way of knowing. He realized how rapidly his depression had been replaced by excitement and apprehension.

He could see her bundled against a stiff, cold wind as she scurried from one pool of light to another, across the huge expanse of the deserted parking lot.

"You're late," he joked as she slid into the front seat. "What's the game plan?"

"I'll just go in and tell him to come outside."

"Now wait a minute. Are you going to tell him I'm here to talk to him? Is he going to come out alone? I don't even know what I should say to him."

"Do you want me to tell him you're here or not?"

"I think he should have the right to know what and to decide if he wants to come out and talk. If he does, I'll be here in the car. I'll even give you a half hour. But, Jean, if you can't get him to come out, please come out yourself…sober."

She smiled and was gone, leaving Jack alone with his memories of the only vigil he had endured here once before. His loneliness was short-lived as headlights splashed across the darkness and a police car stopped a short distance behind him. The distorted, staticky sound of police radio told Jack his license plates were being run. Shortly, a door opened and closed. Jack rolled his window down, and there stood Officer Boles.

"Any problem."

"No, I'm just trying to meet somebody. You probably know who."

"Right, I'd better get out of your way then. Sorry to bother you."

"No problem."

Finally, Jean arrived—alone.

"Strike one, huh?"

"No," she said. "He was coming out here then he saw you talking to the juvie."

"Damn."

"Why was he here?"

"Who knows, just cruising around, I guess. The half hour isn't up. Want to try again? What did he say anyway?"

"He tried to make it seem like it was a big brother, you know, but he was putting his coat on."

"Will he come now…do you think?"

"I'll see…if you want me to."

"Be sure he knows I didn't bring the cops here. He should be able to figure that out."

"I'll be right back."

Jack used the time to turn the car around, enabling him to see Jean enter the house through the garage, and sooner than Jack thought, two familiar figures emerged and made their way through the slush toward him. Jack could notice nothing different about the way Russell walked. The light came on as the door opened, and Russell piled into the back seat from then passenger side.

"You don't give up, do you?" Russell opened. It was a fierce, biting remark in which Jack could find no comfort and no opening for rebuilding or even self-preservation.

Fight fire with fire, Jack thought, turning the overhead light on so the boy could see his steady glare. "You got that right."

"Well, you can leave me out."

"I don't think so…not yet anyway…and I appreciate you coming out here like this. I'm sure it wasn't easy."

The boy shrugged. Jean sat silently in the front seat. "There are three people in this car." Jack continued, switching off the interior light. "Who are all after the same thing. We're each interested—or were—in whatever is best for the other two. I think that really sums up what friendship is all about."

"How many friends you got?" Russell challenged.

"You're asking the wrong person, Rus." The cold wind rocked the car. Jack started the engine for warmth.

Jean's voice brought a warmth of its own. She began. "It just seemed like we had a special feeling—I guess like you say, friendship, and then it all just dropped."

Jack nodded slowly. "Yes, I see that now, and I'm sorry, really sorry. I missed having you guys come in after school, and it bothered me. I guess that article was pretty bad judgment on my part, but that kid can write! You've got to give him that much. I don't know…it was just one of those perfect things…a kid comes forward, wanting to do something constructive like that, and he asked me. Everything just fit together so well, and I lost perspective. It's not that I was trying to ignore my friends."

"It hurt," she said.

"And now I hurt, you know that, and all I can do is offer some feeble thank-you to both of you for letting me try to explain, and that doesn't even come close to the rest of the group. I feel a real big loss."

"Yeah, well, I better get back to my game. I'm glad you like David's writing. You ought to hear him sing. You'll like that too, I'm sure. You comin' in?" he demanded of Jean.

She just shook her head and looked down.

"Well, let me out then." The light flashed on, and Jack impulsively grabbed Russell's arm. "Wait a second…" he started to say, but Russell twisted away and glared at Jack as if he had been threatened. "Just go back to being a teacher." And he was gone.

"I'd have to call that a noncommittal answer," Jack tried to joke.

"We'll, now you know."

"You mean that was the drugs talking?"

"I think so. It will be hard for him to mellow out with you, but I think he'll want to."

"I'm sorry for everything."

"It's our fault. I really don't think it was that article. That just triggered. Win some, lose some, right?"

"I don't know. He'll come around, I hope."

"I hope. Thanks for calling and everything." Jack wanted to end the evening. He sought solitude to hibernate away from depressing problems. With Jean out of the car, he felt a near relief. If only he had Janice to go home to, he thought. He couldn't know it, but he was going home to someone else. A stop at the doughnut shop seemed appealing, but his mind was not relieved of its torment.

Within a half hour, he was heading home for peaceful sleep but was greeted as he stepped from his car by Officer Boles.

"Did you find who you were looking for?"

"Yeah, found him, all right. Didn't accomplish much."

"Mr. Flemming, could I ask you a couple questions?"

Jack was jolted by the formality, the slight change of tone and mood. "Sure, come on up, if you like."

"Oh no, that won't be necessary. We can just sit in my car."

Already Jack felt threatened. Was he trying too hard to be nonchalant? Is everyone uncomfortable sitting in a patrol car, a rifle braced against the dashboard, radio emitting a soft glow and staccato, unintelligible messages? Does everyone feel that those messages are about him? That all the resources, the cool, efficient, faceless voices, the sophisticated equipment are all directed against him?

"Mr. Flemming, have you ever allowed any of these kids to drive your car?"

"No, you got to be kidding!"

A pleasant businesslike smile was all Jack got in return. "Would there be a chance, any way at all, that one of them could have used your car at any time without you knowing about it?"

"You mean just hop in it and go?"

Boles shrugged.

"I don't see how. I would surely have noticed it. I really don't think so. Why, what's up?"

"Oh, probably nothing. This Gilmore kid, you know, being kind of close to that murder and all."

Jack could feel himself perspiring. "Yeah, I know," he finally said in his most sincerely interested tone.

Boles was nodding, his brow showing deep thought but his eye showing that he knew a great deal more, as if toying with Jack. "I know that you knew," he said thoughtfully. "And that's been just a little bit of a bother to me, Mr. Flemming. I guess it just bothers me to think that you knew that Randy might know something and yet not tell us about it."

The following silence was frightening. It told Jack he was expected to explain. He wanted desperately to talk to Jean, to check signals. He struggled to stay and look calm while through his brain rushed thoughts of insisting on his rights, of asking for a lawyer, but instinctively he groped to be back on the offensive. The radio crackled some meaningless tidbit, an unwelcome distraction to him not even acknowledged by Boles. "So you're saying Randy took my car and did what?"

"I don't know. I really don't know." Boles started his engine, signifying, Jack hoped, an end to the meeting. "You don't have a gun of any kind somebody could have gotten hold of, do you?"

"No." At that instant, Jack became aware of how a lie detector works. He realized he had no control over his heart rate; he could feel his palms become moist. He didn't know whether he felt hot or cold.

"Well, I know you work pretty close with some of these kids, and I can see how you wouldn't want to jeopardize any of that relationship by coming to us, but I guess what I'm saying is if you're on to something like these kids' rights. Of course, I could never convince them of it, but, you know, we'd never grill anybody or leave you out on a limb either."

"Okay, I'm sorry." Jack felt himself relax. The man had left him an opening, and he was more than willing to rush in. "I guess I should have told you, but I just didn't think there was much connection, and I didn't want to lose all the trust I'd built up with 'em."

"Sure, I know." The car lurched slightly as Boles moved the shift lever from neutral to reverse. Jack started to swing the door open and step out. "Oh, by the way, did you learn of Randy's business involvement with the victim before or after the murder?"

Jack's knees went weak. He was now outside the car, but he bent down as if to look at his interrogator but couldn't. He had to settle for looking down at the dark pavement. "Well, soon afterwards. I—"

"Thanks for your time, Mr. Flemming. Good night."

★★★★★

Jack sat on his bed in a daze, trying to force himself to relax. The uncertainty caused his heart to pound. What had gone wrong, he wondered. Did Boles know something? Were things coming apart? Flopping back on the bed, Jack thought of how he preferred being in Boles's position and realized, absently, how students reacted when they were made to feel accused of something. He wanted to talk to Jean to find out if Boles had spoken to her or to Randy, but he knew better than to try. "Caution," he told himself. "Don't rock the boat." He then began trying to convince himself that there was no problem.

Boles had just been asking legitimate questions. That's his job after all. The man probably likes kids anyway, but what about the car? Was his car reported? Has he been spotted? Had Jean figured it all out? And so it went until Jack fell off into fitful sleep still fully dressed.

The phone startled him. He was confused by sunshine streaming through the window. He almost wanted to ignore the ringing intrusion then thoughts of the previous night returned, snapping him fully awake.

"Hello," he said.

"Hi, Mr. Flemming, this is Jim. I hope it's okay for me to call you like this, but—"

"Sure, what's up?"

"Well, everything has changed, I guess. They're all back into it just as heavy as ever."

Jack let out a sigh. "How do you know? I mean…are you sure?"

"Yep. I'm sure."

"Now, you said all of them. Do you mean there was a Friday night party? You know, I'm just trying to get a feeling for what's going on."

"Well, the partying started after school yesterday. I don't know anything about last night."

"You were busy weight lifting," Jack teased.

"Monday, Wednesday, and Friday. I tried to call you last night."

"Yeah, I was out for a while. Okay, I appreciate what you're doing. Like you said, I wouldn't want to find this out, but I do have to know. If you come up with any ideas of what I can do about it, don't hesitate to call. If not, I'll see you Monday. Have a good weekend."

"See you Monday."

The click on the line made Jack feel totally isolated again. He longed to fall asleep maybe until Monday, but he knew he faced a long weekend of worry.

★★★★★

Jack felt full and, for the first time in many hours, safe as he and Glenn settled in the Beckers' living room. The rest of the household seemed to be running smoothly; a television could be heard in the den, keeping Tom occupied while Mrs. Becker was in the kitchen. Jack's thoughts flashed back to Janet, domesticity, maybe a fireplace like the one Glenn was poking.

"More coffee?" Glenn asked his guest as he sat down.

"No, no, really. Everything was great."

"Well, where were we? I'm interested in what you were bringing up yesterday afternoon."

"It's kind of a problem, and I've had a little time to think about it too, but it seems like maybe the therapy, so to speak, is more important than the final result."

Glenn smiled and shook his head. "Try that again."

"Well, let's say with whatever amount of effort it takes, we can get a given kid or group off drugs…"

"You, Jack, not we. You're the one getting results, and I mean that. You alone deserve the credit."

"Thank you, but the point is this. It's self-defeating, see. A person in my position can't expand."

"I'm afraid I don't understand that," Glenn admitted.

"Okay, back to what I was saying. I get a kid or a group to stop. Now that they've stopped, they don't have me on 'em all the time, nobody to hassle 'em and show that they care. See, no worry. Mother Henning, if you will." With Glenn nodding slowly, Jack rushed on. "They like the therapy, so they return to the drugs when they feel they have been ignored."

"I see. I wonder, do you feel that during the time that they were not using, were you able to give them as much attention, reinforcement?"

"Well, that's hard to measure. It's easier to show concern than praise since I'd be constantly praising them for not doing something they're not supposed to be doing anyway. Plus, that newspaper thing took my attention too much, I guess. So…anyway, the committee, as I call them, got their nose out of joint."

"What did you call them the other day, the Bridge Committee?"

"It's the best name I could come up with—dignified, you know?"

"I don't remember your derivation," said Glenn, pressing for an explanation.

"The burnouts, mostly ninth graders, all hang out at the bridge that crosswalk down from home ec, so I call 'em the Bridge Committee. Cute, huh?"

"Do they know themselves by that name?"

"I don't know. It seems like I used it the other day. They'd know it if they heard it, I think."

"The Bridge Committee…I like it," Glenn admitted. "So there has been a change for the worse? Recently?"

"About three weeks ago, we had a major breakthrough. The committee came in, en masse, and Russell announced they were off drugs. That same day, as I remember it, Dave Thurmond brought up the idea of the newspaper, but things held until yesterday when the paper came out. Russell was offended by the article, and well, everything fell apart. They were all partying pretty good last night.

"I'm certainly not in a position to argue with you," Glenn said. "But I don't think the article was the problem. It sounds to me like they either wanted to go back to the drugs and needed an excuse, which the article was, or, and this is more likely the case, Russell was just jealous, and the article just released the feeling."

"So…now I start over, right?"

"First thing Monday morning."

"If not before," Jack said.

The change in subject was abrupt, but Jack knew it was bound to be brought up. Glenn began. "What involvement do any of our kids have with this dogfight business?"

"The only thing I heard of, and I guess it's true, was that Randy Gilmore was selling dogs, presumably stolen ones, to some guy for that purpose. Jean was pretty upset about it and told me, but that was quite a while back. The next thing I heard, again from Jean, was the guy was killed—murdered, I guess—so I haven't anything else… until last night when Boles asked me if any of the kids could have ever taken my car and been involved in some way. I really didn't get a chance to follow that up."

"Your car?"

"I don't know. Apparently he knows some of the kids are involved, but I don't know what I'm supposed in liberty to say to him."

"That is a problem," Glenn mused.

"What's a problem?" Tom bounded into the living room.

His dad joked, "The problem is fishing a decent pitcher for the team next year."

"Are you going to be our coach?"

Jack was so relieved at the change in subject that he heard himself say, "I hope so."

✶✶✶✶✶

Finally, by late afternoon on Sunday, with snow melting in the bright sunlight, Jack was able to come to grips with a few basic facts. First, he had succeeded once with the committee, so he could do so again. A direct approach was called for, and he would again meet them on their own turf—at the bridge. As for Boles, what was done was done. Whether the police knew more than they appeared to be was something Jack could not and should not find out. He would try to assume he was still safe and not a suspect in any way.

Monday looked to be another bright sunny day, comforting to Jack; he knew the bridge would be warm and sunny enough to draw the crowd. He walked around the building so as to enter by the ninth-grade locker area. Jean was leaning against a wall of lockers, her back to Jack as he approached. He resisted the urge to hug her.

"Good morning," he said simply.

"Hi," she said excitedly, to Jack's relief.

"I thought I'd wander down to the bridge at noon. You can spread the warning." He winked.

"See you then."

"Good." He passed Jim in the hall and could see that the boy didn't want to stop and talk. "First lunch at the bridge," Jack said. Jim nodded but said nothing.

Jack could not control his nervousness. He tried to analyze it, putting the whole thing into perspective. He had succeeded before; he could do it again. Still there was Boles; which one was really worrying him more? *Only one way to find out*, he thought. *And today is the day.*

The bright noontime sunlight hurt his eyes as he stepped outside, but its warmth was welcome. He now hoped for another welcome but assumed it would not be forthcoming. It was not.

"How's it goin' down here?" he asked of no one in particular.

"No problem," someone said. The remaining silence was painful to Jack. He leaned against the bridge railing, indicating to himself at least that he was there to stay, and surveyed the members and their hostility. Scott sat with his legs dangling over the bridge. He wore only a small bandage now; stitches would be removed soon. Jean sat at the far end of the bridge, Russell's head in her lap. He laid stretched out, jacket lying open, displaying a colorful rock 'n' roll motif on his T-shirt. Occasionally his wrist twitched enough to flick gravel into the water below. Randy leaned near Jack, contemplating his own feet. Pam had just arrived and imitated Scott's posture. Several others clustered about the railing as if in suspended thought and motion, waiting to take their cues from someone else. Only the stream below spoke as the runoff gurgled over and around the assorted chunks of concrete and stone.

"Well," Jack finally began. "Let me take a little risk here. I'd like to talk to you, but if I'm not welcome here, if one person objects to my being here, just say so, and I'll leave. It's your bridge."

"Glad you see it that way," Russell said. "I got nothin' to talk about."

Jack let his shoulders drop, expelled a long breath, and with head down started for the end of the bridge.

"Mr. Flemming."

It was Scott's voice, he was sure. He stopped but didn't turn until Scott said, "Wait up." As he turned, he saw that Jean was standing on the far end of the bridge, leaving Russell lying alone. Scott was walking toward him. "How about after school? Maybe we could get together in you room."

When the boy caught up with him, they were far enough away from the others to talk alone. "Scott, you don't need permission to come in my room any day. You know that." Then he decided to go for it all; he felt the confidence surge within him. If he could just keep talking, he could win, and without winning Russell, it would be a hollow victory.

He continued, "But I feel like I let everybody down. I offended all of you, so I'd like to talk to everybody. I don't know. Do you think you can pull that off? You know, bring everybody with you?"

Scott smiled. "He'll come. We'll all be there…and, in my opinion, you didn't do anything wrong."

"I appreciate that, Scott. See you after school." He had time for a brief thumbs-up sign to Jean and received a nod in return. He realized that she knew there would be no monition of this in class. It was all up to her and Scott to bring Russell.

✶✶✶✶✶

Jack was amused as the room began to fill after school. Desks were being shoved and rearranged so that a large circle formed and filled with subdued, or was it apprehensive, kids. Russell was here and so was Jean though Jack noted that they arrived separately. He quietly sat at one of the desks in the circle just as Greg Posen entered.

"Posen, close the door." Scott seemed to be taking charge, and Jack felt slightly uncomfortable. "Mr. Flemming," Scott began. "I don't know whether you got some already prepared speech or something, but I just want to try to tell you that I didn't like what went down Friday and I didn't like what I did and I think everybody feels the same. I respect you a lot for coming down to the bridge to give us a chance to…I don't know…patch things up."

Seeing that Scott had finished, and sensing that it was now his turn, Jack began slowly, looking at first at the ceiling. "That was one of the hardest things I ever did—coming down to that bridge— so maybe that tells you how lousy I felt all weekend. I don't know whether we lost it all there last week, but I sure felt bad and wanted to try to get things back on the rails."

"Think how bad we felt," Greg blurted out.

Jack nodded momentarily before answering. "I guess that's what we really ought to talk about—feelings. My honest feelings were that I blew it. I felt I had betrayed a bunch of good friends, and then my feelings get screwed up. It seems like because they're mad at me, they go out and do something…shall we say…self-destructive just to get even with me. See, there's nothing logical to talk about. It's been strictly emotional."

Then Scott took over. He declared, "The problem was that we acted as a group last time. We all quit as a group instead of as individuals, so we all felt we had to start up again. That's the part I didn't like."

"I should have foreseen that, but—"

"No, Mr. Flemming, it was a great thing at first. We all felt good. You didn't do anything wrong, and printing that newspaper didn't have anything to do with it."

Russell finally stirred, starting at Scott, but others concurred with his last statement, and Jack saw opportunity.

"Wait a minute. Let's not turn this into a debate. We're all still on the same side. Sure, I have more access to some. They're in my class every day. I'm not ashamed to say it. Russell is a good friend of mine, student or no student. I like the guy. The problem was I took advantage of that, of him, to try to get to all of you. Now I realize that as I should have earlier. If you're going to quit, you're each going to have to make a decision for yourself and not rely on Russell or anyone else to do it for you. There's no pressure from me, but I guarantee I'll respect and fully support any of you who do make such a decision."

"But how will you know?" Pam whispered.

"He'll know," Randy asserted.

"If it's important for me to know, tell me. If you'd rather not, that's okay too. The last three weeks was an absolute luxury, but I really didn't deserve that. I didn't really earn it. You guys made the decision and shared it with me and I loved it, but I can't have that kind of… *luxury* is the only word I can think of and still have each of you as a friend. Like Scott said, it's got to be more individual than that."

Russell finally spoke. "What about that newspaper? Is there going to be another one?"

"I don't know. Do you want to write an article?"

Russell simply shook his head, ending that idea, but Jack pressed on for as much mileage as he could get. "We were talking about all this not long ago," he began. "And I pointed to the big concern of mine, remember? About coping skills. Maybe that article had to be coped with. You chose a certain method of coping last Friday, and by now, you aren't sure you like that method you chose, so you're learning to cope. Trial and error is okay as long as you keep a good handle on your feelings. If it doesn't feel right, reject it and try something else…and that's why we're here."

Jack was smiling as Russell's head slowly turned toward him. The two eyed each other momentarily. Finally, Russell spoke. "You do have a way with words."

"Me and Dave Thurmond, apparently."

"No, I mean it. You lay everything out to where a person can see it all and really think about things, and you're right, Thurmond was good, damn good. Not that I agree with him all the way, but he wrote a hell of an article."

"He engineered the whole thing. How could I have turned down that kind of initiative? Besides, if I had turned him down, he'd have written an article about me." Wanting to catch as many as possible before they left, Jack extended one last olive branch gesture. "So," he started cheerfully. "Everybody is on his own. Those who want to quit or stay that way can and will receive no pressure or recriminations from others. My only role will be as someone to talk to, complain to, brag to—whatever—if you want. Neither my address nor my phone number is a secret, but other than that, you're on your own."

Then Jack was on his own, left by himself to wonder if anything had been accomplished, wishing Jim were her to lend encouragement.

The door opened again, and encouragement walked in. "Got a minute?" Russell said.

"Sure, come on in. Where's Jean?"

"She knows we need to talk alone."

"She's a class act."

"And she's right. We need to talk alone."

"It's your show. I tried at noon."

"I've spent a lot of time on his desk," he began, perching as usual, front row center.

"Mostly good times, I might add," Jack said.

"Really." The boy was studying his feet. "Sorry I let you down," he finally mumbled. "It just seemed like everything ended all of a sudden."

"You didn't let me down any more than I let you down. If anything, you let yourself down."

"I really don't know what I want to do, to be honest."

"It's your decision. I liked you before…when you were a bum… so I'm not hurt either way. And whatever you decide, I'll know soon enough, won't I."

"I guess. I was just thinking of cutting down, you know…just not do it so often."

Jack walked toward the windows. "I don't know, Russell. I always say if you're going to do something, do it right. I'd say all or nothing. If you are going to do drug scene, do it all. Buy, sell, trade, and use it like there's no tomorrow."

"I don't believe you, man. I'm trying to be serious."

"You're being very serious, Russell, much more serious than you realize. So it's not that you don't believe me but that you don't want to believe me. Trouble is I'm just as serious as you are. You simply can't be a halfway drugger." He returned to his desk to see the boy's eyes were tearful. "I'm your teacher, Russell, and hopefully your friend, but I'm not your father. I can't force you to—"

"That's the problem," the boy interrupted before burying his face in his elbow, his shoulders heaving as breaths came in huge gulps.

Jack walked back and closed the door before approaching the boy. First patting him on the back then rubbing his hand up and down the boy's back, he said, "I'm sorry. It sounds like we have something to talk about now, and I've sure got the time when you're ready." He gave Russell a wad of tissues and sat down to wait. Finally, the boy looked up apologetically, rather sheepishly, and responded to Jack's smile.

"I hit a sore spot there somewhere," Jack began. "Maybe we don't know each other as well as I thought." He was groping through recent memory for any clues but could not remember ever hearing about Russell's father. Perhaps a recent death was causing the pain. "I'm sorry. I guess you're the man of the family, and I know that can be tough at times. We've shared good times, remember? We might as well share the bad times too."

"What, do you think he kicked the bucket or something?"

"I use the word *died*," Jack said.

"He's alive and well."

Jack was relieved at that news and seeing Russell return to his old self. "You ended up saying, 'That's the problem.' I don't understand."

After expelling a long breath, he started his answer.

"I'm almost fifteen now, and I've been doing drugs since I was twelve." Another long breath as if he was building strength. "And in all that time, he never even said anything 'bout it. If he had just said something, gotten mad, grounded me—hell, I don't care what—that would have done it. I'd have quit if he'd have told me to or asked me to."

"Have you thought about how you'll handle it with your own kids?"

"Sure, I'll just—"

Jack held up his hand. "The point is you've thought about it. Do you see the disadvantage your father is in? He never had a chance to think about it 'cause he probably wasn't into drugs. How was he to know what to do with his own feelings, much less with yours? He was probably just afraid of making matters worse!"

"You're giving him the benefit of the doubt, I'd say."

"Let's say he deserves it. He's raising a pretty neat kid all in all. Besides, I don't know the guy. Tell me about him. What's his line of work?

"Salesman…sells truck parts…plays golf, comes home, watches TV, and had three beers."

"Fascinating. So when I sounded like I didn't care about your drug using, you thought your dad and I both didn't care."

Russell nodded and looked down at his feet again as if embarrassed at the memory of the recent conversation.

"But see, Russell, my problem is I have to stop thinking of all this in terms of win/lose. I can't keep thinking of each drug…renunciation…as a victory for me. That's all I meant. Sure, I care personally whether or not you screw yourself up on drugs—I proved that Friday night and again at noon today—but whether you do or no, I still like you just the same. See, friendship doesn't enter into it at all…just as I'm sure your father loves you all the same. He simply doesn't know what to do. Let's get out of here. Is Jean waiting for you?"

"I don't know. I'll walk though."

"I'm glad we got to clear the air," Jack said, closing the door to his room. "And I hope you guys will start coming in to talk again. You haven't been over to the apartment in a long time. I miss that."

"Thanks, see you tomorrow."

Jack caught Russell by surprise when he reached out and shook hands. "Hang in there."

13

As he neared his car, Jack saw a small cluster of boys beyond, nearly hidden from view by shrubbery at the end of the parking lot. At first, he paid no attention, then it appeared to be fight. He moved to where he could see what was happening in time to see one large kid grab a much smaller one by the jacket, lift him, then hurl him to the ground where another one grabbed him, yanked him to his feet, and shook him violently before shoving him across a tight circle to someone else who pounded on his shoulder and chest.

"Hey!" he yelled. "Knock it off," but not in time to prevent one last kick as the smaller boy hit the ground and tried to squirm away.

"This doesn't look real even. Are you okay, son?" he asked, helping the boy to his feet. "You're going to have to stop picking on these guys. Are you sure you're okay?" Jack could see this was not a racial problem. Six ninth graders, all White, were obviously settling some grudge with one small seventh or eighth grader, also White. Coming up the hill from behind were two Black boys whom Jack did not recognize. *Spectators*, Jack thought to himself.

He addressed the victim first. "Are you on your way home?" The boy nodded but did not answer. "All right, you go on home now. Whatever this is about is now over and done for. I'll handle the rest."

As the boy moved meekly out of the circle, he was hit in the chest, and he struck back. Jack tried to move into the fray and pull the feisty victim to safety when two strong Black arms wrapped around the attacker and spun him away from the action.

"Be cool, man," a deep voice commanded, and cool prevailed.

"Now we've got a different problem," Jack announced. "I don't know your names, but I'm getting to know your faces. All six of you, be in my room after school tomorrow. Until then, let's hope nobody presses charges."

"We've got basketball practice," the tallest complained.

"Not tomorrow," Jack said, staring the boy down. "Don't forget it. Now go on your way." Then he addressed the Black youngster, "Thanks, I appreciate it."

"That's all right, Mr. Flemming."

"What's your name?" Jack asked, surprised that the boy knew his.

"Larry," the boy said simply.

"Well, Larry, I really do appreciate your help. Do you know anything about the problem here?"

"No, sir."

"Are they on the basketball team?"

"Every one of 'em."

"How come they don't have practice today?"

"Never on Monday. I don't have practice today?"

"Never on Monday…I don't know why not."

"What's the kid's name that was getting beat up?"

"Eric somebody. He's got a mouth…that's all I know."

"Well, thanks again."

"That's all right."

Jack could hear his phone ringing as he fumbled for his keys. "Hello," he said breathlessly.

"Hi. How did your little talk with Russell go?" Jean asked.

"Well, you're coming right to the point, aren't you? We had a good man-to-man talk. Let's just leave it at that. Have you seen him since?"

"No, he didn't come here. I think I'll go over to his house."

"I think you will too," Jack joked. "I need a little research, though, seriously. There was a kid named Eric somebody…"

"Ugh. Eric Sommers."

"Oh? Friend of yours?"

"Nobody is a friend of his."

"Anyway," continued Jack. "He was getting beat up by half the basketball team after school today. I'd just like to know the scoop before I wade into it tomorrow."

"I didn't think you got uptight about fights."

"This is a little different—six against one, for starters. Then after I got them stopped, they started back at it again. That's defiance, I guess. I can't ignore it. Call me back when you find out about it."

"Why don't I just tell you now? It's common knowledge."

"Hang on. Let me take off my coat and close the front door. Now…what's it all about?"

"Do you know Mr. Elridge, the basketball coach?"

"I know who he is—tall Black guy, teaches part-time or something."

"He coaches in the morning at the high school then comes over to West for a couple of gym classes in the afternoon. Anyway, he kicked that Eric kid out of class for goofin' off or something. Then the next day, there was a sign up on the bulletin board somewhere in the dressing room that said, 'Elridge is a n———.' Apparently, everybody likes him especially the basketball team."

"So who is Larry?"

"Larry?"

"Tall Black kid, mellow as can be, has a deep voice."

"Larry Washington. He's nice."

"Really," Jack agreed. "Ought to be a singer."

"You know who really can sing? David Thurmond."

"Oh, yeah? He never mentioned that to me. Well, listen, if you find out anything else about the basketball team hit squad, let me know. I told them to come in after school tomorrow."

"I'll call you later. Bye."

"Goodbye."

✶✶✶✶✶

By Tuesday afternoon, Jack felt that he had all the facts pretty well straight. Pulling Eric Sommers out of class had brought a confession of guilt, and Jack forced a written apology to be delivered to Coach Elridge. Punishment for the others, Jack concluded, would be the missing or being late to basketball practice so that as kids congregated in his room, he graciously talked and joked with them, wanting the room as full and busy as possible. Four of the basketballers entered together and were told to sit down and wait.

"What about the other two?" Jack pressed.

"They're comin'."

"I'm in no hurry." He turned his attention back to the others.

"Okay, gentlemen," he finally said when the room had cleared out twenty minutes later. "The name for what was going on out there yesterday is assault and battery, and it is serious. It has nothing to do with your reason for being there because there was no element of mitigation, no element of self-defense, six guys acted with intent of bodily harm, and it's first degree because you obviously planned it ahead of time. So what you may see as a justifiable act, our society sees as a criminal one. Missing a basketball practice is Little League compared to what would be happening to you now if that kid had been injured. Are you with me so far?"

Nervous shuffling of feet accompanied their acknowledgments.

"Nobody needs this kind of thing on his record. We'll get to that in just a moment. Now I commend you loyalty to your coach, but your method stinks and comes close to jeopardizing your positions on the team, and it compromises his honor as well. It makes a bad situation terrible. Before I even learn your names, I'm going to ask you each one question. Think before you answer. Do you want Coach Elridge to know about what you did? How about you?" he said, starting with the tallest.

The boy shrugged and contemplated the desktop. "No."

"And you?" He turned to the next in the circle.

"I guess not. He'd be mad."

And so it went, all six saying they would not want their coach to know.

Then Jack handed each a three-by-five card with all the particulars—time, date, names, and places—typed in. "Sign it," he said. "Unless you find it untrue."

The boys looked at him in disbelief.

"Need a pen? Here." Jack was leaving no room for argument. "I'm going to keep these in my file drawer until you graduate from high school. If you are involved in anything like this again, out comes your card, and that will make it a second offense.

"Only one more problem left. How do you explain where you have been to your coach? Can you handle that, or do you want me to?" He was collecting the cards.

"We'll explain it," said the tallest. Jack read his name. "And thanks for not turning us in or nothin'."

"Bill, don't make me regret it. John Sargent, stay seated. The rest of you may go."

Drawing another card from his pocket, Jack said, "John, you have another problem. Do you know what I'm talking about?"

"No, sir."

"You didn't stop even when I told you to. You defied my direct order to stop fighting and pounded the poor kid again. It's all spelled out here. Sign this one too, please."

Dutifully the boy signed.

"Ironically, it took a Black kid to bring you to your senses and then only by physically restraining you. Think about that for a while. You may go."

As the door clicked shut on his silent room, Jack sat thinking about his own victims, eliminated as irritants, given no chance to defend themselves. It may as well have been six against one; it's not much of a fight when one man carries a Luger. Jack smiled pensively. Even the motive was not all that different. They were acting for someone they respected. So had he. Jack wondered about the old man who dealt in dogs. Maybe he had been a misfit whom no one liked in school, forced into antisocial behavior, picked on, brutalized until he was helpless and unable to function or cope.

Bringing himself back to the present, he contemplated what happened to kids like Eric Sommers who had no friends, probably no support systems at school or home. Like wild dogs, they had to fend for themselves and never really found satisfaction.

The Bridge Committee

Having confronted the six boys, Jack noticed that he saw them frequently throughout the next weeks in the halls, in the lunchroom, always a cordial nod or hello. John Sargent was usually accompanied by a girl in Jack's second-hour class. There certainly was no animosity.

14

"Spring is upon us, and the sap is running," Glenn said with a shrug.

"I hope you aren't saying this happens every spring," Jack said. "I don't think we could take it. I don't see how he could stand it."

Glenn shook his head. "It's first."

Don poked his head in the office. "What's all the excitement?"

"Smoke bomb," Glenn announced simply.

"In Mr. Headley's room," Jack added defensively then realized how the older man must have felt. Automatically Jack had wanted it understood that it was not in his own room that such a thing could happen. His vision returned of Mr. Headley still standing at his desk as if trying to play down the calamity while students spilled into the hall coughing and leaning out the windows for fresh air. The hurt to the old man's pride must have been even greater than the smarting to his eyes and the burning in his throat.

With Don gone, Jack reflected to Glenn. "I couldn't even get in there to lead him out. I don't know how he could stand it in there."

John Bemis had acted swiftly and decisively in the initial stages. When he learned of the problem, he was heard throughout the school on the intercom. "Mr. Headley's sixth-hour students are to report to the auditorium immediately. Teachers, hold your sixth-hour classes until further notice. Please ignore the regular bells ending sixth hour."

Glenn had decided to let the juvenile officers handle the situation after the custodians had placed fans to air out the room as quickly as possible, and it looked as if sixth hour could end on time.

Jack's own thoughts as he sat in Glenn's office kept returning to Mr. Headley. *Does this have to happen to older teachers?* he wondered. Why do they take advantage of him so? He probably loves kids and knows his subject matter as well as any. He remembered the stories he had earlier dismissed about Billy Tobin drinking a can of beer in Mr. Headley's class and Odell Daniels actually sitting by the window, smoking a cigarette and dangling it and his arm out the window between puffs. It all seemed more credible now. They were simply taking advantage of the man, and it had nothing to do with springtime!

The intercom clicked on. "Teachers, we will resume regular scheduling," John announced. "Sixth hour is now over." A bell sounded throughout the building, and to all appearances, the calamity had passed, most students not even having been aware of it though Jack knew they would soon be talking about it as the rumors flew. He couldn't help glancing into Mr. Headley's room. The man seemed intent upon something on his desk, and Jack resisted the impulse to enter. It would avoid embarrassing explanations.

The amazing part to Jack was the completely overt manner in which the stunt was performed. Seemingly, no attempt was made to avoid detection. Kerry Jenkins had simply lit a fuse and slid it up the aisle. Jack had his suspicions and asked Russell to see him after school. He and Jean showed up.

"Tell me," he began. "And I know you don't like to give out names, but what kind of a state of mind would once have to be in, in your opinion, to light a smoke bomb in, say, Mr. Headley's room and casually slide it up the aisle?"

"You mean like today, maybe sixth hour?"

"Okay."

"Well, without mentioning names, I'd say completely out of it."

"It wasn't one," Jean interjected. "It was four of 'em taped together."

"Terrific…but seriously, Russell, in your opinion, was Kerry Jenkins stoned so bad he did it without knowing what he was doing?"

Russell thought for a moment, and Jack realized the boy was honored at being consulted. "I think it's more a matter of not caring than not knowing."

"I see. Good answer. Now…would you hold equally responsible the guy who brought them?"

The two answered almost simultaneously. "Brought what?"

"How do you know somebody else brought 'em?"

Jack thought silently for a moment. "I'm not trying to trick anyone here, but both your answers are interesting and informative. In the first place, Jean, yours confirms my suspicion that somebody did bring the smoke bomb. The guy who thinks it up, usually, can think enough to know better than to pull it off, but Russell's answer was even more interesting. When I asked about who brought them, he said, 'What.' He didn't seem to know whether I was talking about the smoke bombs or something else. I'd have to guess, what, pills of some kind. Am I right?"

"No, as a matter of fact. Do you really want to know how it went down?"

"I'd like to know whatever needs to be known to help prevent problems in the future." Jack could tell that Russell was surprisingly anxious to talk about this. "Start at the beginning. It will all stay in here unless I have your permission to use it elsewhere. Fair enough?"

"I guess it started yesterday. Somebody said they had the smoke bombs, and you know a dare here, a deal there…altogether he was given six J's for lighting it."

"I see. Would you say that's a pretty good deal?"

"Well, to him, yes. He thinks he's a hero for doing it…the police, the whole bit."

"I take it you don't care for Kerry."

"I don't know him all that well."

"So…back to my original question. If either of you were in a position to do anything about it, would you hold the person who supplied the device equally responsible?"

"You'd also have to include the ones who paid him to do it," Jean pointed out.

"But would you or not?"

"It depends on what you're going to do with 'em," Russell said lamely.

"It shouldn't."

Russell nodded. "Well, if somebody hires someone to kill a guy, he's committed a crime. This is the same thing."

"Yeah," Jean said. "But nobody made Kerry do it."

"So Russell is taking the conspiracy approach, which means that anyone who knew about it was in on it, and if they didn't try to stop it, they are guilty of conspiracy."

"But there's another way to think about it," Russell said. "If the main problem is the smoke bomb, then the guy who brought it is most guilty 'cause he would have found somebody to actually light it."

"Exactly—I like the way you put that. Now here comes the tricky part. Before, you said somebody had a smoke bomb. You know my next question."

Russell smiled. "I pass."

"You won't tell me his name?"

"I don't think so."

"That's okay. I appreciate your input thus far," Jack said, leaving open the possibility for further input. "I realize Headley is not one of your favorite people, but…" Jack thought long and hard, trying to decide exactly where he was going with this line of thought. "Never mind."

"I know." Jean ventured. "We were talking about that. It really wasn't as funny as they thought it would be."

"I noticed your pronoun there. Does that mean you didn't think it would be funny?"

"I was curious"—she smiled—"but equally guilty."

"There's a class statement, right, Russell?"

"It's not like we're trying to…hurt him…but in his classes, people get away with everything."

"I know, I know. Anyway, we're not here to talk about him. What's the best punishment?"

To Jack's surprise, Jean answered, "Apologize to Headley then have to go in after school every day for…a while."

"Doesn't that punish Mr. Headley?"

"Well, it might make him feel like he's in control."

"Good point."

"Listen to her," Russell exclaimed. "Who do you think you are?"

"Who do I think I am?" She had done it again. That razor-sharp look and cotton-soft voice had left him no room for further complaining. He shrugged. "That would be a punishment."

"I said none of this would leave this room without your permission. Do I have your permission to share that one—about the punishment—with others? No one will know where it came from, of course."

"Sure," she answered simply.

"Thank you…and thanks for coming. See you tomorrow."

Jack headed for the office.

"Got a minute or two?" Glenn seemed intent on a file folder but greeted Jack and motioned to a chair.

"In the it's-none-of-my-business category, I was just wondering what was being done with this Kerry Jenkins kid, it being somewhat of a drug-related problem."

Glenn lowered the folder to his desk and looked questioningly at Jack. "Drug problem?"

"I think so, but for now, let's leave that out of it—at least 'til I find out a little more. My question is how is Jenkins going to be punished?"

"The usual suspension. Five days is my maximum. Over that, it is a school board decision."

"I see. Has that already been decided? Finalized?"

"Certainly not. I was just looking in his file—really no problems before this. Seems like a decent kid. What have you got?"

"Well, I asked a couple kids. They said the worst punishment for him would be to have him apologize to Mr. Headley then spend time after school for, I don't know, maybe a week or so. My thinking was let Jenkins know that he comes after school for a half hour or more a day until we find out who supplied the smoke bomb. That puts him in a no-win situation. Then I can find out who put him up to it, and then Kerry won't be such a hero as he thinks he is now."

"He tells us it was his, no one else involved."

"Not true, Glenn. I know it, and by tomorrow I'll probably know whose it was and who else put him up to it. Plus, if we do it this way, it puts Mr. Headley in charge…in control, you know?"

Glenn was nodding. "Good point. For that alone it has merit. As for other people, I'm not real comfortable with that part."

"Well, should I try to find out who brought the thing in the first place?"

"Absolutely…absolutely. I just don't see how all this ties into your area of drugs."

"Payoff, that's all."

"Do I enter that in this file? Are you sure?"

"Give me a day or two," Jack said, standing up.

"Fair enough. Keep me posted. The police didn't get much, you know." He held up the folder. "There's nothing in here to suggest that it was anything but a one-time prank."

"Well, maybe so. I'll see you tomorrow or soon after."

"Thanks, Jack."

It was 4:30 before Jack pulled into his apartment parking lot. There sat Jim, slouched atop his bicycle.

"Howdy," Jack greeted him. "How did you know where I live?"

"I've seen your car here before."

"Come on in. You got time?"

"I just wanted to talk for a second."

"Good, good. I'll split a soda with you. So what's up?"

"I'm walking to school with Dave tomorrow, so be ready, remember?"

"Sure, I'll be ready. Here, enjoy," he said, handling the boy an ice-filled glass of cola. "Talk about Russell Carter. What's he up to?"

"I think he's old. I really do. It seems like the whole group is more, I don't know, independent, you know?"

"Good word, and probably pretty accurate, but basically, you haven't known Russell to be using anything lately?"

"Not at school, at noon anyway, but there's a new customer for you."

"Does he light smoke bombs?"

Jim showed his surprise. "How did you know?"

"You don't want me to ever answer that question. Let me just tell you what I've heard, then you can add or correct as you care to."

Jim shrugged.

"Kerry Jenkins was paid to light the thing," Jack began. "Kind of a dare, but the payoff was in marijuana. What I don't know is who paid him and who provided the bomb." The boy was interested again.

"So…is this basically correct, and do you care to add anything?"

"He was well paid off. I think it got up to six or seven joints."

"That's about what I heard." Then there was a considerable long silence. "So…who brought it?"

"You don't want to know."

"Try me."

"What will you do if I tell you?"

"Shoot him," Jack joked.

"No, really?"

"I don't know, Jim. I don't know that I'd do anything. It's just…I don't know. I thought we had a better line on each other, but I understand if you can't tell me."

"I didn't say I couldn't tell you. I said you didn't want to know."

"I'm a big boy," Jack said. "Let me decide that, okay?"

Jim sighed audibly then blurted it out, "Scott."

"Graham?"

"Right on."

"Ouch," Jack tried to think. Was it really all that serious? Just a prank, after all. No mind the method of payment. "And then there were some other backers, weren't there?" he asked.

"Yeah, I don't know who all pitched in. Like I say, he got six or seven joints to do it."

"But you're sure Scott brought it to school originally?"

"I was standing right there."

"Oh, yeah." Jack tried to keep the topic of conversation alive. "Tell me, as you remember it, did Scott specifically ask Kerry to light the thing, or was it just a general announcement and Kerry went for it?"

"It's hard to say…I think Kerry specifically…but it was because they both have Headley sixth hour. They may have planned the thing earlier, for all I know." He gulped his soda and flopped back in the chair.

"Are you worried about all this? That it is going to catch up with you?"

"It could."

"I realize that, Jim," Jack said, taking the boy's glass. "And you know I'll be careful. You've been honest with me, so I'll be honest with you. Here's what I want to do. I want to put Jenkins in Headley's room after school every day. He can clean blackboards, whatever, and we won't say for how long. Then we let the word get around that he stays there 'til we find out who put him up to it. Now I know Doc won't go along with the second part—he can't—but if we could get the first part, you know, staying after school, then I can handle the tricky part."

"Why?" Jim asked simply.

"I want to blow some of the hero out of his sails. If it even looks like he ratted on Scott, they won't want anything to do with him, and hopefully he'll choose some different direction."

"You've got it all figured out."

"I hope so. Will you help?"

"If it will help me."

"Meaning what?"

"I'm worried about somebody finding out, you know. I'd get killed."

"I'm aware of the danger, Jim. That's why I'll always check with you before I do anything. As for it helping you, if you were the one spreading the rumor, it could at least make it sound like you're on their side."

"Maybe, but what finally happens to Scott?"

"I think he ought to catch all holy hell, but I don't know what specifically…maybe the same thing…after school in Headley's room."

The discussion ended with Jim understanding that if Kerry started appearing in Mr. Headley's room, he could start a rumor that the authorities were trying to find out who brought the smoke bomb. Jack could then make his disclosure and let people assume whatever they wanted to.

✶✶✶✶✶

The first person in Jack's room the next morning was Glenn Becker. "I bounced your idea off Carl Headley," Glenn said, scanning the room to see that no one was listening. "He was receptive, I'd say. I think we'll try it for a week. Kerry Jenkins will be back tomorrow. We'll see how it goes…and thanks for the idea."

"You going to be in your office for a while?" Jack asked.

"Sure."

"I'll be along in a minute. I'd like to share something with you."

"Anytime. I'll be there."

With Glenn's office door closed, Jack could relate the full scope of the smoke bomb incident. He began. "The reason I feel this is a drug problem is that Jerry Jenkins was paid to light the thing. It was not in joints, something on the order of half dozen or so. Of course, the real payment to him was the brag power and social stature he seems to crave."

"You know this?"

"About the joints? Yes, it's true."

"I wouldn't have guessed Kerry was in that crowd," Glenn said though his voice did not challenge Jack's information. "We better call in his parents. What do you think?"

"If I were his parents, I'd want to know, but I'd also want some other information."

"Such as?"

"Well, how long he's been into this—if, in fact, he is. I just don't have a feel for it yet in his case. I don't even know whether he intends to use the stuff or is he just trying to get recognition."

"I agree that the parents ought to know as much as we can possibly tell them…as long as it's reliable," Glenn added, looking directly at Jack.

"It will be reliable. My gut feeling is that the committee doesn't want anything to do with the kid. They just wanted a stooge, and I suppose he's a joke in their eyes."

"Jack, do you know who brought it and paid him?"

"Yes, though I think several people paid him."

Glenn swiveled his chair so he faced the large window; long early morning shadows lay across the courtyard. The place was quiet, peaceful. "I'm not comfortable with all of this. Tell me again what you were wanting to do."

"Jenkins spends some time with Mr. Headley, and then we punish the person who brought it. My aim is to shut Kerry out of that group. He doesn't need to get involved. He'll be less of a hero if people think he told us who is behind it all."

Glenn smiled. "That would do it, but I say we'd be doing more harm to him than good. When do I find out who made the damn thing?"

"Scott Graham."

"And the people who contributed to the pot…or should I say to the pot?"

"That I'm not sure of. A lot of the committee is in that class. I can't imagine anyone else contributing, so we could come pretty close."

"What do we do now?" Glenn asked, swinging his chair around to face Jack directly.

"How about Jenkins's parents?"

"Find out what you can. As of now, they only know about the smoke bomb. They'll be in tomorrow, so anything you know by then will be helpful. Keep your ears to the ground. Maybe we could get you in here to talk to them. Would you be willing to do that?"

"Sure. Sixth, seventh hour, even after school. Whatever would work out?"

"Thanks."

"I'll let you know anything I find out," Jack said, standing. "See you later."

"Hi, Mr. Flemming," Jim said as he bounded through the door. The usual preschool confusion was uninterrupted, but Jack caught the signal and nodded.

"Good morning." But his attention had switched to Kevin. He would not have noticed any difference. He would not have noticed anything. Without knowing what he was looking for, Jack began a close-up examination. No loss of balance, no giddiness. Sentences were coherent, friendly enough—really nothing noticeable.

What was noticeable was an exchange between an unusual early morning visitor, Russell himself, and Kevin, who had taken his seat back by the door just as Russell came in. A brief exchange caught Jack's attention and curiosity. Anger, at least friction, was apparent between the two. Then it ended abruptly, and Russell moved toward Jack.

"I need to talk to you sometime," Russell said quietly.

"I think that can be arranged. Can it wait till after school? You know I'll be here."

"Can you get here during your lunch hour?" the boy was insistent.

"Can't do it," Jack answered apologetically. "Noon duty."

"Well, maybe I can catch you then."

"Is it hot?"

"No, just interesting." Russell smiled. "It will keep."

Jack watched as the boy started for the door and noticed that David's eyes cast downward. *Avoiding confrontation maybe*, thought Jack. *He is a little more subdued, quieter, but then a confrontation with Russell Carter could subdue anyone, marijuana or no marijuana.*

✶✶✶✶✶

By noon the air was warming, drawing everyone outside. *What a paradox*, Jack thought. *Everyone lookin' like he is having fun, relaxing, socializing. Frisbees sailed, climbing and dropping on the breeze, yet everyone would vanish in an instant if told they didn't have to be here.*

Russell approached from the rear. "Howdy."

"What do we do now, hide behind a tree?" Jack teased.

"No, we can talk anywhere."

"So…talk."

"It's about this Jenkins guy. He offered to give Tim a couple of J's and a couple more to me and some to Randy. Thought you'd be interested."

"Yep." They strolled for a while, Jack realizing that Russell enjoyed this level of involvement. "So…you're telling me Kerry Jenkins doesn't do dope, doesn't smoke."

"I don't think he'd know how."

"You don't think he'd know how? So it was all show?"

"Yep."

"Can I ask a question?"

"What?"

"What did you say to him when he offered to give them to you?"

"I told him to shove 'em."

"I will take that as a good sign," Jack finally said.

The bell rang, reminding all the relaxers, socializers, and Frisbee throwers that they had to be there.

"It's more than a sign, Mr. Flemming. See you later."

★★★★★

Jack had time to himself as he walked across the dandelion-covered grass. There's something to be said for this on-again, off-again drug career. The offs sure feel good. He realized he had forgotten to find about the altercation between Russell and Kevin. There was plenty of time for that. He noticed a prim little lass hurrying toward him. He didn't know her name but thanked her when she handed him a note. It was from Glenn asking that he come to the office to meet Kerry Jenkins's parents.

★★★★★

"Mr. and Mrs. Jenkins," Glenn was saying. "We just wanted to bring you up-to-date on everything we have been able to uncover.

209

I've asked Mr. Flemming to explain and try to answer any question you might have. Jack…"

"Well," Jack began. "The smoke bomb part you're familiar with, and that in itself could be written off as a prank or adolescent mischief, serious enough, but once it's over and done, it's over and done." Mr. Jenkins was nodding his head in understanding. His wife, already showing apprehension, held her husband's hand.

"The problem which needs further attention is this. Kerry lit the thing in class in exchanges for an amount of marijuana."

"Oh," gasped Mrs. Jenkins, her husband shifting in his chair, pulling her closer. His body language said, "We're in this together," but it was not sufficient to stem a flow of tears in her eyes.

"What do we do?" she wailed.

Jack pressed on, calmly answering the question as if it had not even been asked. "Now the reason I was in favor of talking to you folks first without Kerry was so that you'd have time to get over the emotional shock, the hurt or anger or whatever, and be able when confronting Kerry to rely on one emotion only—love."

Mr. Jenkins asked the obvious question: "What exactly do we say? What should we do?"

Jack smiled. "Let me tell you what a student of mine said to me in a very private, very emotional, very tearful conversation. This kid is one of our"—he groped for a word—"greatest drug problems. He said to me that if his father had sat him down and talked to him, told him not to use the stuff, that would have done the trick. Sounds simple, I know, but show Kerry that you care. Be sure he knows you understand the prevalence of the stuff and the social pressures but that you'd like your family to be able to rise above it." This was allowed to sink in.

"Now there's more still." Jack noticed Glenn's interest pique and Mrs. Jenkins's eyes drop to her lap. "It seems that Kerry has not used the pot, nor does he intend to. He simply was doing it for show. The problem is I don't approve of the group of kids he thinks he's trying to show off for. Do you follow me?"

"He's just trying to get into the wrong crowd," Mr. Jenkins enunciated.

"Exactly, so your job now is to accentuate the good things he does. Encourage any positive interest. Get to know any of his friends. Without overdoing it, take time to show your support of him as a nondrug user."

Glenn was impressed and showed it. "We're fortunate to have Mr. Flemming's input, and we don't want you to think we're just dropping this on you then abandoning you." Addressing Jack, he said, "If they have any questions, they will call me. I'll relay them to you. Is that satisfactory?"

"Sure, anytime," Jack said, standing.

Mr. Jenkins shot to his feet, thrusting forward his hand. "Thank you very much."

"Yes," echoed his wife. "Thank you."

Jack nodded and left in plenty of time to catch Russell between classes.

"What's goin' on between you and Kevin?" Jack asked, wondering whether he could be heard over the general noise in the hallway.

"He was stoned, for cryin' out loud."

"I see. Maybe we better not get into that right now. We can talk about it later." Then he added as a question, "If you don't mind?"

"Sure."

Later was, as Jack expected, after school, after the halls had emptied, after Jean had arrived.

"So…let me get this straight. You somehow noticed that Kevin was stoned…"

Russell nodded.

"Just how do you know he was stoned? How could you tell?"

Jean smiled and looked at Russell intently as if waiting for wisdom.

"I don't…you can just tell. I can't describe it."

Jean's shoulders dropped from disappointment, and Jack was sure his own did too, but he knew not to press just now.

"So you mysteriously determined, may I say diagnosed, his mental state. Then what happened?"

"I told him not to," he answered matter-of-factly.

"You told him not to…and just why did you tell him not to?"

"Do you like him? Does he mean something to you?"

"No, I hardly—"

'Then you don't need to tell him what to do or not to do. You see you've got nothing invested. If he continues, you feel no pain." Jean's smile disappeared; Jack pressed on. "When you try to get a friend to quit, you're making an investment and taking a risk. You may lose the friend. There will be resentment. It takes time and patience and a lot of worry, and the whole thing could end up in failure. So I don't think it's right for you to come on like a sledgehammer and just tell some kid not to. Know what I mean?"

"Sorry," Russell shot back. "I didn't know we had to leave all that up to you—"

"Hey," Jack interrupted. "We agreed everybody does his own thing. That's the way you guys wanted it. Let's make it work."

Just then Officer Boles walked past the window. Seeing him and Russell exchange nods brought that painful stabbing fear which Jack tried to tell himself was imagined and exaggerated. "You know him?" Jack asked the boy. "I mean, really know him?"

"Yeah, why?"

"I don't know. I just don't feel that I know him at all, and maybe I should…being in the same line of business."

"He's a sharp cookie."

Jack felt it again. "You mean detectivewise?"

"Yeah, he knows what's goin' on…or it seems like he does anyway."

Jean volunteered, "Randy is afraid of him."

"What is that?" Jack asked, feigning nonchalance.

"He figures everything out and everybody."

"Seems like a good friend to have."

"That's the thing," Russell said. "He doesn't make friends. You can't talk to him. He just figures, then he does the talking."

Somehow Jack didn't like that line of conversation and returned to Jean. "So…what's Randy got to be afraid of?"

"You know, the whole dog thing."

"You mean he thinks Boles is going to charge him with stealing?" Jack asked.

"Or murder," she said. "He's certainly guilty of stealing."

"And driving without a license," Russell joked.

"Randy thinks Officer Boles believes he killed the guy," Jean said emphatically.

"Now wait a minute," Jack began. "It's easy when you're guilty of something to imagine the worst, to think everyone is closing in on you." The words sounded good. "It's the whole paranoid trip." Jack turned to Russell. "Boles hasn't talked to you about any of this?"

"No, it just seems like he's been friendlier or something, you know, like he wants to talk but doesn't. Should I go to him?"

"No." Jack was a little too quick, he realized. "No, I wouldn't until he asks you. Let Randy worry a while more." Jack just could not resist, could not let it drop, had to find out about this man he had come to fear. "So…do you really know him very well?"

"Boles?"

"Okay."

"Nice guy, I guess. Never hurt me."

"Is that because you outsmart him?"

"Are we talking about drugs?" Russell wanted to know before committing himself.

'Well, since you brought it up."

"Do you outsmart him?"

"Russell, would you suppose that Boles know of your drug-related past?"

"Seems like he knows about everything."

Jack didn't want to hear that. "So what's his bag? What does he do anyway?"

"He has a way of letting you know that he's on to you…know what I mean?"

"I suppose so. What you're saying is that his presence brings about a changes in deportment."

"Whatever."

"He shows up for school activities, dance, ball games, and so forth?"

"Yeah, and just kind of walks around."

"That's something we never talked about—dances."

"What about 'em?"

"Much of a drug scene?"

"Not at the dances."

Meaning what?"

"We'd generally toke on the way to 'em. I suppose there was some goin' on, but I like to dance, you know, tight."

"Tight." There was a long silence as the two friends looked at each other. Finally, Jack continued, "Do you miss that now?"

"Yeah, some."

"Well, I respect that. What I mean is I respect you. Let's call it a day."

15

Springtime was having its effect upon absences and tardies, Jack was coming to realize. Seventh hour was nearly over before he had contacted all offenders from the week and disposed of their individual cases. He was glad the individuals did not include members of the Bridge Committee—at least he had that to feel good about as he walked toward his room. He saw Mr. Headley straining under an arm-length stack of books and stepped into the older man's room.

"Spring cleaning? Here, let me help." Jack could see that a huge pile of books was growing on a table in the back of the room.

"I'm going to have a helper," Mr. Headley said, leaning against the table as if to catch his breath. He smiled. "And I'm going to keep him busy. How long do you think it will take to check through all of these and erase all the pencil marks and mend pages?"

"I'd say it will keep him busy for a while. Be sure to have him help you put them away."

"Good idea," Mr. Headley said with a nod.

"I've got a visitor of my own I need to deal with," Jack said, remembering he had asked Tim to have his homework complete and turned in before going home. The bell sounded, ending the day and the week, and its echo had scarcely died away when Tim hurried into the room. "Here ya go."

"Thanks, Tim," Jack said, standing up as if ready to walk the boy to the door. Tim was about Jack's height and looked as if he still had at least another foot of growing to do. "Say, I realize I call on you an awful lot to read out loud in class, and if that bothers you or seems unfair, then I apologize. It's just that you read so well and everybody pays attention to you…"

"It's okay," Tim said, seemingly surprised at the extra recognition.

"Well, I feel like I'm taking advantage of you, but I wish I had a Tim in my class each hour. Some of these people just can't read at all. Anyway, I appreciate it."

"No problem."

"See you Monday."

"See you."

"Goodbye."

✶✶✶✶✶

Russell and Jean were a very welcome sight. It was dreary outside, and for some reason, Jack had thought about Janice off and on all day. He really missed her consciously and had dreamed of Friday-night get-togethers, good times. He wasn't aware that he was feeling sorry for himself, so Russell's blunt greeting surprised him.

"What are you feeling so sorry for yourself for? You looks bummed out all day."

"Sorry." Jack wanted to end the conversation before it got started, but the boot pressed on. Pushing the two front desks together, he signaled Jean to join him. "What's wrong? Let's talk about it."

"Well, you're certainly up, aren't you?"

"It's Friday," he announced, as if there could only be one emotional state on Friday.

"Really."

"You are bummed out. What's the deal?"

"Just thinking," said Jack.

"About what?"

"Oh, nothing much." He looked at Jean and smiled, hoping for help.

She held Russell's arm for a moment then spoke. "Sometimes people are reminded of something in the past, and even though they feel sad in remembering, they somehow keep thinking about it because the memories themselves are good, even though they can never be relieved."

Russell said simply, "Oh."

"How do you know so much at age fourteen? You know exactly what I'm remembering, don't you?"

"It's pretty obvious."

"It is? asked Russell. "What are you two into?"

Jack smiled slightly then squinted as he stared at the boy before playfully spitting out his answer. "Love."

Jean erupted into laughter.

Russell blinked. "Jesus."

"We told you," Jean continued, as if lecturing Russell while Jack's mind wandered. "The plane wreck, the stewardess."

"Sorry," Russell said. His sincerity touched Jack and brought him back to reality—just in time to hear Russell's suggestion.

"Go talk to your friend the speech teacher, and we'll all go to a show tonight. You drive. I'll buy the tickets."

Never had Jack been so surprised and speechless. "I don't know," he stammered.

"Russell," Jean spoke, and Jack realized he had never heard her call him by his first name. "You don't just"—she paused—"grab the first person that comes along when you care about somebody."

"Who doesn't? I sure—"

"And what's this about my friend the speech teacher?" Jack interrupted.

"Come on!"

"No, really. I hardly know her."

"Well, what better way to change that?"

"I pass," Jack said with a smile.

Russell turned to Jean. "Well, there goes our transportation."

"I figured as much. Just give you my car, and you'd be happy."

"Funny you should mention that."

"Mention what?"

"I'm driving your car."

"Why, what's up?" Jack felt the conversation sweeping him onward into something, somehow, that he didn't want to hear.

"Boles asked me if you ever let me use your car."

Jean's shoulders slumped slightly as she resigned herself to listening to a long conversation. Jack was anything but relaxed. "When was this?"

"I don't know…the other day. I guess I should have mentioned it."

"Strange," said Jack for lack of anything better, but he had to have something better without showing too much interest. "So a cop walks up to you and out of the clear blue sky asks you if your civics teacher ever lets you drive his car?"

Jean chuckled but was ignored.

"Try to put it into context, for crying out loud. What do you think made him ask that?"

"I don't know. Is it all that important?"

"We'll, I'd like to find out if it is important…and that's what I mean about context. If he was saying something like 'Of all your teachers, which one would you ask to borrow a car?' then he's got a good way to find out how you feel about a certain teacher—see what I mean?"

"Yeah, I don't—"

"On the other hand, if he said, perhaps while standing on the back lot, 'Which of these teachers' cars would you borrow?' Then he's talking more about cars." Jack felt himself encouraged by his own conversation, but it wasn't to last long.

"No," Russell began. "I'd say it was more about."

"Where was this?"

"Shopping center, couple days ago."

"Were you with anybody?" Jack looked at Jean, who was becoming slightly more interested, though, soon to become involved.

Russell smiled playfully at her. "No, I was alone—and clean," he added, holding up his arms.

Jack could see no humor and realized he was betraying more than casual interest. He was indeed being swept along by the conversation.

"What exactly did he say?"

"He said, 'Can I ask you a question?' then he said he wondered if Randy or Jeff ever used your car."

"Randy?" Jean whispered.

Russell pressed on. "When I told him I didn't think so, he looked right at me and said, 'Does Mr. Flemming ever allow you to drive his car?' I said no, then he asked if I ever drove your car without you knowing about it."

"And your answer?" Jack pressed.

"Hell no."

"Glad to hear that."

"How did Randy get into this?" Jean wanted to know.

"I guess," suggested Jack. "We ought to get everything out in the open so everybody knows what everybody else knows. Any objections?" There being none, he continued, "It started when Russell came to me with the news that Randy was borrowing his dad's car late at night and driving around town. Jean then came to me, saying Randy was involved in some scheme involving dog stealing, dog selling, and ultimately dogfighting. I had to assume there was a connection, but I didn't know what to do. Then…let's see…Jean told me the guy, the buyer of the dogs, had been killed or found dead…I don't remember which…"

Jack approved of the way he was lying. "Then what happened next?"

"Randy got scared." Jean ventured. "But whether Boles talked to him or not, I don't know."

"He did," Russell said. "And the guy was murdered. Randy was lucky he wasn't there that night, but he had been there the night before—that I do know."

"So how does my car fit into it all?"

"Boles is trying to figure out how Randy got the dogs and how he delivered them," Russell suggested.

"Oh, he doesn't know about your dad's car?" Jack asked.

"Not from me."

"Not from me," Jean added.

"Russell, here's what I'd like you to do. Tell Boles about how Randy was using your dad's car. Will you do that?"

Russell shrugged, not to be committed.

"Come on," Jack urged. "Don't you want to help catch a murderer? Let me know if you get a chance to talk to him."

"I think he's in the office. You want me to talk to him now? I could bring him in here if you want."

"Well." Jack paused. "That would be interesting."

Russell slid off the desk, and Jack knew it was out of his control. The die was cast, and events would have to play themselves out. Left alone with Jean, he tried to relax. He smiled. "What is the latest on this anyway? I haven't gotten to talk with you much about it. Is Randy really scared or even concerned? Does he talk about it much?"

"He really doesn't talk about anything much—not to me anyway—but I don't think he cares much one way or the other except the money he was making."

"And you? Are you satisfied that the dogfighting problem has been eliminated?"

"I hope so. I don't care for the way it ended, but I guess if it had to be, I'm glad it's over, you know?"

"We were lucky Randy wasn't involved more than he was and that he's still alive."

The door swung open, and Russell sauntered in, rolling his eyes. Officer Boles followed, his three-piece suit exquisitely fitted, shoes glossy, and jewelry flashing from both hands. Jack knew about the importance of looking and feeling in charge and could tell that this man had it all down to a science. Anxious to see if the man's razor-sharp creases would bend, Jack offered him a chair. Even seated, Officer Boles seemed far above the others in the room.

"Am I supposed to ask questions, or do I get to answer them this time?" His slight smile only slightly softened his manner.

Jack was comfortable. "We were just talking here," he began lamely. "And Russ mentioned that you had asked him if I had let him drive my car or"— he looked at Russell for support—"if he had ever used it without my letting him. Naturally, I'm curious to know whether my car is involved in anything." Then Jack felt like taking the offensive. "You can consider that a question." And he stared at the man until an answer was forthcoming.

"Mr. Flemming, your car was, at some time, parked in front of Mr. Caruana's home. Can you explain that?"

"Who is Mr. Caruana? Where does he live, and when was my car seen there?"

"Mr. Caruana was the murdered subject. His home was out beyond the city limits, and I know of no one who saw your car. Let's just say I'm sure your car was there at a time reasonably close to the time of the murder."

"I see. Are you unable to tell me how it is known that my car was where it was, or do you just prefer to be mysterious?" Jack saw Russell smile, which faded fast as Officer Boles asked to speak with Jack alone.

Jack fought to calm himself as he acknowledge Jean's and Russell's departure, and he determined to match with his man just as he had done so often with students. He took the offensive.

He began, looking firmly at Boles. "Can you understand how I might feel learning that you are accusing me of allowing an underage kid to use my car—a student of mine, no less?"

"I wasn't exactly accusing you. I was carrying on—"

"If you have questions about my activities—and that is legitimate for you to have questions—then you should ask me, not my students." Jack was relaxing as he fit into his role as teacher.

"That is a good suggestion, Mr. Flemming. Let me ask you a few questions…if that's all right."

"Sure. I'll tell you anything you want to know." Jack bluffed.

"As I said, I'm sure your car was at the Caruana residence at a reasonable proximity to the time of his murder." Jack felt himself losing the offensive. "So…let's start from that point. If you are equally sure that no one else drove it there, may I ask you the obvious question. Did you drive it there?"

"The obvious answer is yes."

"Could you elaborate?" His manner seemed so friendly, open, that Jack's confidence rose. "Or would you rather talk with your attorney," Boles added, throwing Jack off guard.

He forced a smile. "You know Jean Gilmore, I'm sure. Jean approached me some time ago regarding a problem with her brother.

It seems Randy was selling dogs to his guy for dogfighting. At nearly the same time, maybe even slightly before, Russell had mentioned that he was aware of Randy's sneaking out at night and taking the family car for joyrides. I assumed that it wasn't joyrides at all. He was stealing and delivering dogs. My assumption proved correct because I followed the kid one night—one morning actually—from the Carter home to the house where he delivered the dogs…or so it seemed. To make certain, I went back out there either that afternoon or the next." He paused as if thinking, trying to give authenticity. "Anyway, I went out there to see what was there, and it did, indeed, appear that Jean's story and Russell's account fit together."

"Have you been out there since that time?"

"No."

"When was all this investigation taking place in relation to the murder?"

"Well, it was before the murder. I'm not sure when the man died actually."

"How did you learn of his death?"

"It was in the papers. Jean called me up saying that her brother was real scared because the guy was killed."

"The only problem I have now, Mr. Flemming, is why didn't you tell me about all this when we talked earlier?"

"I don't know. They trust me. That's important. Can I ask a question now?"

"Surely."

"How was it determined that my car was at the scene?"

Officer Boles stretched his legs as if stalling, savoring his knowledge. "Your right front tire was plugged. It leaves a mark in soft dirt." He rose as if to end the discussion, but as he pushed open the door, he turned to Jack. "It leaves the same mark everywhere. Have a good weekend, and thanks for your time, Mr. Flemming."

Jack's knees weakened. "Thank you," he managed to say.

He felt hot and mad. As the door swung closed, he sat back down, his mind swirling like the windblown rain around the corner of the building. He was sure Boles knew everything. Anger, fear, and indignation rose within him. He wanted to have the whole committee here in his room again. He would gladly fight the drugs, the insecurity, even the racial tension if only he had not gone so far. For the first time, he thought of his acts as murder. *But it wasn't that for me*, he rationalized. *I was solving a problem.* He removed the index cards from his desk and read them, remembering the positive influence he had over the young basketball players who had also acted selflessly, motivated by their affection for someone else. He tore the cards and began to write.

★★★★★

The rain was letting up as Jack raced to his car.

"Mr. Flemming, wait up," someone called.

Jack had his car door open when Dave Thurmond caught up to him. "Hop in, David."

"Have you got a minute?"

"I've got…an eternity. It's Friday. What's up?"

"Oh, it's just Russell. He seems like he's still mad…I guess about that article."

"He admits that you're one hell of a writer, and I agree."

"Thanks, but I shouldn't have done it that way just to make fun of somebody."

"Well, now you know. I don't think you did any real harm. You guys could be pretty good friends in my opinion. Russell is a sharp cookie like yourself. He was talking about you as I recall."

"I'm sure he was."

Jack started the engine. "Can I give you a ride home?"

"Sure, if you don't mind. What was Russell saying, or was it just about the article?"

"No, no. Singing. Which way to your house?"

"Turn right here and keep going. Singing? What does he know about singing?"

"That you're good at it. Are you?"

"I like to. Grab a left here. I like to sing except—one more left, fourth house."

"Jack pulled to a stop. "Except what?"

"Well, I'm in the choir, and she wants me to do a solo for the spring concert, you know?"

"I think I know what a solo is. You scared to?"

"No, she just wants me to sing 'Old Man River.'" He paused, looked over at Jack. "Dressed like a slave."

Jack chuckled, "That reeks of ethnicity. How do you dress like a slave?"

"Bare feet, tattered pants, no shirt, dirty, and sweaty looking."

"So what's the problem?" Jack teased, and Dave laughed.

"The problem," he said. "Is the no-shirt part. I can't get up in front of the whole school like that."

"What, you think the girls would storm the stage?"

"Mr. Flemming!"

"David, think of it as show business. I say do it. What the heck. If you've got the talent…you know what I mean. At least think about it. And about Russell, just go up to him and talk. If you're sorry, say so. You can pull it off."

"Right," said David, opening the door. He looked at Jack.

"I'll think about it. Thanks for the ride. See you Monday."

"Yeah, listen. You've got a lot of talent, my friend. Don't waste it, okay?"

"Thanks."

Jack's route home took him past the shopping center. His mind started to wander back to that first hot lonely night when Jean had appeared, as if out of a mist, to bring purpose once again to his life. Where had things gotten off the rails? He was almost lost in thought until his attention was grabbed by the blond hair and the trumpet case and the boy dashing across the street through a break in the traffic. Scott appeared to have a purpose and a specific destination as Jack tried to maneuver into the parking lot without losing sight of the boy. Following on foot, he could see that Scott was heading through the mall toward the back parking lot where Jack had spent so many hours in waiting. He now knew where he wanted to be.

Rushing back to his car, he pulled in next to a trash dumpster and was able to peer between it and a huge air conditioning unit without being seen. He could see Scott sitting on a short flight of steps as if waiting. Jack's heart pounded with anticipation, but he only had time to find a pen and some paper when a car rounded the far end of the building and Scott descended the steps.

The trumpet case was opened ever so briefly, and an exchange was made. The car hardly stopped. The driver nodded, Scott turned to retrace his steps, and Jack jotted down a license number.

Jack's mind raced. Should he follow the car, confront Scott, or let Officer Boles in on the amazing discovery?

Self-preservation took over momentarily, and the inclusion of Officer Boles had an instant appeal. Then Jack thought more could be done if he did it himself. Consciously forsaking rationality, he started his engine and slowly drove to the front lot in time to see Scott emerge.

"Hey, what's up? Want a ride?"

"That'd be great…if you don't mind."

"Hop in. Where to?" asked Jack after the door slammed.

"Well, which way are you going?"

"I was going home. I live right over there in those apartments. Got time for a soda?"

"Sure. Sounds great," Scott answered, his arms folded across the trumpet case on his lap.

"Second floor. Follow me," Jack announced, setting the parking break. As an afterthought, he said. "I guess we'd better lock it with that trumpet, huh?"

"Well." There was a long pause. "If you don't want to close up your car, I can just bring it up with me."

"Sure thing. I promise not to make you serenade me again."

They both laughed. "Do you remember that day?" Jack was fumbling for his keys. He felt nervous.

"I remember. I'll bet Headley does too. He didn't seem pleased."

"Well, maybe he just doesn't like good music. He's really a good old guy," Jack added, latching the door shut. "You know who else wasn't pleased? Jean. She accused me of assuming there was pot or something in your trumpet case and that that was why I wanted to look inside. Can you imagine? What do you want to drink?"

"Surprise me."

"I'm about to," Jack said offhandedly. "Let's go with root beer."

Seated, facing Scott, the trumpet case on the table between them, Jack began his finale. Slowly, cautiously, he told himself.

"So…you're into music in a big way. Any other major interests?"

"Oh, anything and everything. You mean, like, hobbies?"

"Okay."

"I've been through dozens of hobbies, I guess."

"Do you like guns."

"They're neat, don't really know too much about 'em. I guess I like pistols more than rifles or shotguns."

"I've got one I'll have to show you," Jack said, a plan fast developing. "Ever heard of a Luger?"

"You've got a Luger? Of course, I've heard of 'em. From World War II. They're German."

"Right on. Let me get it." He brought the shoebox into the living room, and Scott had scooted up to the front of his chair. "This is the ammunition," Jack said, handing a single bullet to the boy. "I've only got half a dozen or so left, but I guess I could get more. Anyway, here she is." He unwrapped the pistol and lovingly polished it before handing it to Scott.

"Just think what this has been through. I wish it could talk. How'd you get it?"

"My dad took it from an officer. He got lucky."

"I'd say. It must be worth a fortune."

"I don't really know, but it would do the job if needed."

"I guess!"

"Do you like it?" Jack asked simply.

"It is beautiful."

"Well," said Jack. He paused before rushing on, knowing he would never be able to turn back once started. "I tell you what…I'll give you that gun if you give me what's in that case."

"My trumpet? That's a tough—"

"I wasn't really talking about the trumpet. As a matter of fact, I don't know whether the trumpet is in there or not, do I."

Scott's eyes fell to the floor.

"Do we have a deal?"

"I don't know what you mean."

"Then let's open up the case."

"Why, Mr. Flemming. I can't trade. I got to get going."

"Scott…" Jack held up both hands, motioning the boy to remain seated. He smiled as he continued, "The game is a little more serious now, but I think we can still win—and we have to win because losing is just going to be too painful, too…total. If you want to win, we've got to both be on the same side. If you want to win, open the case and give me what I want. Then we'll deal with the problem and see where to go from there."

"Am I going to get in trouble?"

"You already are, my friend. We've got to try to get you out of trouble."

Scott flopped back in his chair. "How'd you know?"

"Lucky, I guess," said Jack. "But I'll tell you there are several juvies who would give anything to know what I discovered accidentally. Let's say fate is on your side. You'd have gotten caught eventually anyway. May I?" Jack asked, turning the trumpet case so that the snaps faced him.

"Go ahead."

The snaps clicked open, and there lay a plastic bag of marijuana.

"I'd rather be looking at your trumpet. Come here." The two walked to the bathroom. "I'll flush. You pour." And as the dry, powdery weed tried to float before being swirled down the toilet, Jack asked, "What did you pay for this?"

"Three hundred."

"And what would you sell it for—in the halls of West Junior High?" The last came out a bit overpowering, but Jack liked it.

"Five…six."

"So by now you're rich."

"I figured I'd be able to pay for college."

Jack expelled a long, slow breath—*almost a whistle paradox*, he thought. "I can't let you do it that way. Sorry. It hurts too many others and you as well. Now comes the important part," Jack continued as they returned to the living room. He spotted the pistol gleaming atop the trumpet case. "And I'm not losing sight of the fact that you just lost three hundred bucks, believe me, but the problem is to get you to turn your back on all that and rise above it what to do with your supplier so that it stops there and you don't get hurt."

"I'll be okay."

"Well. You're saying we can handle this strictly between ourselves?"

"Yes … please."

"Then what if something happens to me?"

"Like what?"

"I could get fired or have an accident. Would you be able to stay above it?"

"Yes."

"I realize you have to say yes. How does this sound? Boles gets the guy's license number, his name if you'll give it to me, but that's not too important. I get your assurance that you'll stay clean for the rest of your life, and you get my assurance I'll never tell of your involvement to this point."

"Sounds easy," Scott finally said.

"It won't be, but we have to start somewhere, don't we."

Scott asked, "How do we know…we're getting what we bargained for?"

"Well." Jack had been anticipating this. "One solution is sitting there on the table. If I shoot you, I know you aren't dealing. If you blast me away, you know I'm not telling. Plan B is to trust each other."

"Let's go with plan B."

"Amen." Jack walked around the coffee table and extended his hand. While they still held hands, Jack asked, "So…what's the guy's name?"

"Wayne."

"Yes?"

"That's all I know…just Wayne."

"How did you meet him? Just curious. It has nothing to do with anything really."

"Russell."

"Figures. So here's where we stand, and correct me if this is not your understanding. You will do no more dealing, buying, selling, trading, manufacturing—whatever the hell you've been doing—for the rest of your life. I will tell no one of your involvement to this point for the rest of my life, and three, Officer Boles finds out a license number and the name Wayne."

Scott nodded and started to say something, but Jack cut him off.

"That's the best I can do, Scott."

"I know… Thanks."

The two stood facing each other for only a moment, then Jack threw both arms around the boy and hugged him tightly. "Don't betray me."

"I won't. I promise."

"I guess I should drive you home, but maybe you need a little time alone to think." With his hands now on the boy's shoulder and looking him right in the eye, he continued, "I respect you because I respect your mind. You're a straight thinker, and you'll go far, so don't blow it." He fastened the clasps on the trumpet case and handed it to Scott. "Save this for the trumpet, okay?"

"I don't know what to say."

"What we say isn't all that important. It's what you do. If you got class, you'll know what to do."

He opened the door and felt the warm evening sunlight hit his face. "Goodbye, good friend."

"See you Monday, Mr. Flemming."

Jack couldn't answer.

✶✶✶✶✶

Jack realized as he switched on the television that he really didn't care what was on the news. It was just a habit. When he ate, he watched the news. For that matter, he was not hungry and guessed that he was eating from habit as well.

The phone rang.

Jack thought for a moment, trying to decide whom he hoped it was though he assumed it was Jean. He caught it on the fourth ring. It was Jim.

"Mr. Flemming, I never know whether to call you or if you want to hear this, but—"

"Jim, you can call anytime, and I asked to be told, remember. I appreciate what you're doing. What have you got?"

"Well, it was just kind of lucky. I was waiting for it to stop raining and I was at my locker and Jean and Russell came from somewhere. I'm sure I saw them take some joints out of a locker and stuff them into her purse."

"I see. This was after school today?"

"Yeah, I just got home and thought I'd call you."

"Here's what I'd like you to do. Figure out some way to let them know that I know they had the joints…like maybe ask them how I could have found out and that I was asking you about it. You know what I mean? Don't tell them that you told me. Just let them know that I know, okay?"

"I'll try but—"

"Jim, I appreciate it, and by the way, I really admire the way you have stayed clean. I respect you and what you're doing…and I mean that."

"Thanks, Mr. Flemming."

"Have a good weekend now."

"Okay, goodbye."

"Goodbye, good friend."

16

Jack felt the car's quick response to the accelerator and liked it. Gliding in and out of traffic was effortless, the spray of water off the pavement making his speed seem even greater than it was. At seventy, he was passing everything. At first, he fought with the urge within him to push to the maximum. He knew he could handle it if it started to fishtail, and with a long straight stretch ahead, he fought no more. With his foot to the floor, he could hear the engine speed increase and saw the odometer shoot quickly into the red zone, telling him the rear wheels were spinning. He knew that at this speed, none of the tires had contact with the pavement; the front wheels would be planning above the highway on a sheet of water. The thought thrilled rather than frightened him. Onward he pressed, delighting in swishing past the slower-moving cars around him. Even as the car's rear end began to slide to the right, he did not feel fear but enjoyed seeing the beams from his headlights sweep toward the left, the car angling down the highway but holding a steady course.

In those fleeting seconds, Jack had time to think about the sensation he was getting. This brief flirtation with danger, he realized, was giving him a great deal of enjoyment. Knowing he could control this danger gave him a sense of pride. Others in the same situation would overreact, would freeze, or would in some way endanger themselves and others, but here he was speeding down the highway, his rear wheels swerving from side to side, and all controlled by his deft touch upon the steering wheel. If these were reasonable thoughts, they were among his last. What would course through his brain in the next fleeting instant was the same chemical reaction as thought, but it was not monitored by reason. Too many stimuli crashed in through his senses—too many in too short a time. He was aware of them all, but his brain could not sort them out and react correctly.

He saw the left-hand curb. He felt the car jolt against it, but he was not certain which had come first. Somewhere he heard a horn; it could have been his own. He saw his own hand jerk the steering wheel to the right, but he could not know why; and in that splintering instant, his leg stiffened against the brake pedal, but all that he was fully aware of was that the car kept speeding onward. Water swirling around the front of a culvert flashed into his view; his brain, so overwhelmed, refused to think, and a strange euphoria seized him. For the time that it takes two and a half tons of automobile plot hurtle itself, twisting and rolling into the air and settle again into a sliding stop, Jack felt only the carefree, humorous, delightful, feeling given by a brain turned off to reality. There was no pain, no sound as his body was wedged beneath the steering column in a space less than inches wide between the rear wheels and the engine.

Onlookers gaped as steam rose from the rain splashing upon the hot metal of the engine. The gruesome job of prying metal to release flesh would be left to those more tempered to this work. Untangling a stretcher full of battered limbs so as to find a wallet with identification was a job none of the first to arrive could quite handle. They could only stare and assure themselves it could never happen to them.

✶✶✶✶✶

Glenn pulled out of his driveway, not knowing for sure what to do, how to handle the news he had just received from Jack's father. He considered calling an assembly to make the announcement. He thought of talking to the staff before school and asking them to use first hour as a time to explain the loss. Maybe a personal contact with the students closest to Jack would be best before making a general announcement.

The creek was running high under the bridge as Glenn's car splashed across the parking lot. He still had not reached a decision on his own course of action. He wished he could just stroll down to the bridge and talk to whomever was there. It would surely be the right ones, but he knew they would all see him coming and disperse before he had begun. Oh, how he wanted to cushion this blow. He felt an urge to touch those to whom he spoke, to put his hand on a shoulder and tell them that their closest friend would not be among them anymore. The distance between him and the committee was especially painful now, but the distance was real and would prohibit his telling this most horrible of news the way he thought he could do it best. He would, therefore, use the most difficult way.

In the solitude of his office, all other problems seemed insignificant. First, he had to call the central office and arrange a substitute. It was then that he realized the finality of the situation. It was not a substitute he was requesting but a replacement. What a difficult assignment, he thought. He scrawled a note to his secretary as he did each day a substitute was to be in the building and returned to his office. The passage of time escaped him until he heard the eight o'clock bell. The outer office was its usual hub of confusion and activity. He eyed the microphone to the school's public-address system. In moments, he would use it to convey words whose cruelty he could not measure nor imagine. The tardy bell brought relative calm to the outer office, and he could hear lockers slamming in the usual frenzy to be not too late to class. Allowing ample time for teachers to begin attendance routines, he clicked on the microphone.

"May I have your attention to this morning's announcements?" How many meaningless times had he said this? "The cheerleader practice scheduled this afternoon has been cancelled." In another building, the news was a surprise to the girl's physical education coach. She had not been told of a cancellation, but it suited her fine. "The final varsity baseball game will be held this afternoon. It is a home game and will start at four o'clock…"

Don noticed something different in Glenn's voice and glanced around his freshman class to see if others might have as well. Many students were looking at the wall-mounted speaker; indeed, they had noticed something. All seemed to be paying attention as if anxious for something they all felt.

There was a pause which would have been a signal for overall commotion, but today everyone was still. Glenn's breath could be heard over the speaker then finally, "In this morning's early storm, we all suffered a very great loss…" Glenn's voice cracked, causing him to release the switch on the microphone. He stood up as if to gain control of himself. In each room, as well as in the halls and other offices, that click and the one which followed it as Glenn turned the microphone back on punctuated what Glenn had to say more than he could have with a cannon.

"Mr. Flemming was in an automobile accident which took his life…" A pencil dropped from Mary's hand as she stared blankly at the speaker on her wall. A bell clanked as Pam, who had been aimlessly playing with the carriage on her typewriter, folded her arms and lay her head on them across the machine.

"I am sure there is nothing I can say now that will do even a fair job of expressing the sorrow that we all feel and the loss that we will feel. When more information is available to me, I will pass it along to you without delay. Teachers, we will follow our regular schedule, but I leave it your judgment as to how this day and each period will be spent. If an assembly in the auditorium seems appropriate later in the day, this information will be announced by second lunch period."

Glenn had scarcely put down the microphone when his door opened and Rose entered, mouth open, eyes wide, speechless. "Now you know," he said simply. "I'm going to need some help."

"I don't know what to say," she offered lamely, almost apologetically.

"Could you get out to the public telephone? If anyone wants to use it, ask them if they will come and see me first. Tell them they can make their calls on my phone." As he sat with elbows on his desk, his hands holding his head, it seemed everything was a swirl of confusion. His mind was on a number of kids, wondering how they were doing—more important, what he could do. He wanted to go somewhere but couldn't establish any priorities as he usually could. Aimlessly he began flipping through the file of student schedules until he realized he was looking for Jean Gilmore's. It told him her first-hour class was home economics. At least he had a place to go, and he did want to go someplace.

He hadn't gotten to his door before it opened slightly and Mr. Headley asked if he could come in for a moment.

"I really thought we had a good thing going there," the older man offered as he sat before Glenn's desk.

"I don't understand what you are getting at."

"This man taught us all a great deal—not only the kids around here but, I think, all of us. Of course, the younger you are, the more tragic things like this seem…maybe not tragic but defeating."

Glenn was nodding, aware for the first time that the man had something to say. "I agree that it's harder on the kids. It's going to be a hell of a final two weeks."

"Yes," Mr. Headley continued slowly. "I don't know what you have planned or what would be the best thing to do at a time like this, but I just wanted to ask if you decide to have one." The words came out so apologetically that Glenn was not sure the silent figure seated before him was finished. His expression was of simple hopefulness as the two men stared at each other. "Not that I am any better at this sort of thing than any of the rest of you. It's just something I would like to do."

"How can I say no to an offer like that?" Glenn reached out his hand toward Mr. Headley's firm clasp. "I'll let you know as soon as I can figure out when to fit things in, but yes, I'd appreciate a few words, and I think you could help a great deal."

Through her doorway, Mary saw Glenn walking down the hall, head bowed, looking neither right or left. If she had ever wondered about the authenticity of the news she had just heard or hoped that it was not true, the image of the man who just plodded by told her the hope was not realistic. Glenn was aware that there was not the usual traffic in the halls; all the rooms were quiet, subdued. A few sewing machines were running as he entered the home ec room. No one looked up to notice his entrance which would normally have created a minor stir. He scanned the group until he found Jean standing at window overlooking the creek below. The carpeting silenced his approach so that his "good morning" startled her.

"You probably knew him best. I could use your help. I'll be at the bridge."

Mrs. Packer exchanged a knowing nod as he left, and Glenn felt certain his suggestion would be taken, but he did not look back to see if she were coming. The bright sunlight blinded him momentarily as he started down at the scrawled writings on the bridge. The railing needed paint, and he knew he would get rust on his suit from leaning against it, but that is what he did.

He didn't have to wait long, however. Jean paused at the edge of the bridge as if waiting for permission to come upon it. This was the first time Glenn realized the softness within this girl. There was a quiet courage in her graceful stance even though the clothes she wore did nothing to help make her look so delicate.

"Things will be different now." He began walking toward her. He could see that she was trying to hold back tears. She would not speak, and as he reached to toss the hair from her shoulder, her attempts dissolved, and she pressed her forehead against his chest and flung her arms around his waist. For the first time, that morning he felt worthy. *Why did it take tragedy like this to bridge the distance?* he thought.

Before her voice was lost in sobs, Glenn heard her say, "Everything was going so great. I feel so hollow."

"We have to keep things going great, Jean. That's what I think I wanted to talk to you about. It's hard now, I know, but just try to listen to me." He led her across the bridge to the shade beyond. Leaning against a tree, one arm draped delicately across her shoulder, he began, choosing his words carefully, speaking very slowly.

"Jean, you know what…Mr. Flemming was most interested in. You know it, and I know it. Whatever he was able to get started must not be allowed to fall apart now. I have always been sorry that I couldn't do what he was able to do. I was the goat and always will be and that's as it should be, but I think you have the right to know what was happening here and how Mr. Flemming was trying to do an almost impossible job. I don't know much about this drug business, but I know how he felt and how he felt about you, you meaning… the committee. What, I guess, I need you to do is help keep things alive…the way he would want them to be. In other words, Jean, let me know what I can do or if some other teacher can help in any way. I realize it's a long shot. None of us can hope to fill his shoes, but let us know if we can help. Promise?"

Jean shook her head, but her face was buried in Glenn's chest. For a long time, only the creek nearby broke the silence, its muddy waters anxious to join other runoff before thundering into the sewer far behind them. Finally, Jean relaxed and withdrew to the path where she sat down, never looking at the man who was to her an enigma.

Her words tumbled out softly. "It's all too much of a shock for me to know what to do. I think I know what you are saying, but you're right. If Mr. Flemming got some people…off…then, I don't know, it might be a problem to keep it up with him gone."

"You know he'd—"

"And he did get some of us off." She looked up for the first time. "And some of us will stay off, but you also want a continuing sort of thing, right?"

"I'm talking to you right now."

Jean reached into her purse and drew out a wallet. Glenn watched intently as she flipped through several school pictures. She stopped at a picture of Jack. "You talk like Mr. Flemming."

Glenn half chuckled. "If that's good…you must bring out the best in people."

"While I was crying, I was thinking about myself…hollow. I'll tell you, I think the guys will have the worst problem. What you're talking about anyway…for what it's worth, that's what I think."

"It's worth plenty. Thanks, Jean, and thanks for coming out here. I got to get going."

He started back toward the building then turned and said, "If you like it here, stick around." A step later, he added, "You meaning the committee."

She looked back into her purse. "Here," she said, holding a small bundle wrapped in tissue.

"I think I can get rid of this for you," he said and silently departed.

The bell sounded, ending the first period. "One down," Glenn said to himself. His curiosity made him want to go into the halls to see what general reaction was. He resisted, though, fortunately, because his office was filled with teachers poking their heads in, all curious to know what exactly had happened.

Glenn watched with more than usual interest as the attendance slips piled up during second period. The committee was, just as he had hoped, gathering doubtless on the bridge. From first look, it appeared others were getting to class, perhaps more so than usually. By fifteen minutes into the period, the pattern was clear. Seventeen reported not in class; fourteen of them were definitely of the committee. Glenn marveled at the efficiency of their communication. He smiled within. These kids would make it, he knew. They could lean on one another. He figured a half hour more would tell him whether they planned to come to him or if he would have to go to them. It would be a long half hour's wait, but during that time, he would have to decide what, if anything, could be done to salvage all the good that Jack had accomplished. He went over the options in his mind, but the thought of somehow involving the students in planning a fitting tribute kept returning to him. He picked up the phone and dialed the superintendent's office.

"Good morning," said the businesslike voice on the other end. "I was just about to call you. How they doing?"

"Much better that I thought. I think shock is the big thing right now. He had a following."

"It's more of a shame than any of us can say. I just ask myself why. We've got to pull something out of it. Have you got anything on your mind?"

"That's why I called. What are my choices? I'm going light on a few of his closest followers. About a dozen of them are out of class, but they aren't going anywhere. I hope they come to me soon. If they do, what can I suggest? I'm not sure I can force anyone to go to class."

"Well, Glenn, we can't close off the afternoon. That's out. You can use me on that one if you need to. I'm sorry."

"No, I understand. I'll have to admit that answers my question. We'll work something out. I'll get back to you."

"Thanks, Glenn."

He had scarcely hung up when he noticed someone standing outside his door. He couldn't make out who it was, but he beckoned to the person to enter.

Russell Carter looked more ill at ease than he had on his many other visits to this particular part of the school, but he ended up in the same chair as always. His hand fidgeted with the hat which had become his trademark while his eyes seemed to search the floor for the right thing to say. Glenn waited him out and forced a smiled when their eyes finally met.

"We were just wondering if there was going to be anything more than an announcement. We thought your idea of some kind of an assembly or service or something would be all right."

"Yes, a service or something I would like to have. I thought about tomorrow afternoon. What do you think?"

"Tomorrow?" His head was shaking slowly. "I don't think we want to wait 'til tomorrow."

"Russ, you're always…I think you're right. We can shorten the afternoon classes and go for two or two thirty or just cancel sixth hour and hold it then. Which do you prefer?"

Russell pulled himself up in the chair and leaned forward on the arms, striking a pose very similar to Glenn's. "Uh, I don't know. Whatever is easiest? It doesn't really matter, does it?"

"Let's see if it does. If cancel sixth hour and hold it then, how many people are going to skip? If we shorten the classes, hold the assembly, or service, at say two o'clock then return to sixth hour, will we have better attendance at the service? Or does it matter?"

"I can't see anybody skipping." The boy was bewildered but seemed to respond to being included in such high-level decision-making.

"I can't see people skipping pep assemblies. I can't see skipping Christmas programs," Glenn said.

Russell's eyes found the floor again, and he was now slouched in his chair again. "Let 'em skip…if that's all it means."

"Now you have it. I'll give you that much. It will be like dismissing at two thirty, and we'll just see what happens. You may be the only ones there."

Russell's fists clinched, and he sat silently.

"But if you think it best to hold it today, I'll back up your decision," Glenn continued. "I'm going to put Mr. Headley in charge of it, and I'll get word to him right now. What I need to know is…do you…do you want to participate in any way?"

"Mr. Headley, what does he know about this?"

"All right, I'll be honest with you. He asked if he could be. I've got lots of sides to think about, Russ, and this is one I'd like to stick with. If you like, I'll tell him to meet with you, or I could tell him to help get things started then turn the meeting over to you. Whatever you think—"

"Yeah, well, we just…a couple of 'em wanted to read some poems, you know? And we sorta thought we might say something that would mean something to everybody, and that would be it."

"Fine, fine. Let's let Headley start it, then you people take it on. We'll go for two thirty, and I'll want to see you in here at two o'clock…you and anyone else you think should come…just to check signals." He stood up, noticing for the first time the youngster stood at almost eye level. "You know what John Steinbeck said? He's an author. 'A boy becomes a man when a man is needed.' We need some men around here today, don't we?"

"Sir?"

Glenn's vision became blurred through tears he knew were visible to the boy, and his voice sounded far-off as he said, "Now you call me sir." He extended his hand across the desk but could not see the limp, clammy hand he finally felt. "Seems like you're the man. Thanks, Russell. Two o'clock."

The door closed, and Glenn collapsed into his chair, overwhelmed with warm feeling of respect. Holding his head in his hands, he allowed tears to cascade down his cheeks onto his desk. This brief luxury he afforded himself. He would talk to Mr. Headley after second hour and not call the superintendent until all plans were final.

★★★★★

Jean had her shoes off, one leg dangling in the cold water of the creek before it bounded against the end of the bridge. She reflected over the times she had sat here or nearby under the shelter the bridge could give from rain, snow, or prying eyes. She was the first of the group to see Russell hurrying down the steps toward them. "What's the matter?" she asked.

"I don't know." He took his time about sitting down, and the others gathered nearby. "If we have a service at an assembly, do you think many people will skip?"

No one seemed to want to tackle the possibility until Tim finally ventured an answer. "Hell no, how could they skip out on something like that! There's certain things you gotta do."

"Doc says we can hold it, I think, at two thirty," Russell continued. He had everyone's attention. Perhaps that was what made him sound more nervous, Jean thought. "Headley is in charge though. I don't know how that happened. Anyway, he wants me to come in about two o'clock, so whatever it's going to be, we'll have to be ready by then."

"Headley? Forget it." Tim punctuated his indignation with the splash of a rock he fired into the water. Jean watched the expanding ripple until it played upon her foot.

Her understanding of the various feelings within the group became lost in thoughts and all-consuming sadness. She heard the pros and cons of having Mr. Headley in on the service but made no effort to reach a decision or take sides herself. She pulled her shoe on and stood up. "If I write a poem, will you read it?" she asked Russell.

He nodded without looking up to see her leave.

"It will be lousy if nobody shows up," Randy was saying. "Maybe tomorrow would be better."

"No, that won't make any difference. Where the hell is she going?" Everyone could feel the edge in Russell's voice.

"Cool it. You know how she feels," Joan said. "She'll go off somewhere by herself, and in ten minutes she'll whip up a poem that says everything she wants to say. She does it all the time. It's unbelievable."

"So…what have we got? Nothing." There was a new note of panic in Russell's voice. "A half hour. Hell, I can't think of anything to do for a half hour."

Joan was more hopeful. "All right, get some paper. Who has a pencil?" Positive action brought the group together. "You gotta have a plan," she continued as paper and pencil were brought forth. "Half hour, right?"

Russell nodded his head, relieved that things were out of his hands at this crucial stage.

"Okay, so we put down '2:30 to 2:35'…" Her hand was waving in the air, showing desperate thought. "Enter," she blurted out and scribbled this down. Everyone chimed in in agreement. It certainly took five minutes to enter. "Then…then let's see, '2:35 to 2:40—Headley.' How…" she addressed the group. "Who'll talk to the Head? Tell him he can have the first five minutes."

"Jeez, five minutes. How can anybody get up there and talk about this for five minutes?" Tim was bewildered when confronted by the reality of the situation.

"Oh, these teachers know about this kind of stuff. Now who'll talk to him?" Joan pressed.

"I will," said Shelly. "I've got him next hour."

"Good." Joan was still presiding. "Just ask him if he'll start things off and use maybe five minutes or so."

"Jeez," was Tim's repeated offering.

"Okay, 2:40…now what?"

"Can't somebody read the Bible or something?" urged Scott.

"What do we read?" Russell wanted to know, but he fell silent when he saw Joan writing "Bible reading" on her sheet of paper.

"What's that thing, 'The Lord is my shepherd…'? You know they always read it in church."

Again, the creek dominated the stillness as the committee's limited exposure to church was revealed.

"It's a good idea, I think," Joan insisted. "Now can anybody go home and get a Bible. They can't have any around here. I don't think. If we had one, we could go ask in the library what we should read."

Tim finally spoke up. "We got one. I'll go get it."

"Okay, you check into what should be read. Will you read it? You can practice all day."

Tim was in the spotlight, and having everyone counting on him caused him to agree. "I don't need any practice." He was on his way home as Joan wrote his name on her growing outline.

"Make it about a minute's worth," she called after him.

There was restless shuffling in the group with the realization that all this had only brought them one minute closer to their goal.

"Who'll go talk to Mrs. Jackson about some music? The choir maybe. Pam, you're in it. Is there anything you could do?"

"I don't know. I'll try to find out."

"Go now," Joan insisted. "We need to know, and, Scott, go see if the band can do anything."

"What?"

"Go ask what's-his-name…go ahead." Everyone seemed to be urging him. Hopes rose and enthusiasm built.

The two left, Scott's doubtfulness displayed in his gait, but the committee felt itself regaining control. Each member felt sized by a fear of idleness. Everyone wanted to be doing something and saying something now. In this confused effort, though, even less was being accomplished. Joan sensed this and turned to Russell.

"You're going to read anything. How could she? What's the use of all this anyway? You're all making a big deal out of this program thing. The guy's dead." Russell was on his feet as if to move away from the group, but he did not. "What's the difference whether we have an assembly or read a goddamn poem or the Bible or anything else? It's not going to change anything. He's dead, and that's all…"

The shocked silence of the rest of the group stunned Russell as he sat down again, his face in his hands, the bill of his cap pulled low. It was quiet enough to hear his sobbing. It became contagious.

Joan was speaking slowly. Her voice cracked. She gulped for breath, but she continued her firm answer, not caring whether anyone else listened but Russell. "One thing I learned, and he taught me it, was that you make up your mind then go with it. Maybe that's what he means by class. Just because we've never had to before…" She could say no more. No one spoke nor even looked at one another, but each understood, and each suffered in their own way. They were all acting out of character, yet they realized they were not acting at all. There was comfort in the feeling of sincere honesty.

Minutes went by, and Russell's tirade was somehow ignored, at least bypassed, when Pam returned to say that the choir would do two numbers. "They'll arrange it fifth hour in class," she said. "Jackson said she'd play the piano at the beginning while everybody's entering if we want her to."

"Okay, two songs. I hope one of them is Gwenn's solo thing." Joan had her paper and pencil going again. "Do we want them both together or separated?"

"One near the beginning and one near the end," John ventured. "Okay…"

Scott ambled back and tried not to show that he noticed there had been crying while hers was gone. "He said most of the band instruments were checked back in and there wasn't much they could do. I can play 'Taps'…if you want." He shrugged and sat down, plucking a blade of grass which he slid between his teeth.

"Okay, we got two songs. 'Taps,' I don't know." Joan's pencil was thumping the paper rapidly, inviting suggestions.

"Hell, he was in the service. 'Taps' is kind of…military, but that was a part of him."

Joan nodded thoughtfully. "Scott, the very end, okay?"

"No problem."

"You'll just keep playing while people are leaving."

"What if there aren't any people to leave?" Russell said, his sarcasm unhidden.

Joan fired back, "Damn it—what is your problem?"

"Jeez, it's like Mr. Flemming used to say, 'If you can't think of anything better, don't criticize.'" John was clearly on his sister's side, and she was pressing her point further.

"Come on, say what's wrong. What do you got against this anyway?"

There was a painful silence as Russell's and Joan's eyes met. Then he spoke. "What if it wasn't an accident?"

Jean was moving down the walk toward the gathering and was caught by the total silence there. It was not until she had slipped off her shoes and sat down that she broke the trance. "I wrote a poem," she announced simply.

Scott had been fondling a mud ball, which he fired into the water. His words came out with equal force. "What the hell are you talking about?"

Jean looked up, stunned until she realized it was not she to whom he spoke. Scott was glaring at Russell, and all the others were intently awaiting his reply.

"You've ridden with him. He's a good driver, a great one. It doesn't make sense that he'd get a new car, take it out on the highway on a night like last night, and lose it. It just doesn't make sense."

"Do accidents have to make sense?"

"Accident, hell. We're going to think accident, and we're going to have this program thing, then we're going to forget all about it." Russell noticed Jean's head drop into her folded arms as he spoke. "It will all be wasted if we don't realize he's trying to tell us something now. Jack Flemming loved every one of us. He had one thing he wanted to accomplish and nothing else to live for if he couldn't do it. One more week of school left. Don't tell me it's an accident."

"Jeez."

"Okay, you knew him probably as well as anybody," Jean said, rolling over on her stomach and with her body pulsing as she lay there crying, not caring about what appearance she made nor how dirty it would make her.

"All of us," Russell continued, his voice much softer now. "Liked having him try. It made me feel good to see that he cared. He worried, and that bothered me, but I still liked it. But I never really made a decision to stop." Russell's voice became weak as he tried to mask his emotions. He was almost whispering. "I guess if I stopped, I was afraid he might not worry about me anymore." He crawled over to Jean and stroked her hair, which fell across her back. "Now I've got no choice." He reached into his pocket, pulled out a joint, looked at it. He bent it enough to break the paper then tossed it into the creek. He heard someone say, "Blow my mind," but soon others were floating after his. Small quantities of loose grass, packets of papers, brightly colored capsules all met their doom in the swirling murky water.

Russell nodded his head. "Now," he said. "Let's get this program going."

★★★★★

"Looks good," Glenn said after scanning the neatly typed script which Russell Carter had handed him. Mr. Headley nodded his agreement and folded the carbon copy he had been given. "Okay with you?" he asked the older man.

"Certainly. Five minutes is good. Janice had spoken to me about it. I'd just like to say something to sort of set the tone"—he was looking at Russell now—"but you people will carry the weight. So far you've done excellently."

Glenn needed to check on the particulars; he simply could not believe all this would happen, but he could find no flaws. "What is Tim going to read? Do you know?"

"Yes sir, the…Twenty-third Psalm."

"And Scott and Gwenn? In the words, all these people know what they are to do?"

"Yes, sir, they know what they are supposed to do and who they follow. That's all they need to know."

"That's all they need to know." Glenn repeated in bewilderment. He fixed his gaze upon the lad seated across from him and forced himself smile. "I know of someone who would have been proud of you, and if he ever told you you got class, he sure knew what he was talking about." He stood, and the other two did likewise. He extended his hand first to Russell then to Mr. Headley. "Thanks, both of you. See you at two thirty."

★★★★★

So quiet, so orderly had been the entrance to the auditorium that only those students near the back had seen Dr. Becker and Mr. Bemis walk in together and simply sit down. A ripple of sympathy, almost embarrassment, flowed across the silent audience as Mr. Headley slowly climbed the five stairs at one side of the stage and limped toward the podium at the center. Before it stood a huge arrangement of yellow chrysanthemums flanked by pots of lush ferns. The flowers had been ordered by the superintendent, with the ferns procured, on loan, by the janitor from his friend who operated a funeral parlor. He had rushed out during his lunch break to do his part.

Mr. Headley grasped the podium with both hands and leaned upon it for comforting support. A half smile may have indicated his comfort, or it may have said much about how the older generation understands the pains of growing up, how it sympathizes with youth as obstacles are met and finally conquered.

"I want to tell you a story," he began slowly. "About a football player. He was from a small college down in the southern part of our state. He played a long time ago. He didn't play very much either. In those days, he would be called a mediocre football player. Now he'd be called lousy.

"But the coach always got him into every game though he never started. Maybe the coach knew he had potential. Maybe the coach just felt sorry for him.

"This football player lived in that small college town. He lived with his father. His father was blind. Each evening, the father and son would be seen taking a walk either around the town or, perhaps, across the campus.

"He played that first year but never really distinguished himself. As I said, mediocre.

"He started his second year about the same way. Seemed like he almost didn't care about football, and then one day, he wasn't seen taking his father for a walk. By the end of the next week, the old man died.

"Well, our football player hung in there, and as usual, the coach put him in late in the game."

Mr. Headley stood erect and walked around in front of the podium, his disheveled brown suit a marked contrast to the beauty of the flowers behind him. "He was like a new player," he continued.

"He made key blocks on offense, tore up the quarterback on defense, made tackles and blocked a punt.

"After the game, the coach pulled him aside, 'Tell me, how come you finally played the way I always knew you could?' He wanted to know.

"'My dad was blind,' he said. 'Do you remember?'

"'Sure, I recall seeing you leading him around the campus in the evening, and you know how sorry I am…'

"But the boy didn't want any sympathy. He just looked up to his coach and said, 'Well, I guess I played better today because now I know he can watch me play.'"

A long all-encompassing scanning of the darkened auditorium ended Mr. Headley's offering. He then turned and began his slow departure. Russell could only faintly see him through tears which melted the brightly lighted stage, the explosion of color in front of the podium, and the almost stationary old man into one gossamer image he wanted never to lose sight of.

Glenn saw John's head bow, but held his own up to see Tim cross the stage from the other side and assume the exact stance and posture Mr. Headley had used. The latter, using the wall for support, was letting himself down one step at a time.

Tim turned toward him. "Thank you, sir. Thank you very much." The audience barely heard his words above his crying. Glenn reached for his handkerchief just as Tim ran his arm across his face and fought to regain his vision. Glenn could not tell whether he was reading or had memorized. Probably both, he decided.

"The Lord is my shepherd, I shall not want…"

Oh, Tim could read. This kid is going to make it, Glenn thought to himself.

Then the stage went dark momentarily before a voice could be heard singing "Old Man River" as a spotlight switched on, showing David Thurmond in tattered pants, shoeless and shirtless. Glenn clinched, expecting screams and catcalls, but the audience was silently respectful. "He must know something. He don't say nothing. He just keeps rolling along."

Far on the left, three others were moving also, rolling along toward the door. Glenn could not recognize all of them in the darkness, but the swaggering pace and low-pilled hat of the first one told him it was Odell Johnson leading the exodus. A faint red glow shone down from the Exit sign above the rear door. This light fell upon Larry Washington's broad shoulders. The threesomes were still fifteen feet from the door when Larry pointed dramatically toward some vacant seats. The three stood still for a moment. Something was said, barely audibly. Then they turned and disappeared in the darkness toward the seats.

"I'm tired of living…" David's voice cracked. He paused, but the piano music continued. "But I'm scared of dying…" Glenn felt John's arm move. "But that old man river…" David dropped his voice to a near whisper. "He just keeps rolling along."

The program went like clockwork. "That's all they need to know," he remembered. The chorus was polished, devoid of the usual squirming, face making, and gum chewing. Gwenn's voice as she trilled "The Reason That I Love You" sent a warmth through Glenn which he knew was shared by everyone in the room. Here was a girl singing with all the meaning, all the devotion she possibly could possess. Here was a child with purpose.

Glenn felt nervous as Russell approached the podium, a sheet of paper in his hand. "I want to read a poem written by someone who was very close to Mr. Flemming.

> I want to touch you, to know you are near.
> I want to talk to you, I want you to hear.
> Now, I am lost. You have gone away.
> You have given me so much. I long for yesterday.
> I want you by me to wipe away my fear.
> I want you back, to wipe away my tear.

There was to be no wiping away of tears now. They blotted out Glenn's vision, and he assumed everyone else's, but they couldn't blot out the trumpet tones which came as Russell's words faded. Slow and crystal clear, each note right on the money. Scott was giving it his all from the gut. The volume built then faded, with Scott holding his last note until the trumpet and echo were indistinguishable.

The houselights were brightening. The stage was empty. No one moved. Many of the seats seemed empty from where Glenn sat. One by one, then in more rapid succession, faculty members got to their feet like the first kernels to pop in a batch of popcorn. As he stood, Glenn saw the reason for the apparently empty seats. Many students bent over double with their heads on their knees. Others, their spines even more contorted, had slid down in their chairs as if seeking their own privacy. These did not see the growing parade of faculty which was spontaneously descending the center aisle, toward the front row where they shook hands or hugged the ragged warriors who had just proven themselves.

The outpouring of emotion was more than enough to erase the faculty-student barrier, enough to force Irene Hedgepeth to tousle Russell's hair lovingly then throw both arms around him, enough so that he could allow it.

Mr. Headley had made it as far as Jean, and if she had been in need of a shoulder to cry on, she need look no more.

Don was patting Tim on the back then extended his hand, waiting for Tim to free his own hand of its unfamiliar load. No one said anything—no one needed to. Long before the thirty-plus teachers had been able to privately convey their feelings to each and every one of the performers, the auditorium had emptied. Glenn looked at his watch. It was three after three.

At ten after three, Mrs. Carter was surprised not to have heard the basement door open as Russell and his friends tumbled in the usual manner. It was not until almost three thirty that the door opened, but the entry was noticeably more subdued. She called down the stairs, "Russell, you've got a letter, honey."

Russell climbed the stairs, leaving the others behind. He tore open the envelope.

The Bridge Committee

Dear Russell,

You've probably got enough class to have things
figured out by now. I hope you stick with the
right game plan.
Goodbye, and good luck to all of you.

Yours forever,

JF

About the Author

M r. Kim Westrup earned his degree in elementary education in the spring of 1960. That fall, he found himself with a class of forty-two fifth graders and an army of angry parents. By the next school year, President Kennedy's education advisor, who was writing a book titled *The Mis-Education of American Teachers*, interviewed the new teacher to determine how his year-end achievement test scores were so high. Westrup remembers saying, "We just had a good time…every day." To teachers everywhere, Westrup has always said, "Yours is not a *job* but a *life*. Enjoy living it." He adds, "If you find yourself not looking forward to every day, become a dentist."

Blurb

The Bridge Committee is a novel. The only nonfiction aspect is the title itself, which is derived from a dignified-sounding name applied to the growing group of drug users whom the author managed to become close enough with to try to modify their behavior while teaching American history in junior high school. Other labels at that time could have included druggies, druggers, and burnouts. Using a nonjudgmental, individual approach, a teacher of fifteen-year-olds can and did have considerable impact. The stress is enormous, the setbacks frequent, and the frustrations painful. The reader is asked to avoid or at least resist allowing the fictitious plot to interfere with the aim of believing in the character of young people struggling through adolescence. They need positive role models. The sixties was a decade of turmoil. Against a backdrop of unpopular war, there were protesters of almost everything. The most influential of these topics for the school-aged population was the forced racial integration of public schools. "Bussing" became a swear word. Those reaching puberty seemed the least ready for this kind of adjustment. The plot shows how well-meaning sanctimonious action can spiral out of control.